VAMPYR?

VAMPYR?

KEVIN RANDLE

FIVE STAR
A part of Gale, Cengage Learning

GALE
CENGAGE Learning™

Detroit • New York • San Francisco • New Haven, Conn • Waterville, Maine • London

GALE
CENGAGE Learning·

LIBRARY OF CONGRESS CATALOGING-IN-PUBLICATION DATA

Randle, Kevin D., 1949–
  Vampyr? / by Kevin Randle. — 1st ed.
    p. cm.
  ISBN-13: 978-1-59414-921-4
  ISBN-10: 1-59414-921-6
  1. Vampires—Fiction. I. Title.
PS3568.A534V36 2010
813'.54—dc22   2010036701

First Edition. First Printing: December 2010.
Published in 2010 in conjunction with Tekno Books and Ed Gorman.

Printed in the United States of America
1 2 3 4 5 6 7 14 13 12 11 10

VAMPYR?

CHAPTER ONE

Thomas Johnson was standing there, in the literal sense, with the smoking gun in his hand as the police entered the room. He was stomping on flesh-colored insects that seemed to move with a slowness borne of extreme cold. He didn't listen as the police shouted at him to drop his gun. The insects must not escape. He feared them more than the police who were pointing a variety of weapons at him, including two shotguns that would shred his body if fired.

Lying on the floor, near the overturned coffee table with the broken leg, was an unconscious woman. She was dressed in dark blue slacks and a white shirt that was knotted above her abdomen. There was blood staining her blond hair and a bruise on the side of her face, under her left eye.

Near Thomas Johnson was the other, a dead woman. There was a single, ragged hole in her forehead, and a fan of blood under her, spreading out and staining the carpet. There were tiny cuts on her face and tears in her clothes but little blood from those wounds. She had lost one shoe and her hose were torn at both knees, looking as if she had fallen heavily before toppling to her back. Had she not been dead, had there not been so much blood near her, had her skin not looked so white, so bleached, her pose on the floor might have seemed erotic. Her skirt was pulled high, showing long, tapering thighs that looked as if they had been chiseled from the finest tanned marble.

"Drop the gun," yelled one of the police officers. "Put it on the floor and get down on your belly. Drop the gun. Now!"

Johnson still acted as if he couldn't hear. He stomped with his right foot, leaping back, as if afraid of splashing himself. He stomped and stomped, leaving small, bloody smears on the cream-colored carpet, the pistol forgotten in his hand.

"I said get down. On your face. Drop the gun."

Without thinking, Johnson let the pistol fall to the carpet, turned and knelt. He touched the face of the unconscious woman and leaned close, searching for signs of life at the throat, probing with his fingers.

"Get away from her," ordered another of the police officers, advancing into the room, his shotgun pointed at Johnson's head. With the toe of his shoe, he kicked Johnson's pistol away from him, out of reach. With that threat gone, the other four police officers swarmed into the room, almost surrounding Johnson, shouting at him, giving conflicting orders. One of them shoved him at the shoulder, pushing him away from the unconscious woman.

He seemed to awaken then, looked into the barrel of a shotgun and was surprised. "You're here," he said.

"Get on your belly, hands out from your body."

This time he complied. As he got down, he said, "She'll be okay. Maybe you should get an ambulance."

"You shut up. You have the right to remain silent and I'd advise you to use it."

Johnson stared at the cop. He was a slight man with light hair. He looked young, as if he had just escaped from high school and certainly not old enough to be a police officer.

The cop moved in, his shotgun still pointed at Johnson. When he was close, he put the weapon down on the carpet, out of Johnson's reach. There were two others, standing to the side, their pistols pointed at Johnson so that if he twitched, they could protect their fellow officer.

The young cop handcuffed Johnson and then lifted him to his feet. "You're going to jail," he said unnecessarily.

"You have to burn the body."

"What?"

"The body. You have to burn it. Quickly. Now."

"Sure, and destroy the forensic evidence on it."

"You don't understand. You have to make sure. You have to burn the body."

"That'll be up to the family."

"Christ, Davis, why are you talking to this guy? Get him outside and into a car."

Davis pushed Johnson toward the door and then opened it. He shoved Johnson outside, onto the porch, but Johnson dodged right, around the cop and ran back into the house. He stopped at the edge of the living room and looked at the two cops kneeling near the body.

"You have to burn her. You have to burn her completely," Johnson pleaded.

One of the cops looked up and then stood, moving forward, as if to block Johnson's path.

"Get out of here," he said. "You're not giving anyone orders here."

Johnson, his hands cuffed, tried to force his way back into the living room. "You don't understand," he said, his voice rising. "You have to burn the body. It's the only way."

The cop reached out, put his hands on Johnson's shoulders and shoved, throwing him back into the entry. Johnson stumbled and then sat down, hard. He stared at the police officer, looking as if he was going to cry, as if his world had been shattered and no one would listen to him or understand him. He looked lost, pitiful, almost as if he was unable to think clearly.

Davis grabbed him under the arms and lifted him to his feet.

"You're just making it harder on yourself. We'll charge you with resisting arrest."

"I'm not resisting. I'm trying to warn you. The body must be burned."

Davis forced Johnson to turn around so that he was facing the door. With one hand on his head and another grasping Johnson by the belt, he forced him outside, to the porch, and then down to the steps, toward the police cars.

Johnson jerked once, to the right, trying to break Davis's grip, but the young cop held on. They stopped near the police cars, one of them parked on the lawn, its red and blue lights flashing. Two cops stood near it, looking up at the house but making no move to cordon the area, stop the curious, or help Davis. They might as well have been tourists out for an enjoyable evening for all the good they were doing.

Tentatively, Davis let go, but Johnson didn't move. Davis opened the rear door and put a hand on the top of Johnson's head, to protect him from bumping it, and as a way to feel for any tenseness in Johnson warning of more resistance.

Johnson ducked his head but failed to turn so that he could get into the cruiser. He said, "You'll make sure they burn the body, won't you? They have to burn her."

"Why'd you do it?" asked Davis, aware that he had not advised Johnson of his rights and the question was inappropriate.

"Had to. She was going to kill Sarah. Had to shoot her."

"Get in the car."

"Only if you'll tell them to burn the body. Only if you'll make sure they burn her."

"I'll tell them," said Davis. "Now get into the car before I get pissed."

Johnson hesitated, not sure if he believed the cop or not.

Finally, he turned and sat down carefully, sliding across the bench seat.

Davis didn't close the door immediately. He looked down at Johnson, thinking that he didn't look high on drugs, that he didn't look drunk and that he didn't look crazy except for that crap about burning the body. That struck him as a little crazy.

In fact, had he not been standing in the living room with the pistol in his hand, Davis would have thought he was a helpful neighbor and not the perpetrator.

"What were those things on the floor?" he asked, finally.

Johnson smiled and nodded, as if Davis now understood. "They were offspring."

CHAPTER TWO

Johnson was taken into the station, up a flight of stairs that looked as if it belonged in the nineteenth century, down a narrow corridor that was gloomy, and finally put into a room that looked as if it belonged in the next century. It was brightly lighted, with green walls, a darker green carpet on the floor, and a table set in the exact middle of the room. There were two chairs, one on each side of the table. There were curtains on one wall that were an aqua, and a huge mirror on the other that Johnson knew was one-way glass.

The cop removed the cuffs, and Johnson was directed to one of the two chairs. He was ordered to sit down and stay quiet. He walked across the carpet to the table but was tempted to pull the curtains aside, because, if he hadn't gotten turned around, there could be no window on that wall. The curtains were more for the psychological show.

As Johnson sat down Davis said, "You wait right here and don't move. You want something to drink?"

Johnson stared up and said, "I don't think so. Thank you." He grinned and thought about an attorney, but said nothing about it. Let the cops think that he was going to cooperate.

He wished he knew the time. He had only about sixty hours before the situation changed radically. If he couldn't convince the police, then maybe his attorney would understand that the body needed to be cremated. He turned the word over in his mind. *Cremated.* He should have been telling them to cremate it. Make it a religious thing. Then they might comply. They didn't need it for forensics because they didn't have to solve the case. They had all the information they needed to prosecute. Hell, he had been standing there with the gun in his hand.

For ten minutes, Johnson sat quietly in the chair, knowing that the cops were standing behind the one-way glass, watching him carefully. He thought about the things he could do to annoy them such as tapping on the glass and waving, or looking behind the curtains to prove there was no window, but in the end, he just sat quietly, looking at a spot of blood on his khaki-colored trousers. He hadn't realized that he had been splashed with the blood, and figured, at some point, the cops would notice, and that they would want the blood for DNA comparison with the victim. That was going to be interesting because, if he was right, there would be lots of DNA from lots of different people in that spot of blood. They might be able to isolate the blood of a half dozen of her victims.

Johnson folded his hands and then stared at the blank wall, understanding fully what was happening. Standard interrogation technique. It would be wasted on anyone who understood it, but the cops rarely dealt with anyone who understood interrogation or the psychology of the situation. All he needed to do was remain calm and rational. He had gotten himself under control now that he was out of that house and away from the body. He just had to be patient for a little while longer, and he would be able to take control of the situation.

The door finally opened, but it wasn't Davis who entered. Instead, it was an older man, maybe fifty, maybe a little older, who carried two cups of coffee. He was dressed in a suit and tie. A suit and not a sport coat and gray trousers that seemed to be an almost uniform for police in plain clothes.

The cop's shirt looked fresh and bright, as did his face, indicating he had recently shaved, even at the late hour. It meant that he had been called from home, dressed carefully, and was probably a senior officer, called because of the strange nature of the crime.

"I brought some coffee," he said, setting one of the cups on the table near Johnson.

"Thank you, but no. I don't drink coffee."

The man smiled. "I just can't function without it. Wakes me up."

"That's the caffeine in it," said Johnson without thinking about it.

"True enough. I need my caffeine fix."

"Funny to hear a police officer talk that way, Lieutenant . . . ?"

"Steve Mitchell and it's captain."

"So, they brought in the big guns," said Johnson, smiling weakly.

"Can I get you anything? Anything at all?"

Johnson sighed and said, "How is Sarah? She was badly injured tonight."

Mitchell dropped into the chair on the other side of the interrogation table. "I'll check for certain, but I do know that she was taken to the hospital. You sure you don't want the coffee? I had it brewed fresh."

"This the good-cop routine?"

"We don't have to play that game tonight. We have you pretty much dead to rights here. Jesus, I don't remember another case with the guy standing there with the smoking gun in his hand. The actual, real smoking gun, right in his hand. Ballistics can tie the bullet to the gun and our case is made."

Johnson sat quietly, forcing himself to remain calm, to think clearly. Time was running, but not that fast. He had nearly three days.

He said, "Providing that I didn't just pick it up when I arrived on the scene. You haven't even bothered to give me a paraffin test."

"You think we need one?"

"How else will you establish, forensically, that I fired a weapon?"

"Well, you know, if you fertilized your lawn today, the paraffin test will come back positive, even if you haven't fired a gun. Then, if you wore a glove, it might come back negative. Besides, we have your statement made spontaneously at the crime scene."

"Without benefit of counsel or *Miranda*," said Johnson.

"Admissible as a statement against self-interest and a crime scene utterance that was not induced by the officers present or during an unlawful questioning. I think we can get it in, if we need to. You are in it deep and smelly."

Mitchell sipped at his coffee and asked, "You sure you don't want that other cup?"

"No, and please don't offer cigarettes because I don't smoke either," said Johnson.

"Can I get you a soda? Water? Anything?"

"No, thank you."

"So, you want to tell me why you did it?"

"Nice. Smooth. Get me talking and then slip into the interrogation."

Mitchell raised his eyebrows and nodded.

"Of course, I want an attorney."

"We were getting along so well," said Mitchell. "I thought that we could hammer this out, between the two of us, and not bother a lot of people so late at night. Save everyone a lot of extra work."

"You realize, of course, that now I have officially asked for an attorney that this interrogation must end. Anything I say after this point is inadmissible."

"Did you have someone special in mind?"

15

"Of course. Rachael Goldberg."

"She's not a criminal attorney."

"How could you possibly know that?"

"I am familiar with the attorneys in the area who are involved in criminal work. Her name is unfamiliar to me."

"She is my attorney and is certainly competent enough to tell me not to talk to you."

Mitchell took another sip of his coffee and said, "You are guilty. There is no question that you murdered a fellow human being."

"That is your first mistake, Captain," said Johnson. "I did not murder another human."

CHAPTER THREE

There was a quiet knock on the door to the interrogation room. They hesitated, neither Johnson nor Mitchell saying anything, and then the door swung open slowly. A woman, dressed in a light gray suit with a very short skirt, holding onto a briefcase that had a purse-like strap rather than a handle, stood there. She had raven dark hair, with an oval face and small, delicate features and bright brown eyes. Although she looked very good and seemed to be sexy, there was an air of professionalism about her that stopped most of the off-color comments. She looked like an attorney, though no one could explain just how that worked. No one would challenge her professionalism.

Johnson turned to look and then stood up. "Rachael, how good of you to come."

"Christ, Tom, this isn't a party. I came, summoned as your attorney by the police."

"I seem to have mistimed the events tonight. I need some help."

She entered the interrogation room, set her briefcase on the table, looked casually at Mitchell and dismissed him as unimportant to her mission. To Johnson, she said, "I am not a criminal attorney."

Now Mitchell spoke. He stood up, held out his hand and said, "I'm Captain Mitchell and I suggested a criminal attorney. Someone on hand here for the basics before we began waking people all over town."

Goldberg ignored the hand. "I would like some time alone with my client. Is there a room around here that doesn't have an observation room behind the one-way glass and microphones planted all over?"

"I'll clear out the observation room so that you can stay in here."

"I'm going to have to insist on something a little more private."

"Insist away, Ms. Goldberg, but Mr. Johnson is under arrest, has been booked and will be kept in this room until we decide to put him into a cell or move him to another location for either his safety or ours. You can confer in here, or you can wait until later."

"My client has a right to an attorney."

"That he does, and here you are. But you have no right to demand where and how you will conduct your conference and our duty supersedes your desires. So, you can use this room, aware that I have promised that you will not be taped or observed, or you can wait for another twelve or fourteen hours, until we finish our work. Not that there is anything he could say to you that would be of help to us. Your call, counselor."

Goldberg sat down in the chair that had been vacated by Johnson. She crossed her legs, sat quietly for a moment, but when Mitchell added nothing, she said, "Anything overheard in here, or recorded from this meeting would be inadmissible because of the violation of attorney–client privilege. You must be aware of all that."

"Counselor, we have this guy dead bang, and I will not allow sleazy tricks that would jeopardize the prosecution. You may confer, but, as I understand it, there will be an arraignment later this morning. That's how confident we are in the case we have against him."

Goldberg ignored that and said, "We have work to do here, if

Vampyr?

you'll excuse us."

Mitchell nodded, moved to the door and said, "Push the button here when you're through, and an officer will come to escort you from the building. This room will be locked so you can't just walk out." He closed the door on his way out.

"You didn't have to be so rude," said Johnson.

"Rude? What in the hell are you talking about?"

Now Johnson grinned. "You telling him what you wanted and giving orders."

"Let me clue you in, pal. I was sound asleep with not a worry in the world. I was warm and snug in my bed, dreaming of my vacation. Then I get this cockamamie telephone call to come to get you out of the slammer and it isn't drunk driving or even armed robbery, but murder. You killed someone?"

Johnson sat back in his chair and took a deep breath. "This is going to take some time. I didn't kill anyone. I didn't kill a person."

"I don't think I like the way you're qualifying this. What the hell happened?"

"Sarah was attacked and I ended it."

"You're claiming self-defense?"

"No, because I didn't kill a person."

Goldberg rubbed her head and said, "I don't understand what is going on here. And I don't want to play games with semantics this early in the morning."

"The police have arrested me for . . ."

"I'm not stupid, Tom. I'm confused. Does this have to do with Linda Miller?"

"Rachael, this has been a long night . . . and I would like to know that Sarah got to the hospital and that she'll be okay. The cops haven't told me much because they said that they ask the questions."

"I can find out about Sarah later. First, I need to know what

19

in the hell is going on in here."

"We don't have to worry about Miller anymore," said Johnson. "I took care of her."

"What, exactly, does that mean?"

Johnson, his hands folded on the table, leaned closer, as if to whisper. For just an instant he looked like a little kid who had been caught with his hand in the cookie jar, but for just an instant. His features hardened and he said, "I eliminated her. She won't cause any of us any more trouble, that's for sure, provided we all move quickly enough."

Goldberg pulled her briefcase close and opened it, taking out a yellow legal pad that looked as if it had never been used. She took a fountain pen from the case, unscrewed the cap, and then wrote both Johnson's name and the date at the top of the pad. She looked up, expectantly.

"I'm not sure that you should write any of this down," said Johnson.

"There is no way that the police or anyone else can get their hands on my notes. Attorney–client privilege applies and they know it."

Johnson nodded and said, "That's just my intelligence training taking over. Commit as little as possible to paper and when finished, destroy all notes and records as completely as possible. Saves everyone from having to answer awkward questions later."

Goldberg looked at her watch. It was a tiny, gold thing that was paper thin, looking more like a twisted gold tennis bracelet than a timepiece.

"It's approaching four in the morning and I'm not in a very good mood right now."

"Okay."

"Tell me why the police have arrested you."

"Because I shot Linda Miller in the head with a large-caliber pistol and they ran into the room about ten seconds after I pulled the trigger. I have no idea how they got there that fast or even why they were there in the first place."

"Christ," said Goldberg.

"The police saw you kill her?"

"No. But they saw me standing there with the pistol in my hand and her lying on the floor."

Goldberg shook her head in disbelief. "Talk about a smoking gun."

"That's what the cops all said."

"I'm going to need help with this," she said. "I'm going to need a lot of help and this is going to cost you. Big time. Piles of loot."

Johnson smiled and said, "I'll give you a defense that'll get me out of this, but I need one promise. You have to make sure the cops burn the body. You tell them that they have to cremate it. They only have sixty hours or so to get rid of it. Less now. It's been a couple of hours."

"Tom, you're not making any sense here. You trying to establish an insanity defense? They almost never work and when they do, you end up in a hospital."

He looked at her and kept his voice low. He said, "Miller has no family. Maybe you could get a court order saying that her religion demands that she be cremated. She has to be created by sundown the day after death or something like that for her religion."

"Tom, this isn't going to work." Then, a moment later, she asked, "Why does the body have to be cremated?"

"Because if it's not, the trouble gets deeper."

CHAPTER FOUR

Police Captain Steve Mitchell stood in the darkened hall of Mercy Hospital at night. The lights had been reduced, and the noise had been quieted to an occasional bark from one of the televisions, the quiet, distant bong of the nurse call button and a low murmur of voices.

He stood outside the partially closed door of Sarah Hartwell who had been brought to the hospital by ambulance and who, according to the doctor, had yet to regain consciousness. Her vital signs were being monitored carefully by both machinery and the nursing staff, and she seemed to be in no real life-threatening danger.

"So when can I talk to her?" Mitchell asked a man who had come from her room.

The doctor, a young man with short, dark hair, a wide face with hard, sharp features except for a rounded and somewhat large nose, said, "I would expect her to awaken this morning, but I don't think she'll be in any shape to talk."

"Meaning?"

"With this sort of a head injury, in fact with many severe injuries, there is an amnesia that follows. The victim might not remember anything in the hours leading up to the injury. Those memories have been wiped out, never fixed in the brain. I think that this facilitates the healing process."

"That still hasn't answered my question," said Mitchell, his voice slightly louder.

"When she awakens, she's going to be confused, and it will take her some time to sort it all out. She'll be groggy and probably need more sleep."

"I have to talk to her as soon as I can."

"Then check in with us later this morning or early afternoon. That's the best I can do."

Mitchell thanked the doctor and then walked down the hall to the elevators. He touched the button, glanced up to see where the elevator was, but the door opened immediately, almost as if it had been waiting.

He rode down, walked along a brightly lighted corridor, through an emergency room that was vacant and out into the parking lot. There was a hint of gray in the sky, telling him that the sun was about to rise. Even at that point, just before dawn, the air was heavy with humidity, and it was slightly uncomfortable, though the temperature had to be around seventy.

He found his car, unlocked the door and climbed in. For a moment he sat, quietly, looking down at the dirty floorboards. Finally, he put the key in the ignition and started the engine. With that, he closed the door, adjusted the radio, setting it on a classic rock station, and then turned on the police radio, setting it so that it was just slightly louder than the music.

Slowly, he drove over to the crime scene. He wanted to see what it looked like. He wanted to see if he could tell anything from the evidence at the scene. Something that Johnson had been reluctant to mention, or something that might provide some insight into the crime. It was his way of connecting to the crime and sometimes helped him when it was time to assemble the evidence. Of course, this was different because it wasn't a "whodunit." They had the perpetrator in custody.

To him, the murder made no sense, but then few of them did. Oh, he could understand a man shooting his wayward girlfriend or a wife killing an abusive husband. He didn't condone it, but he could understand the motivations behind it.

He could even understand, in an abstract way, why a serial killer would commit those crimes. In many of them it was some kind of compulsion they couldn't resist, and they saw everyone in the world as the players on their stage. The killer could eliminate those who had annoyed him or intrigued him and not worry about the act. His desire, his pleasure, took precedence over the lives of the victims.

But he had never, not once, been involved in a crime in which the killer had demanded, not asked, but demanded the body of the victim be burned. He seemed to be frightened by the fact he had been unable to burn the body. What strange compulsion made him want the body burned, now, with the police standing in the room with him? It certainly wasn't to destroy evidence.

He slowed for a red light, saw no other traffic on the streets around him, and drove through. There was no reason for him to stop at five in the morning with the streets deserted. The lights should be reset so they flashed at night, not require a full stop until a machine decided the traffic could begin to move again.

He turned down the street and about halfway down the block he saw four police cars. One was parked in the driveway, one on the street, and two on the lawn. Only one had its lights flashing, almost as if a beacon to draw in other cops. There was no need for the lights now.

Mitchell pulled up behind the car parked on the street, and then stepped out. A police officer, young, small, female, came toward him and then recognized him.

"Morning, Captain."

"Crime scene here yet?"

"No, sir. Anytime now. Jeffords is around back, watching that door, and Davis and Hamilton are back and now inside with the body."

"Coroner?"

"Been called but she probably won't arrive until after eight or something. The victim isn't going anywhere."

"Okay. Turn off the flashing lights, will you? We don't need them now."

"Yes, sir."

As she walked off toward the patrol car, Mitchell stepped onto the lawn. Grass was short, recently mowed. He stepped over a short, dense hedge that lined the sidewalk. The porch had three steps and was wide. The light was on, as if they were expecting visitors. He noticed that the newspaper, if they subscribed, had not been delivered, though police officers would probably have intercepted it if it had.

He opened the door, looked at the entryway. It was wide and long, with a rug over tile, maybe marble. There was a narrow table set to the right that held a plant, the mail and a set of keys. Nothing extraordinary about that.

To the left was the dining room that was so clean that it looked as if a meal had never been eaten in it. Directly ahead was the living room, or great room, which was very bright. He could see the overturned table and one foot of the victim.

He walked in, slid to the left, and into the kitchen. There was an officer sitting at the kitchen table and another sitting on a stool nearby. All the lights were on and it was bright enough to film for television.

Mitchell moved around without a word to either officer and looked down at the body. They had not covered it, pulled down the skirt, or touched it in any way. They knew, from hundreds of hours of police training and constant reminders on the job that the crime scene was not to be touched. A blanket was not to be put over the face of the deceased, and the body not to be touched, other than to make sure that it was dead. There would be no contamination of a crime scene by rookie cops who had more enthusiasm than brains. Besides, anyone who watched television would be aware of these simple procedures.

The blood near the head had begun to dry and turn black. There was a faint odor of shaved copper. Mitchell walked to the edge of the carpet and crouched down. He looked first at the face that was only slightly disfigured by the bullet hole in the forehead. There was little blood near it and a smudge of black stippling that suggested the barrel of the weapon was no more than three feet away. Johnson was not about to miss at that range.

She might have been a pretty woman. Certainly she was good looking, with long, dark hair that was now matted and stained with her blood. Her figure was good, maybe a little lean, and her legs were fine.

He shook his head and said, quietly, to himself, "What could she have done?"

The officer slid off the stool and asked, "You say something, Captain?"

Mitchell stood up and said, "Officer . . . Winters?"

"Yes, sir."

Winters was an older man, close to forty, with graying hair, a long, fleshy face, narrow eyes and large, jug-handle ears. Not ugly, but certainly not overly attractive. He was a good family man with two teenage daughters who gave them no trouble. A solid family man with a solid family.

"What can you tell me?"

"When I got here the party was practically over. I backed up the first units, saw the man drop his pistol to the carpet and then saw him handcuffed and taken out. Ambulance crew arrived, checked the injured woman, Sarah Hartwell, and determined that the other woman, Linda Miller, I think, was dead. Once the ambulance crew and the Hartwell woman were out of here, I secured the scene, awaiting the arrival of the techs and the coroner."

"You know what happened?"

"My best guess is that the suspect shot the Miller woman once in the head."

"You know why?"

"Nope. Only thing, he was getting hysterical, demanding that we burn the body. Yelled that we knew what happened so we didn't need the body."

"Takes all kinds," said Mitchell.

"You going to stay here, Captain?"

"Why?"

"Well, if you're going to wait for the crime scene guys, I could get back out on patrol."

"Go. I'll make sure that no one screws up the crime scene before the techs get here."

"Thanks, Cap."

"You have any idea why he shot her?"

"Nope. He only said that we needed to burn the body, and that just ain't going to happen."

Mitchell watched as Winters and the rookie officer walked the long way around to the door, avoiding the crime scene. They closed the door, and a moment later he heard a car engine start as they took their cruiser.

Now he stepped back and sat down at the kitchen table. It was wooden, with no tablecloth but with green-gray placemats. There was some kind of dried flower arrangement set in the center that matched, somehow, the placemats, adding a hint of color to the table.

Mitchell studied the crime scene, looking at it from the point of view of one who didn't know who had shot the woman. He was pretending that this was a fresh crime with the shooter long gone. This would be a "whodunit" if Johnson hadn't been caught in the room. So, what is out of place? What would give him the hints about the shooter?

Mitchell stood up and walked to the edge of the carpet. He crouched there and examined the dead woman carefully. Nothing to indicate a sexual assault, though her skirt had been flipped up, exposing her long legs.

There was a single gunshot wound to her forehead and a number of tiny cuts or abrasions to her face that didn't look like anything he had seen before. They didn't look like knife wounds, and no knife had been found.

There were some minor tears to her blouse and a little bit of blood staining it. Near the body were a number of splotches of red, looking as if someone had stamped on something that bled or someone had stamped on drops of blood. He didn't understand what those signified, but that might be cleared up as he talked to the first officers on the scene and to Johnson.

The front door opened and two men and a single woman entered. They stood still by the door, studying the scene, one man making notes while the woman took photographs of everything that she could see.

Mitchell left the kitchen, watched the technicians work for a moment and then stepped into the hallway. They didn't stop their work. They ignored him.

For a moment, Mitchell thought about giving them an order or two, to make sure that certain things were photographed or that certain evidence was collected, but he knew that they knew their job. He would just be in their way and probably annoy them by suggesting areas to collect. Instead, he moved past them and stepped out on the porch.

The sun was now up, the sky bright blue with only a few clouds. The ground was still wrapped in long shadows and there was a hint of heat. It was going to be a long, hot day.

CHAPTER FIVE

Thomas Johnson stood up and then began to pace, first toward the door and then toward the curtains. He felt tired, dirty and there was stubble on his face that had the roughness of sandpaper. He wanted to get some sleep but knew that wasn't going to happen for hours. Now he wondered if that knowledge, that he couldn't possibly catch a nap, made him feel more tired and more ragged than he was.

"Sit down, Tom," said Goldberg.

"I would like my breakfast."

"As would I, but that's not going to happen. You have to tell me about last night."

Johnson walked back to the table and sat down. He leaned forward on his elbows and looked into her eyes. He wanted her to understand that he was going to be telling her the whole truth and nothing but the truth. Unfortunately, he knew that she wasn't going to believe him.

"Do you think I could get something cold to drink?" asked Johnson.

"I don't think the cops are going to provide us with much of anything, given the nature of the case."

"Well, maybe you could bribe someone to find me a Coke or something. I think I'm suffering from terminal low blood sugar."

Goldberg stood up, walked to the door and touched the button there. She heard nothing and didn't know if it worked until the door opened and a man in civilian clothes appeared.

"Yeah?"

"Can we get a couple of Cokes in here?"

"Cost you four bucks," he said without hesitation.

Johnson grinned and said, "Go ahead, Rachael. You can always add it to the bill."

To the officer, she said, "How about I give you six bucks and you buy one for yourself? Then maybe find us a Danish to go with it."

"Are you attempting to bribe an officer of the law?"

"Yup."

"Done," he said and closed the door.

Goldberg returned to her chair, sat down, and then pulled her pad around so that she had it where she wanted it. "Now, what happened last night?"

"If you are going to understand any of this, I can't start with last night. I have to start long before last night."

Goldberg put her pen down and looked at him. "Did you kill that woman?"

"I killed Linda Miller," said Johnson.

Goldberg wasn't sure that she understood the distinction, but it was one that Johnson had been insisting on since she had arrived. "Okay."

"You want the whole story?"

"Yes."

Johnson sat quietly for a moment, as if gathering his thoughts, but he didn't say anything. He just sat there, looking at the curtains that hid the wall.

After a minute or so, the door opened and the plainclothes cop entered. He set a Coke in front of Goldberg, another in front of Johnson and then waited.

"You need something else?" asked Goldberg.

"There was a discussion of money?"

"There was a discussion of Danish, too," said Goldberg.

"They are making the run for donuts a little later this morning."

Goldberg smiled and said, "I'll have to owe you the money until I'm finished here."

"Listen, I'm not going to buy sodas for someone accused of murder. I don't care how pretty the attorney might be or how flimsy the evidence might be, I'm just not going to donate to the defense fund." He seemed to be genuinely angry that she hadn't produced the cash.

Goldberg reached into her briefcase, took out a wallet and found a five and a one. She handed the money to the cop and said, "That should take care of it."

"It surely does. If you need anything else, you know where the buzzer is."

"Thank you."

When the cop was gone and the door closed, Goldberg said, "Now is the time."

Johnson opened his Coke, took a sip and then set it back on the table. He scrubbed at his face with both hands, hoping that would wake him up. Finally, he leaned back in the chair and said, "Linda Miller arrived in town about three years ago. I think it was May."

CHAPTER SIX

Linda Miller, traveling on a Canadian passport that was forged, exited the Boeing aircraft into the jet way and thereby avoided the steady rain falling. She hurried forward, dodged around an elderly man and walked out into the terminal concourse. She blinked at the bright lights and held a hand up to shade her eyes as she studied the scene in front of her.

Although it was late, just after midnight, the terminal was crowded. There were even couples with small children, either walking toward the baggage claim area or moving down the concourse toward the departure gates. The tile floor and sterile walls bounced the sound around, creating an unpleasant undercurrent of noise.

Miller, dressed in a short T-shirt and a hip-hugging short skirt, caught a number of the businessmen staring at her as she walked by. Most of them were older, with graying hair and expanding waists. She ignored them, just happy that she could still turn heads.

At the baggage claim area she stood in the rear, wondering if those crowding forward believed it would make their luggage arrive faster. She'd seen the same thing in a hundred airports or on the docks, or anywhere else that travelers congregated. She smiled, thinking that humans never changed.

When her suitcase appeared, she shouldered her way through the crowd, snatched it from the carousel and then walked out of the terminal. There were taxis lined up waiting, and she got into one, setting the suitcase on the seat next to her.

The driver looked back over his shoulder, then grinned as he ran his eyes over her.

"Piedmont Hotel," she said.

"Piedmont it is."

The taxi pulled out of the line, slowed and then shot forward, slipping into a break in the traffic flow that seemed too small for it. Miller settled back in the soft seat of the taxi, amid the stale odors of Chinese food, someone's illegal cigar and a hint of perfume that might have been the aftershave of the driver. She closed her eyes, not interested in the bright lights or the freeway signs. She was tired from the long trip and the effort of hiding. She thought that she had gotten away clean, but sometimes, in the modern world, there were indications that couldn't be seen with the unaided eye. She'd had to move too fast to worry about any of that.

The cab slowed, stopped for a moment and then started again. They were now downtown, and even at the late hour there were people on the street. Not the kind of people that you would want to invite home to meet mom, but then, not all of them were hustlers or hookers or out to turn a fast buck. The club kids, those slumming, and the social anthropologists were out there too, maybe in numbers greater than those of the first group.

They turned a corner, onto a brightly lighted street that seemed to hold dozens of people, some in strange costumes, others in abbreviated costumes, and some looking as out of place as the palace guard at a hockey rink.

"How much farther, driver?"

"Couple of blocks, up on the right."

"Pull over. I want to walk now that the rain has finally stopped."

"Excuse me, ma'am, but I'm not sure that is such a good

idea, this time of the night."

"Just pull over."

There was a moment's hesitation and then the cab dived from the middle lane to the curb. The driver stared at the meter and then said, "That's twenty-two fifty."

Miller paid with a twenty and a five and told the driver to keep the change. She didn't wait for a receipt as she threw open the door, grabbed her suitcase and climbed out. She stood on the sidewalk for a few seconds, taking in the sights and the sounds and tasting the air around her.

A young man with spiked hair and more tattoos than found in a parlor stopped, looked her up and down slowly and nodded his approval. Miller turned a cold shoulder and began to walk toward the hotel.

The man, smoking a tiny cigarette, ran around to block her way and asked, "New in town?"

She glanced at the suitcase in her hand and said, "Brilliant deduction."

"I can help," he said.

"I don't need your help. Get lost."

"That's not very friendly."

Miller stopped walking, set her suitcase down on the sidewalk and immediately regretted the action. She didn't know what might have been thrown, dropped or spit onto the concrete. She studied the young man in front of her. He was wearing a dirty black T-shirt, grimy jeans that were torn in several places and scuffed boots. There was dirt under his fingernails, he needed a shave and he didn't smell all that great, proving that he was a hustler and not slumming. He just wasn't worth the effort, and she didn't know how contaminated he might be.

"Why don't you just go on your way and leave me alone. Before you get hurt."

The man flipped away his cigarette, grinned revealing broken, yellow teeth, and asked nastily, "And just how am I going to get hurt?"

Without warning, Miller stomped down on the top of his foot with her spiked heel, driving it deep and feeling one of the bones break. The man shrieked, the sound like tires on dry concrete, and dropped to the sidewalk. Blood stained his boot.

Miller grabbed her suitcase and stepped over the moaning man. Had he been a little cleaner, maybe a little nicer, she might have suggested something, but there were so many other men, and even a few women, who would be happy to help her.

She walked down the street rapidly, looking right and left, but trying not to seem the tourist. She got a feel for the neighborhood and then found the Piedmont. The front was narrow, almost invisible between the doors of a restaurant and a bar and grill, proving the hotel was exclusive. A man dressed in what looked to be a red and orange uniform touched the bill of his cap and then opened the door for her.

She walked through the narrow entrance, down a short, wide hallway, and then out into the open lobby of the first-class hotel. The floor was marble with dark green carpets scattered about. Each was anchored by two chairs, a sofa, end tables with lamps and a coffee table. The colors complemented the carpet and ran from dark to light.

She walked across the lobby and stopped at the reception desk. Suddenly she felt underdressed. She wished that she had worn a blouse and maybe a skirt that was a little longer. She felt like a hooker masquerading as a respectable lady.

The registration clerk glanced at her, apparently thinking the same thing. The clerk was a young woman dressed in a charcoal blazer and dark maroon pants. She looked elegant, understated and more than a little annoyed. With a voice filled with sarcasm, she asked, "How may I help you?"

"I'd like a suite, for about a week."

The clerk smiled, showing white, straight teeth. "They are quite expensive."

Miller pulled a small wallet from her skirt pocket and gave the clerk a platinum American Express card from it. "That cover it?"

The clerk looked at the name on the card, looked at Miller and said, "I'll need a driver's license."

"Will a passport do?"

"Certainly."

Miller handed it over, waited while the card was processed, and then accepted the plastic key inside the paper wallet. She glanced at the room number.

"Is there anything else?" asked the clerk.

"Nope. How late do you have room service?"

"I'm afraid that the kitchen closed at midnight."

Miller picked up her card, passport and the key. She grabbed her suitcase before a bellhop could be summoned, and walked from the lobby to the elevators and rode them up. She got off, found her room and opened the door. She had expected the interior to be dark, but there was a dim glow from a nightlight set off to the right, near the bathroom.

She entered. The sitting room had a short couch, probably a love seat, two chairs, a small table with two more chairs, and a big-screen, flat panel television hung near the floor-to-ceiling windows. Outside she could see the city, flashing, sparkling and glowing. There was an aircraft moving silently, slowly, across the night sky, looking like something from a futuristic science fiction film.

She went into the bedroom that had a large bed, a short sofa and an armoire that contained a second TV. There was a bathroom off to the right there too, but this one had a large tub and a long, two-sink vanity.

"Yes," she said out loud. "This will do quite nicely for now."

She set her suitcase on the bed, opened it and looked at the clothes. She wasn't sure what she wanted to wear, thinking in terms of the coming hunt. Her short skirt and short T-shirt would attract young men, but something more sophisticated might attract the older, more mature and certainly more well-off men. Someone who could supply money as well as energy.

She decided that she wouldn't change and wouldn't make a real effort. Tonight would be to learn the city, learn the right spots and she would begin her hunt tomorrow. There was no need to hurry now because she was in the clear.

She transferred some money into the small wallet, left her passport in the suitcase, figuring that she could pass for an American if the question came up, and if not, she could get her passport to prove she had legally entered the country, if that became necessary.

She walked back to the elevator, took it down and then left through a side door, out of the view of the desk clerk and the doorman. Out on the sidewalk, she saw a small group of people and followed them as they strolled along, talking, laughing, kissing and drinking. They would take her where she wanted to go.

The club was hidden behind a brightly colored door that had no sign, no hours of operation and nothing to indicate that it concealed a club. She followed the group through, saw the bouncer sitting on a stool looking bored and slipped into the gloomy interior. Music blasted from a band on a slightly raised stage at the far end of the huge, cavernous room. The dance floor was filled with gyrating people and opposite the band was a bar where people waited four and five deep to pay for overpriced drinks.

Miller shoved her way in amongst the dancers, and then began to move with the beat. There were so many people that no one could tell who was dancing with whom, so she didn't seem out of place. When the song ended, she left the dance floor and pushed her way toward the bar.

"Damn, it's noisy," said a voice in her ear.

She turned. A tall man, with broad shoulders, short hair and a narrow face was grinning at her. She smiled back and said, "Yes. Very."

"Can I buy you a drink?"

"Yes. That would be nice."

"What are you drinking?"

"Bloody Mary."

"You wait right here," he said and then forced his way to the bar.

Miller stood there and turned back so that she could look at the dance floor. There were so many people jammed together that it didn't seem that anyone could move. The whole crowd seemed to dance together almost as if it was a military formation.

Miller felt a tap on her shoulder and glanced back. The man held a drink up for her. She took it and sipped at it, staring up into his dark eyes.

"I haven't seen you around before," he said.

"I haven't been around before."

He grinned and said, "New in town, sailor?"

She looked at him blankly.

"It's a joke."

She raised an eyebrow but still said nothing.

He wiped his hand on his hip and held it out. "My name's Travis."

"I'm Jane," she lied.

"Well, Jane, it's awfully hard to talk in here. The band is too loud."

She lifted her drink to her lips and gulped it down. She grinned broadly and handed him the empty glass. "I'm ready to go whenever you are."

Vampyr?

They exited the club together and walked down the street, toward a lighted deli that was open, even that late. Travis held the door as they walked in and then found a small table toward the back.

"You hungry?" he asked.

"Yes," said Miller, "but not in the way you think. I'd just like a cup of coffee."

Travis walked back to the counter, ordered, turned and looked at Miller. He grinned broadly. When the order was ready, he paid and then made his way back to the table.

As he set the coffee in front of her, he asked, "So, where are you from?"

"Here and there. Depends on the time of the year and the mood that I'm in."

"Must be nice," said Travis.

They talked on, Miller sipping her coffee and Travis eating his sandwich. After thirty minutes, they left the deli, walking along the street that now held fewer people. Travis, impatient to conclude the evening, pushed Miller back into a narrow alley that smelled of garbage and urine. There were huge dumpsters, a dozen silver garbage cans and trash thrown everywhere. There might have been a couple of people there, sleeping or it might have just been tricks of the light playing across bundles of rags.

Thirty minutes later, satisfied by the target of opportunity, Miller emerged from the alley. Without a thought, she turned to the right and began the walk back to the hotel. Now she thought that she would sleep through the day without cravings waking her every hour or so. Now she could get some rest.

CHAPTER SEVEN

Goldberg looked up from her legal pad and asked, "Just how in the hell do you know all this?"

"I have been studying her for the last two years. I am going to do a book about her. It's a fascinating and unbelievable story."

"Well," said Goldberg, "I wish we had this Travis guy's last name."

"Travis Bonham."

"We'll need him for a witness, and I want to talk to him to make sure you have these events down in the right order. That'll provide some corroboration."

Now Johnson laughed, though there was no mirth in it. "He's dead. I thought I had made that clear. Miller had killed him to feed her hunger."

"You just said that she left the alley."

"And Travis remained behind. The police found him a day or so later."

Goldberg sat for a moment and then asked, "She killed him?"

"Deader than hell."

"There should be police reports and an autopsy report, of course."

"There are police reports and the autopsy said that he died of a combination of drugs, alcohol and blood loss, though they didn't explain the blood loss very well."

Goldberg stopped writing again and looked up, surprised. "Blood loss?"

"The police theory was that he injured himself, or he might have been mugged. There were two small wounds on his chest, neither of which should have been fatal, except for the combination of drugs and alcohol. With his blood thinned by the alcohol, and his heart racing because of the drugs, the wounds were of sufficient size and depth to kill him, they claimed. Case closed."

"That doesn't make any sense," said Goldberg.

"Sure it does. Bonham was a petty thief, part-time rapist or sexual abuser, and drug user. He lived, hand-to-mouth, never with more than twenty dollars in his pocket. He sponged off the girls he met, used them at his whim and then discarded them when he grew tired of them. I think the police were happy that the problem had been solved for them."

"I can verify this?" asked Goldberg.

"You can pull the police reports, you can get the autopsy and you can talk to the cops. But there is nothing to link Miller to his death. Nothing to suggest that she had caused it, or was responsible for it. All the police could learn was that he had coffee with a good-looking, slender, dark-haired woman about an hour before he died. They never did find her, though I don't think they looked very hard once they had the coroner's report in hand. That solved the case."

"So why didn't you give the lead to the police?"

"And tell them what? They could establish that she arrived in the city the day Bonham died, and they could verify that she checked into the hotel late on that day, but they couldn't connect her to him in any way. I had nothing to tell them that would have been of use to them. And, as I said, the case was closed."

"This isn't going to help you," said Goldberg, looking up from her notes.

"I thought you were interested in why Linda Miller is dead. I was giving you, am giving you, the reasons. But you have to

41

understand the whole story."

There was a tap at the door and the cop who had brought the Cokes opened it. "We've got to take this guy over to the court for the arraignment."

"I'm not finished here," said Goldberg.

"Not my problem, counselor."

Goldberg flipped the pages back on her legal pad so that the cop couldn't read them. Then she slipped the pad into her briefcase.

"Okay, Tom, I'll meet you over at the courthouse. We'll plead not guilty of course."

The cop snorted. "Why not plead guilty and save everyone a lot of work, time and effort?"

"Thank you for your legal expertise, but our trial strategy is none of your concern," said Goldberg.

"Defense attorneys. Never interested in the truth. Just want to get their guy off."

"Officer," said Goldberg, "the accused is presumed innocent unless and until proven guilty. Hell, at this point, you don't know the situation, so I will thank you to keep your legal opinions to yourself."

"And, I now must take your innocent client to the holding cell until we move him to the courthouse. You can resume your work when that has been accomplished."

Goldberg reached across the table and touched the back of Johnson's hand. "Tom, you say nothing to these people. You don't engage in conversation about the weather, the time of day, or the latest movie. They are not your friends, though they'll try to convince you that they only have your welfare at heart. They are the enemy team on this. They have a different agenda than I do, so don't trust them."

"Sure, Rachael, I understand that."

"Most people don't. And remember too that these guys are a

lot smarter than they seem. They'll trip you up in a minute, and you'll find yourself in more trouble."

"I don't have anything to hide," said Johnson.

"Christ, Tom, haven't you been listening? They think they've got you cold here . . ."

"But they . . ."

"Shut up," she yelled. "Just shut the fuck up. You are not to talk to these people about anything. You just sit quietly and do not engage in conversation with any of them. I don't know how to make this any clearer."

"I understand, Rachael," he said, surprised by her tone, anger and obscenity.

She stood up, straightened her jacket and then snapped the catches on her briefcase. "Okay. I'll see you at the arraignment. You don't have to speak unless the judge asks you a specific question. You don't answer until I tell you that you can, and then you say as little as possible. We're not going to hand these people anything. You understand?"

"Yes."

When Goldberg was gone, the cop motioned Johnson to stand. He said, "You come with me and if you try anything, I'll make sure that you can't walk for a long time. I'll kick your kneecap into next week."

Johnson, following his instructions, stood but said nothing to the cop.

They walked back down the hallway and then entered another room, this one larger, filled with desks and detectives sitting behind some of them. A few of the detectives were on telephones. Others were standing near a long, narrow window that looked out and down on the street. They were standing there not to look out, but because the coffee pot and a box of donuts were sitting on a small table pushed into a corner under the window. They were talking quietly amongst themselves, unaware that Johnson had been escorted into the squad room.

They crossed the stained carpet to the holding cell that was as far from the door and the windows as it could be. Johnson caught a glimpse of the street and was surprised to see people walking around. He thought it was early in the morning, and then noticed the clock. It was nearly ten.

Time was running and he felt a momentary sense of panic. He swallowed it, telling himself there was more than two days left. He could get something arranged in the next two days.

The cop unlocked the cell door and Johnson stepped in. He sat down on the hard wooden bench as the cop closed and then locked the door. He leaned back and closed his eyes, wondering how long it would be before he could catch a nap.

He was aware of someone standing close, near the cell door, and opened his eyes. The man was big, wearing a sport coat and brown trousers, a dusting of powdered sugar on one lapel. He looked mean and he looked unhappy, but he somehow didn't look like he was a detective.

"You Johnson?"

"Yes."

"Okay. We're going over to the courthouse. I'll be taking you. Me and two uniformed officers. You try anything and these young guys will run you down, if I don't shoot you first. You got that?"

"Yes, I understand."

The cop opened the door and let Johnson out. He put a hand on Johnson's shoulder and said, "Put your hands behind you."

"Is this necessary?"

"Standard procedure. You know how people get fucked up? They ignore procedure. Figure the little woman can be no danger and the next thing they know, they're hanging onto their nuts while the little woman is running down the road waving bye-bye. So, yeah, this is necessary and I don't want no lip about it."

Johnson, without another word, complied. Then he stood there, waiting. Finally, the cop pushed him toward the door, and about the time they reached it, two uniformed officers entered. Johnson recognized one of them as the young cop, Davis, from the night before. He was about to greet Davis when he remembered what Goldberg had told him, so he said nothing.

The big cop, with his hand back on Johnson's shoulder, steered him through the door, down the hall, down the stairs and out onto the sidewalk. Across a narrow band of green, which had a couple of trees and one concrete-surrounded flower bed, was the courthouse, looking like a gothic castle complete with a turret. It was all made of huge blocks of rough-cut gray stone. It was the appropriate building for all this, Johnson decided.

They took him down a narrow set of stairs, into the basement area of the building. They were among a series of cells, most of them open and empty. One woman sat on a wooden bench at the rear of a cell crying softly. No one paid any attention to her.

Johnson was put into a cell by himself that had nothing in it other than the wooden bench. It was clear that the cells had been designed simply to hold prisoners waiting to go to court and not for an extended period of imprisonment.

He turned, felt the cuffs removed, and as the door clanged shut, Davis stepped forward and asked, "You need anything?"

"Restroom."

"On the way upstairs," said Davis.

"How long?"

Davis looked over his shoulder and the big cop said, "Shouldn't be more than twenty minutes."

"That work?" asked Davis.

"Fine."

Johnson walked to the rear and sat down. A moment later, thinking that it made no difference, he laid down, an arm over his eyes to block the bright overhead light. Somewhere he could hear water dripping and wondered, just for a moment, if that was some sort of psychological device to make the prisoners more uncomfortable. He decided that there was no one in the police department or the prosecutor's office who was smart enough, or devious enough, to set up something like that.

What seemed to be an instant later, he heard his name being repeated over and over, and sat up.

Davis was standing there. Johnson slowly got to his feet, groggy, his eyes filled with sand and his mouth dry. He shouldn't have fallen asleep. It just made him feel worse.

"Let's go. We just have time to stop off at the restroom," said Davis.

Johnson waited until the cell door swung open and then stepped out.

Davis said, "You give me any trouble, and I'll shoot you full of holes."

They then walked down a narrow hallway with a stone floor and white-painted plaster walls. They moved through a door, climbed a set of stairs and exited into a much larger hallway that was, more or less, the foyer to one of the courtrooms.

Davis pointed him to a restroom, but followed him in. Johnson used the facility and then walked to the sink. He ran water, washed his hands and then washed his face. He wished he could shower and then lay down for a few hours. The next time he shot someone, it was going to be in the early morning so that he wouldn't have his day turned upside down, or end up being awake for thirty, thirty-five hours.

Davis escorted him into the courtroom, and a moment later the bailiff called the case number. Johnson was pushed forward through the gate and toward Goldberg, who was already at one of the two tables facing the judge, sitting high on her bench.

The bailiff read the charges, which included resisting arrest and illegal possession of an unregistered firearm. He also mentioned capital murder.

Johnson leaned close to Goldberg and asked, "What's this crap about capital murder?"

Goldberg turned her head and snapped, "Be quiet."

The judge asked, "How do you plead?"

Goldberg, not waiting for Johnson, said, "Not guilty. Request bail."

"Prosecution?"

"This was a heinous crime with one woman dead, shot in the head by the defendant. There are eyewitnesses and forensic evidence that put him at the scene of the murder and make him the trigger man."

Johnson said, "They haven't had time to develop the forensic evidence."

Goldberg ignored him and said, "Your honor, my client has strong ties to the community, is not a risk to anyone and has been a model citizen for his entire life. There is no risk of flight. Bail is requested."

"Your honor," said the prosecutor, "he resisted arrest and has traveled extensively in Europe and South America in the last several years. He has enough money to leave the country immediately if he is so inclined."

"Bail is denied," said the judge. She looked at the prosecutor and then at Goldberg, as if waiting for one or the other to say something more.

"Well," said Goldberg quietly, "now you know why they charged capital murder and resisting arrest. Hard to get bail under those circumstances."

"So what's next?"

"I'll appeal and try to get a reasonable bail set. You'll go back to the jail for the time being. The police are going to want to talk to you, but you say nothing to them and make sure they all understand that you are represented by an attorney. You are not required to answer any of their questions."

"Okay, Rachael. Can you get me out?"

She shook her head. "I don't think so, Tom. At least not today, but I'm sure going to try."

CHAPTER EIGHT

Captain Steve Mitchell stood in the cold, stainless steel world of the morgue and watched as the pathologist, Doctor William C. Blanchard, circled the body, almost like a predator looking for the soft tissues. The body of Linda Miller was naked, the sheet having been removed so that Blanchard could do his work.

Blanchard was an older man, within a few years of retiring. He was short and stocky, with salt-and-pepper hair and a van Dyke that he thought gave him an academic appearance. His wife was long gone and while he let people think she had died, she had just left him, taking their only child with her. He'd seen neither in more than a decade and that suited him fine because it gave him the opportunity to pursue his own work. He thought of himself as a biologist and was just waiting for the one case, the one body, the one sample that would propel him into the scientific spotlight.

The morgue was the most modern of the rooms in the building that held a police laboratory, an investigator's room, a half a dozen offices and one small lunch room. The morgue had bright lights, two hanging down from the ceiling that could be maneuvered by the pathologist and bright enough to illuminate the moon. The table, just over waist high, was of stainless steel and had a small trough around it to drain away bodily fluids. The table could be lifted, lowered, or tilted at the whim of the pathologist, giving him or her access to the body and its various structures and internal organs.

Blanchard, having already given his name and provided the time and the date, began the narration of the procedure. He would talk all the way through the procedure, using the recording to take his notes, and then using the transcript of that record to prepare his final report.

To Mitchell he said, "I see one gunshot wound to the head, an entrance wound, but I see no evidence of an exit wound." He reached down with a gloved hand and then added, "I misspoke. I feel a wound in the back of the head, but it seems smaller. Not at all like an exit wound."

"He used a jacketed round. Jacketed in silver," said Mitchell. "We looked at the rounds left in the weapon."

"Silver," said Blanchard, grinning. "You know what that sounds like?"

"Of course. It takes all kinds."

Blanchard then turned down the lights in the morgue and used a black light to scan the body, finding traces of fluids and a couple of fibers, tiny little threads, that he collected into evidence envelopes. He also took samples of the fluids for later analysis, though he didn't believe they would reveal anything of value.

With the lights back on, he began to examine the wounds carefully, beginning with the gunshot to the head. It was centered on the forehead about half an inch above the eyebrows. There was stippling around it, telling him that the barrel had not been more than two or three feet from the victim and that the power used in the round was not of commercial quality. It seemed to be a low-grade black power that suggested the round had been hand loaded. With what Mitchell had said about it being silver, it indicated that Johnson might have made it himself or had it made for him by someone who was capable but not expert in the creation of ammunition.

He carefully probed the wound and then lifted and turned

the head so that he could look at what he thought was the exit wound. Normally, the exit wound would be larger, shattering part of the skull as the forces of the bullet passing through the brain and creating hydrostatic shock were transferred to the bone. This round had punched right through without creating the normal, massive damage. At first Blanchard thought, because it was a hand-loaded round, it had been hot, meaning overly powerful. It had punched through everything so quickly that the forces had not built up properly to smash the skull, but that didn't seem quite right.

He bent down, pulled the light around and used a magnifying glass. He said, for both the digital recording and for Mitchell, "The skull is exceptionally heavy, more than a quarter inch thicker than normal."

Mitchell asked, "Is that significant?"

"Only in that she could take a blow to the back of the head with a baseball bat that would kill a normal human. Her skull is exceptionally strong."

Blanchard laid the head back facing up, making it look as if she was attempting to sun herself. He used the magnifying glass on the face, looking at the wounds there. They seemed to be surface scrapings, shallow gouges in the flesh that in some cases didn't even reach below the surface of the skin. He had no idea what could have made them.

He pointed at one and asked Mitchell, "Do you know what might have caused these?"

"No clue."

"I've never seen anything like them. A little painful. Maybe a little annoying, but that would be all."

"She has a couple on her right side and one on her belly," said Mitchell.

"I'll get down to those."

He moved down the body carefully but found no other wounds except for those that Mitchell had mentioned. He examined the scrape marks but they were identical to those on the face. One of them might have bleed heavily, being just a little deeper than the others, but Blanchard didn't know, and it was obvious to him that the gunshot wound was the cause of death.

He did examine each limb carefully but found no signs of trauma to either with the exception of a small scrape on the inside of the left thigh that was indicative of nothing at all, other than a small, normal-looking scratch. He noticed that she had shaved herself so that there was no trace of pubic hair.

Blanchard continued to dictate his findings as he examined the body, occasionally glancing up at Mitchell who looked disinterested. Finally, Blanchard stepped back from the table and said, "I'm going to open her up now."

Mitchell grinned because Blanchard always made that announcement to frighten the rookies. Mitchell had seen so many autopsies that the sight of a body being cut open in such a gross fashion no longer bothered him. It was all as if it was a giant Hollywood special effect designed to make the teenagers faint.

Blanchard made the long cuts in the torso and folded back the skin. A stench, an almost visible cloud of odor, rose from the body. Even Blanchard took a step back, giving the stink a chance to dissipate.

"Wow," said Blanchard. "Was that foul or what?"

Mitchell had turned his head and taken a deep breath from the little clean air that remained.

Blanchard looked down into the incision and said, "Well, this isn't right."

Mitchell took a step closer but saw nothing but the mass of tissue that filled the inside of a human chest. He recognized the lungs and thought he saw the heart, but there were a couple of lower organs that didn't look quite right and that he didn't recognize at all.

Blanchard reached up for the light and pulled it around so that it was focused directly on the chest. He probed with his fingers, pushed a mass to one side and then leaned forward, looking down.

"Looks as if the stomach has atrophied a bit. Looks like a vestigial organ that wasn't used much. I can't find the gall bladder, but I didn't see any scars to indicate surgery. The liver is shriveled and hardened. I see that the heart is enlarged and the lungs are well developed."

He kept probing rather than conducting the autopsy because the chest was odd. More than odd. It was almost impossibly different from that of other humans. He could find most of the organs, but their orientation was shifted around slightly to make room for a couple that he didn't really recognize. He thought of elementary biology and the studies of mutations, but this seemed to be far beyond this.

Blanchard looked at Mitchell and said, "If we were in an anatomy class in which the assignment was to reproduce the human chest with the proper organs in the proper place, this would be a failure."

"Meaning?"

"Meaning I don't know how this woman lived as long as she did. The digestive system, and I only glanced at it, is all out of whack. The liver is misshapen and hard. The heart is enlarged, as are the lungs. The arteries are oversized as well. Her chest is a real mess. She must have had a history of chest trouble. Of medical trouble, but I don't see any attempts to correct these problems surgically. This woman should have died in childhood. In fact, she would have been lucky to survive infancy."

"But the gunshot is what killed her," Mitchell said, suddenly afraid that Blanchard would create the reasonable doubt that would put Johnson back on the street. He didn't like complications, and this autopsy was becoming quite complicated.

"Well, until I look into the skull, I can't give you a finished opinion, but the lack of injury to any other part of the body would suggest that. I mean, from what you said, she was alive until she was shot, so the conclusion is that it was the shot that killed her. I'll also run the tox screens, but she doesn't look like a drug user, so I doubt that we'll find anything there that would have killed her, and I seen no signs of poison, though some are very difficult to detect."

"But the gunshot killed her, right?" repeated Mitchell.

"Yeah, the gunshot killed her," said Blanchard, "I'm pretty sure of that."

"Not pretty sure. Sure," said Mitchell. "I'll need a complete report as soon as you can get it."

"Certainly." Blanchard hesitated for a moment, and then to complicate things even more, said, "You realize, if I didn't know better, I'd say that this wasn't a human body."

CHAPTER NINE

With the arraignment over, with his mug shots and fingerprints taken, with the paperwork completed and with no detective wishing to question him about anything, Johnson was taken to the jail and assigned to a cell. It was a modern cell with bright lights, plumbing that not only worked but looked as if it had been cleaned recently, a single bunk bolted to the metal wall that held a thick mattress, a blanket and a pillow. There were earphones so that he could watch the television mounted high on the wall, outside his cell where neither he nor the other prisoners could get at it to smash it. This was a modern jail built to convince the prisoners to behave so that the staff would have as little trouble from them as possible.

He used the toilet and then washed his hands. He sat on the surprisingly comfortable bunk, and realized that he still hadn't eaten, but he didn't care. He wasn't hungry at the moment. Not thirsty either. At the moment all he could hear was the bailiff, or the judge, or someone saying, "Capital murder."

That meant he could get the death penalty if they could prove he'd killed a human. If they could prove the special circumstances, and if they could make the resisting arrest charge stick. Lots of ifs.

And with that, he realized he didn't know where the body was. He didn't know what they were doing with it. He stood up and walked to the cell door. He leaned against the cool, smooth bars and tried to see down the hallway to the central desk where the guards and sheriff's deputies sat watching everything on closed-circuit television.

He yelled, "Hey. I want my attorney."

There was no response from the guards. There was a grunt from the cell next to him, but Johnson paid no attention to it.

"I want my attorney."

He kept shouting every ten or fifteen seconds until one of the large deputies lumbered down the corridor, moving slowly, looking from side to side as if he were an elephant surveying all that he ruled.

He stopped in front of the cell, put his hands on his hips and stared. He had short-cropped hair, a heavy brow ridge, a large, bulbous nose, but a small mouth with thin, almost invisible lips. His shirt was stretched tight across his massive chest, and he had narrow hips and almost spindly legs, looking as if he had been assembled from spare parts. The silver nameplate said, "Richard Sheffield."

"Now, Mr. Johnson," he said in a rather high, thin voice. "We don't shout down the hallway here. We use that nice little red button, over there, near your bunk, so that you don't disturb your friends. Now, I'm going to overlook this transgression because you are new to our facility and might not have been aware of the rules here."

"Yes, yes. I'm sorry about that. But I really need to see my attorney."

"You may call her, during our scheduled exercise activity." He looked at his watch. "In three hours."

"I need to talk to her now. I have the right to a telephone call."

"Well, I'm not sure that it's a right but, as a matter of courtesy, we allow you to make a telephone call. Now, you had yours this morning. You have the right to remain silent, but I don't notice you using it."

"I want to talk to my attorney and you have no right to stop me."

Sheffield laughed. "Mr. Johnson, you're in a cell. You have been charged with a crime, and I am under no obligation to do anything for you. Now, let's just keep that in mind."

"I have to talk to my attorney."

"And talk to her you shall, but you must wait until the exercise period to use the telephone. Now, no one is attempting to interrogate you, no one is abusing you and you have been provided with every luxury available in this facility. I don't want to have any trouble with you that will, of course, result in the revocation of some or all of your privileges. Have I made myself clear?"

"Could you pass a message on to her that I need to see her now?"

"Why in the world would I do that after just having explained to you, in great detail, our procedures here?"

There was a quiet crackle, and the small radio attached to Sheffield's uniform announced, "Hey, Dick, if you're down there near Johnson, bring him up. His attorney is here."

Sheffield grinned and said, "See? Good things come to he who waits patiently. Now, step back from the door."

When Johnson had complied, Sheffield ducked his head and keyed the mike on his small radio. "Open twenty-one, please."

There was a subtle pop and then a loud buzz as the door slid to the right. Sheffield took a step back, out of the way, but kept his attention focused on Johnson. He said, "Come forward and turn right."

With Sheffield a step behind him, Johnson walked down the corridor to the central control area and then was directed to a bright red door that was in stark contrast to the muted tones and colors of the rest of the facility. He was told to go in and to have a seat. A moment later the door opened again and

Goldberg, carrying her briefcase, entered. When she sat down, the door was closed and locked.

She opened the briefcase and said, "Okay. Here's the deal. I haven't been able to get bail set or the charges reduced, but I'm still working on that."

"Which means," said Johnson, "I remain here."

"For the time being, yes, but at least you have a cell to yourself, and they'll be giving you three meals a day."

"They wouldn't let me call you."

Goldberg stopped shuffling the papers and said, "No, they have strict telephone policies. I asked them about that already. Just checking on the procedures here."

Johnson sat back and seemed to slump into the chair. He looked smaller, tired and defeated. His skin was gray and his eyes were cloudy. He looked like he was sick and might not survive the night if something wasn't done.

Goldberg reached out, touched his hand and said, "You've got to hang in there, Tom. These things take some time. We'll get it all resolved."

"What have they done with the body?"

"It's undergoing autopsy."

For the first time he grinned slightly. Then, almost as if speaking to himself, he said, "Okay. That buys us some time. When they're finished, they've got to burn it. Not bury it, but burn it. They can't hang on to it as evidence. They have got to destroy it as soon as they can."

"Why? What makes that so important?"

"We have to destroy the body so that she doesn't come back," said Johnson, sounding reasonable with his completely unreasonable statement.

"I'm afraid that I don't understand that."

Johnson realized how it sounded and added, "Disease. Burning destroys the virus." He realized how lame that sounded.

"She was infected with something?"

"Yeah. It's not real contagious, but there is a possibility. Burning will destroy the virus."

Goldberg made a note and said, "I'll pass that along, but it really will be up to the next of kin."

"She doesn't have any. She was traveling in this country with a Canadian passport. She was using it for identification, but she isn't Canadian. She was from Europe."

Goldberg held up a hand to stop him. "This is getting confusing, and I'm not sure that it's relevant."

Johnson said, "I'm just trying to save us all some trouble. We can stop this thing now."

"Look, Tom, you're in a great deal of trouble here and these digressions aren't helping the matter."

"But you have to understand what is going on. If you understand that, then I can get out of this thing. I can get out of jail."

Goldberg shook her head. "I think you'd better get used to the idea that you're going to spend some time in here. You were standing over the dead body with the gun in your hand. I can't tell you how bad that makes you look."

"But I saved Sarah. She's okay, isn't she? She'll back up what I say."

"Ms. Hartwell is in the hospital and the police have yet to take her statement."

"Okay," said Johnson. "This will all get straightened out when Sarah talks to the police. Then I'll go home."

Goldberg took her pad out of her briefcase. "Tom, we've got a lot of work to do here, and I don't want to get sidetracked on all this trivia. I need to know some more about Miller's background so that I can start building the defense."

"You just write down the names I give you. That and the locations, and you'll be able to verify all this and that'll change the strategy."

"How did you meet Miller?"

CHAPTER TEN

Johnson took a deep breath, as if he was about to plunge into a cold lake and really did not want to make the jump. He began his narrative:

The hotel made a good, temporary quarters, but Linda Miller knew that she couldn't stay there forever. The bill would become huge, forcing her to tap into her reserves, and that would cause someone, Interpol, Scotland Yard, the Mounties, or the FBI, to begin to take a look at her, especially in a world that was full of paranoia about terrorists and terrorist plots. That would involve the INS and Homeland Security and maybe even the CIA and certainly the IRS, not to mention the FBI. Such attention would focus the spotlight on her rather stateless existence, her fake passport and her fortune that was more than seven hundred years old. All of that would cause questions that she would rather not answer and in some cases couldn't answer.

Sitting in the chair, the curtains opened so that she could see the sunlit city, it was no longer so easy. Life had been simpler before everyone had a computer that could cross check everything in a matter of seconds, searching worldwide databases for any information that related to her. Immigration would see that she had not entered the United States legally, because they would learn that she had not entered Canada legally. Her exit, if it could be traced, would show that she had left Germany illegally on a Belgian passport that belonged to a little girl who had died a few years earlier and that she had stolen. In other words, that passport was illegal as well.

Oh, it would take the police agencies weeks to trace everything, but they would be able to do it because today's world left a paper trail and an electronic trial and there was no way to avoid it. Cash, which once had been king, was reduced to the point of unimportance as plastic took over. Plastic credit cards, plastic driver's licenses, plastic passports, all geared to magnetic strips that contained way too much personal information that sometimes included a DNA coding. There was no longer an easy way to remain in the background.

The old days, which weren't all that long ago, had allowed her to move through parts of the world with little notice. Sprinkling cash here and there, and giving men a little bit of a hard luck story, and she could vanish for months at a time. Now, cash sometimes called attention to her, and she still had to provide some kind of identification to the hotel clerks so that they would give her a room, to banks so they would surrender her money to her, and to any police official who asked. There were tougher customs regulations, airline clerks drunk with power to deny seats and government officials at every turn searching for the slightest taint. Names on "no fly" lists, and locked into computers and passed around to police and intelligence agencies. Soon, she would have to explain her age, her fortune, her heritage and her very existence.

She stood up and walked to the sliding glass door that looked out on the small balcony. There were two chairs and a small table out there, both looking as if they could stand to be hosed down. They looked dirty, which surprised her. It was a high-class hotel, and she would have thought they would routinely maintain the furniture on the balconies.

She opened the door and listened to the sounds of the city. The understated roar of the traffic, the periodic horn with a shrill blare cutting through, and the sound of a hundred air conditioners all fighting the beginnings of the morning heat. Sounds that were now familiar to her, just as familiar as the different sounds of routine had been in a different time and in a different place.

Finally, she closed the door and walked back into the bedroom. She finished dressing, opting for a conservative suit with a knee-length skirt and a light jacket with a tiny gold pin stuck on the lapel. Elegance with a hint of wealth. Just the image that she needed now in the bright sunlight.

She left the room, took the elevator to the lobby and then had the doorman signal for a cab. She handed him a bill for his trouble, trying to make the tip large enough that he wouldn't feel slighted, but small enough that it wasn't memorable.

She rode to a real estate office, talked to the manager and told him that she wanted a small house with easy access to the city but with some privacy. She wanted something where she might entertain close friends, but nothing that was too large because she just didn't feel like finding the proper staff. Something where she could hire a cleaning service and a yard care service, and let it go at that. No live-in maid or cook. Just some temporary help on the inside.

They toured a number of neighborhoods, looking at houses that needed repair, houses that stood surrounded by their neighbors that looked more like fish bowls than houses, at places that were too small and others that were too large. It seemed that there was nothing in the city that would meet her needs until they came to a house on a cul-de-sac that had trees in the back, and no real way to see the neighbors' houses without an effort. It had four bedrooms, a formal dining room, a large great room, a medium kitchen and more finished space in the lower level. Miller liked it almost immediately. It had an elegance that was understated and suggested a hint of wealth but nothing that stood out or called attention to her.

"This is home," she said to the realtor after they had walked up to the front door. Although she didn't need to see the interior, she went through the motions to please her companion. They wrote an offer, she paid cash, transferred by wire from Germany to the Bahamas and then to the mortgage company. With the transaction completed she then had nothing more to do with either the bank or the realtor, not realizing that although she had used only cash for the house, she had alerted various government agencies that didn't like ordinary citizens moving money around electronically. She had found her house, and now she attempted to sever all ties with those who had helped her find it, buy and pay for it and who might identify her later.

She ordered some furniture, but only the basics. She didn't bother with a telephone, though in a world of cell telephones and Internet telephones, it didn't matter much. She didn't order cable or satellite television because wireless connection gave her everything she needed, and only contacted the electric company and the water company because they would send people around to cause trouble if she didn't.

With her hideout finished, with furniture delivered, she took a taxi to the Ford dealer and bought herself the latest Taurus, paying for it with cash. Well, a check really, and having the papers, once signed and documented, sent to her. She didn't want to do that, but she couldn't take possession of the car without some of the proper documents, no matter how much cash she was prepared to spend. Besides, the banks wouldn't clear the check for five working days, though they admitted that her account had plenty of money to cover it. Local laws said that she had to give them proof of insurance as well. More bureaucratic meddling that opened her life up to public scrutiny.

Now she had everything that she needed to begin. She was in the city, she had transportation, a base, and was as anonymous as she could be in the electronic world where everything seemed to be within easy access of the Internet. She had wiped away as many of the traces as she could, and if she learned that someone had found them, well, she could find a new identity just as easily as she had found the one she now held.

Johnson fell silent, having given Goldberg what he believed to be a detailed description of the movements of Linda Miller when she first arrived. He closed his eyes for a moment and wished that he could go to sleep, at least for a few minutes.

"How do you know all this?" she asked.

"Put it all together while I was investigating her. It wasn't hard. Talked to realtors, talked to the Ford people, talked to the various companies, and I talked to her. Didn't tell her what I was doing, just talked to her casually."

"Then you knew her?"

Johnson seemed startled by the question. "Of course I knew her. You don't think I would have shot her if I didn't know what I was doing, do you?"

"Just what were you doing?"

"I was writing a book. I wanted to write about how people could get into the country, establish themselves, and no one would be the wiser. We all worried about terrorists coming in from all over, especially if they were young Arab males, and that they could sneak across the border and disappear into the undercurrent of society. There were others who came in, on aircraft, who actually went through customs, or just drove across the border legally and never bothered to return to their homes. I thought it an interesting story."

"How did you meet her?" asked Goldberg, realizing that Johnson had never answered the question.

"At a small dinner party that Sarah held. She wanted to get some of her single friends together, hoping that she could get them hooked up. Sarah was always the matchmaker. I was at the party as a place holder and began talking to Miller. I noticed she had a slight accent. Not much. Her English was very good, but once in a while she would say a word with a definite Eastern European flavor to it. So I began to talk about immigration with her."

"You thought this was an interesting story?"

"Given all that had happened in the world, I thought that I could interest any number of magazines in just such a piece. The INS had already said they really had no idea who was in the United States illegally. Students just overstayed their visas and no one came looking for them. Thousands crossed the borders from Canada or Mexico, legally crossed, but then remained here. Thousands more, those poor souls, tried to cross illegally and were preyed on by vultures on both sides of the border. But those who came in, established themselves, had money, seemed to be the story that no one else was investigating. And terrorists, if nothing else, are well financed."

"You thought she was a terrorist?"

"No, I thought that she might be an illegal immigrant and I wanted to learn more about her."

"And she went along with this? She helped you point your finger at her?"

Johnson laughed. "Of course not. I didn't tell her I was writing a story. I just got friendly with her and we would chat. Maybe have lunch."

Goldberg shook her head. "And then you shot her?"

"Well, it wasn't quite like that, but yes. There was no other choice, because I learned what she really was."

CHAPTER ELEVEN

Mitchell returned to the station and walked up the stairs to the main reception area with its bulletproof Plexiglas protecting the desk sergeant. The desk sergeant still sat at a high desk, but now there were metal detectors and other sensors arrayed across it for him. There was also a computer monitor, a keyboard and mouse, not to mention an audio input, digital cameras, and access to all law enforcement databases around the world through the computer. There should have been two officers at the computer station, but at the moment there was only one.

Mitchell waved and then shoved open the door to the stairwell. Sometimes, just for the hell of it, he walked the three flights up to his office. The elevator was a hassle and the exercise would do him good. He had read that taking the stairs would strengthen his heart, increase his circulation, lengthen his life and reduce his waist. It did so much good according to so many people that Mitchell wished he could find a way to bottle it and make himself rich.

He entered his office, which was small, barely large enough for his desk, computer, credenza, telephones, and a short, narrow bookcase that held few books but lots of paper. He opened the blinds, blinked at the bright sun, but left them open. It just seemed jollier with the blinds open, except on an overcast or rainy day. Then it was depressing.

On his desk was a single-page report. The computer printout gave the basic information, and if he wanted to see everything, then all he had to do was access it on his computer. The tox screen and the preliminary DNA of Linda Miller had already been completed. There were no drugs or chemicals that suggested Miller had been an addict of any kind. But the DNA test was a mess.

Mitchell sat there for a moment, trying to figure out what it meant. Finally, he turned, pulled the mouse around and began to work his way through the various windows, reading bits and pieces of the DNA report. If he understood the report, there were a dozen or more blood samples. He could have believed three, Miller, Johnson and the unconscious woman, Hartwell. But where did all the other blood samples come from? Obviously there had been contamination, either at the scene or in the lab. Too much DNA for so simple a case and Mitchell didn't know what it meant.

He reached out for the telephone, dialed the number that was printed on the computer screen DNA report and wound his way through the voice mail and computerized answering service. He grinned as he realized that whoever had invented the software that created answering programs should be shot. It took a job away from a human, but were so easy to install that everyone had them. It was the curse of the century.

Finally, he heard a human voice and said, "This is Captain Mitchell. Who are you?"

"Denise Douglas at the lab. How might I help you, Captain?"

"I have the DNA results on the Miller case."

"Preliminary results," said Douglas.

"All right, preliminary. What I don't understand is that you found a dozen different blood types and DNA?"

Douglas said, "Hang on for just a moment, please, Captain." She set the phone down and came back nearly five minutes later. "Sorry, I had to search. Now, what is the problem?"

"The number of DNA, what, strands, you found."

"Yes. I see that we have isolated DNA from fourteen individuals here. Quite a mess, actually."

"How can that be?"

"The samples that were provided contained the DNA from fourteen individuals," said Douglas reasonably.

"At most, there should have been three, but in reality, probably only one."

"What can I tell you? We isolated the DNA. There is no question about the accuracy of our tests. We ran them twice to make sure."

"Could the sample have been contaminated at the lab?" asked Mitchell.

"Of course, it could have, Captain. But the reality is that it wasn't. The blood contained those fourteen different DNA samples. I can tell you, based on the simple genetic tests we ran, that you have two black men and an Asian woman in the mix somewhere. That's along with the samples from your standard European population."

"What?"

"Based on racial traits and gender markers, we could tell that there were two African men and a single Asian woman. We can also tell you that we have the blood of nine men and four women. All the blood samples were quite clear on this. Oh, we did find a blood type that is extremely rare, which might help you identify the donor."

Mitchell rocked back in his chair until it squeaked in protest and stared up at the ceiling, as if looking for divine inspiration. He said, "I need someone to go through this with me, carefully. I don't know what I have here."

"Well, I would say that your crime scene was contaminated in some fashion. There were a lot of people bleeding in that place, at some time."

Mitchell seized on that. "Can you supply a time frame? When

each sample was left?"

"It's all mixed in together. Give me a clean sample, that is, give me a sample from a single person and one that hasn't been bled on several different occasions, and I might be able to tell you how long ago the blood was left. But this is just one large conglomeration."

Mitchell was silent, his mind racing. If there was that many different DNA donors, and all the DNA had been left in that one room, then there might be other evidence in other rooms. No one had looked very hard at the rest of the house because they had everything they needed. Miller was obviously killed in that one room. The blood samples were taken from that one room, and there was no evidence of a struggle in any of the other rooms. Mitchell needed to revisit the crime scene and take a close look at everything left behind. He needed to understand exactly what he had here.

Suddenly the case was more confusing, and he was afraid of what the defense might make out of the multiple blood samples. He wasn't sure what defense strategy would work, only that the defense sometimes believes that its mission was to confuse the issue enough so that the jury would acquit the defendant, and often they didn't care how they get to that point.

"I do have a strange question," said Mitchell. "Let's say the person received a blood transfusion. Would more than one DNA sample show up?"

"I wouldn't think so," said Douglas. "They remove the white cells so there is little in the way of genetic material left in a transfusion."

"But," said Mitchell, "if they used whole blood, then there could be a contamination of the DNA? You could get two different DNA samples?"

"Certainly. Even with a transfusion, it is theoretically possible. Is that all, Captain?" asked Douglas.

"For the moment," said Mitchell. "When will all the results be posted?"

"We'll have the final report on the Net before six tonight. Seven at the latest."

Mitchell said thank you and hung up. He had no idea what all that DNA meant, but someone was throwing it around his crime scene and that had to stop.

CHAPTER TWELVE

Thomas Johnson drank half the can of Coke in a single, long, sustained pull and then burped. Not loudly. Not obnoxiously, but quietly. He rocked back against the hard red plastic of the chair and said, "I need to get some sleep."

"Of course," said Rachael Goldberg, who was almost as tired as Johnson but who needed more information. She said, "If we're going to have a chance to beat this thing, I need everything you can tell me."

"I'm trying."

"So, who was the first person she killed?" asked Goldberg, sitting with her pen posed, ready to write it all down.

Johnson shook his head. "I don't know who she killed first. I know that she killed a man the night she arrived. That fellow named Travis."

"I have that. Who was next?"

"Well, she had several opportunities, but each of those people could be traced back to her. She'd learned that it was not good to be the last person known to see someone alive. If a trades-man was coming to fix the toilet, rewire a plug, paint, garden, whatever, and he, or she, was not seen again, suspicion would be directed at you."

"Naturally."

"The place to go was into the clubbing world. Get out among the anonymous in strange costumes who hooked up and then never saw one another again. Get into that mix, make the selection carefully, and the trail would end at the body. A little care and no one would be knocking on her door."

"So she went hunting?"

"Yes . . ."

Linda Miller knew that her body was among the best in the city. She worked to maintain the muscle tone, worked to keep herself from turning a pasty white with chemicals that produced a golden brown from the inside, and stayed out of the sun, which could wrinkle the skin and create brown spots for the average human. She seemed to be immune.

She exercised in the small gym she created in the spare bedroom, using the equipment first thing in the morning and then in the middle of the afternoon. She had installed mirrors along one wall so that she could watch herself work out. She wanted to see the effort, and when she exercised in the nude, she could see every little flaw. It provided an added incentive, as if she actually needed one.

She rested in the late afternoon and sometimes got up to watch the sun sink below the trees in her backyard. She enjoyed watching the sunset because, well, it was sunset. It meant that night was coming on, and she could, at last, come alive. She was a night person.

Three days after she moved into the house and a day after the last of the furniture arrived she dressed for the night. She wore a tight shirt and a short skirt. She put on ankle socks and high-heeled shoes. She walked into her mini-gym, examined herself from all angles in the mirrors and decided that she looked very good. There would be no trouble.

Her car had been delivered that afternoon, so she drove downtown, found a parking place in a self-service lot that required a twenty-dollar deposit and operated with a plastic card and a machine to dispense change. Then she joined the crowds milling around on the sidewalks, circulated through a couple of the clubs that opened early and finally began to make the circuit of the best places.

The bouncer stopped her at the door of one, demanding to see her ID. He didn't want some nineteen-year-old bitch screwing up everything for him and his boss. Miller showed her passport that listed her as twenty-six. The age was wrong, but no one would challenge a passport.

"Lady, you sure don't look it," he said, grudgingly.

She smiled, touched him under the chin and said, "Thank you very much."

The interior looked like an electronics convention gone wrong. Lasers danced on the ceiling and along the upper parts of the walls. Videos flashed on screens on each of the walls, showing people dancing, kissing, undressing and even making love. In some places the short videos looked downright pornographic and were wildly cheered by the men and women.

Miller moved, carefully, slowly, toward the bar and found a stool. She sat down and waited until the bartender, dressed in the style of the 1890s complete to garters around his arms, slipped closer and asked, "What'll you have?"

Miller said, "Bloody Mary and hold the salad."

The bartender grinned, nodded and slipped to the right to make the drink. He returned a moment later and said, "Here you go. You're new here. I haven't seen you in here before."

"First time," Miller confirmed.

"Then this one is on the house. All first-timers get a free drink."

"Thank you, kind sir," she said.

He grinned, nodded and then slid away to take the orders from a dozen other people who were sitting at the bar.

Miller sipped her drink and watched the crowd, looking for a target. There were lots of men, but they seemed to be with women, or were attached to groups of both men and women. She didn't want to target someone who would have a girlfriend to remember her, or who was the member of a group who would have friends that might remember her. She needed an unattached victim, preferably male, but that didn't matter all that much.

She watched the door as people entered. She watched couples head for the dance floor and watched groups that swirled about the room. It seemed that everyone was attached, in some fashion, to someone else in the club. No one entered solo, though some of the groups were small and of a single gender.

She nursed her drink, wondering if the bartender might be a good target. He was tall, rugged looking with broad shoulders and nearly perfect teeth. But the women, and a few of the men, seemed to have the same idea. They all would notice who he left with and that was a trail that she didn't want followed.

She sipped her drink and watched the people dance. She was asked a couple of times, but when the music ended and her partner wanted her to join his group, she would decline. She didn't want to be part of a group. She wanted a single target who would not be noticed as he, or she, left the club.

She noticed single men enter a couple of times. Once, a man, who looked over fifty, had a large stomach, a long beard and little hair on his head, looked as out of place there as she would in a football locker room. He stood out in the crowd because he was so different from the others. She didn't want to draw attention to herself by joining someone who simply did not belong inside.

Yes, she understood that people would notice her, but she wasn't that different. There were other women in the club, dressed as she was, and some were prettier than she. She would have to find herself a hunting partner because single women in the clubs were a rarity. A hunting partner to fly interference for her and to help her get out without being noticed.

She watched two men arrive, both about six feet tall, both with dark hair and both dressed in T-shirts and jeans. As soon as they walked into the main part of the club, they separated, clearly looking for women and clearly operating independently. The one closest to her would make the best target.

Miller pushed herself off her stool, leaving the remains of her Bloody Mary behind. She shouldered her way through the crowd, getting bumped around and groped by those who thought grabbing at her was the height of sophistication. She managed to catch the man before he asked anyone else to dance, cut around him quickly and stopped, almost like a guard in basketball trying to draw the charging foul.

He looked at her, grinned with nearly perfect teeth and said, "I guess you'd like to dance."

"To start."

"Okay," he said, "but no names yet. Let's just keep it anonymous."

"Is there another way?" she asked.

They slipped deeper into the crowd toward the center of the dance floor and began to move and gyrate in time to the music. The beat of the music rarely changed, except to get faster. This wasn't a spot where they played slow music so that the dancers could hang onto each other. The plan by management was to keep them moving fast, make them work up a thirst and then sell them overpriced drinks that kept the money flowing.

Miller joined right in, moving with an ease and grace that suggested she was at home in her body and didn't mind that others, especially men, were looking at her, watching her. She believed that those would remember her as a body rather than as a person, and there would be no connection between her and the sudden disappearance of this man. They wouldn't see them as a couple, but as dance partners who probably went their separate ways when the music died.

After thirty minutes, with the man sweating profusely and his shirt soaking wet, she grinned and asked, "Had enough?"

"Just getting started."

"Let's go outside for a breath of air," she said.

Without a word he turned and worked his way toward the door. Miller trailed him, a step or two back so that it wasn't obvious that she was with him. They looked like two people who were leaving the club, but not together.

Outside, they stopped on the sidewalk, watching the traffic circulate, listening to the late-night sounds, the distant horns and a deep rhythmic thumping that came from the club and was transmitted through the ground.

"Now what?" asked the man.

Miller said, "I have my car. Would you care to take a short ride?"

"I have my car as well," he said.

"Well, it'll be all right for a couple of hours. If we hadn't hooked up in the club, then you probably would still be inside. No one will think twice about your car."

"True," he said.

They walked down the street, watching the swirl of people around them. Miller was walking close enough that her hip bumped the man every couple of steps. She was well inside his circle of intimacy, letting him know, silently, that she found him attractive, hinting at what would be coming just a little later.

They found her car and she opened the driver's side, using the button to unlock the other door. He climbed in, took a deep breath and said, "New?"

"Couple of days."

"I like it. What did it set you back?"

She glanced at him, surprised by the question, but then many now grew up without even the basic manners. She said, "More than enough for basic transportation," which meant nothing, but answered the question, sort of.

They drove out to her house and she used the garage door opener so that they could drive directly into the garage. No one would see her companion that way and there would be no difficult questions later when he didn't emerge normally.

She got out of the car, walked around and unlocked the door into the house. Before she could move, the man was behind her, standing close enough that she knew what he had on his mind. He pressed against her and she pushed back harder, suggesting that she had the same idea. She could tell that he was more than ready for her.

They entered into the kitchen and she turned on more lights. The man looked around, grinning, and said, "This is very nice. Expensive. You live here alone?"

That was the sort of question a woman alone usually didn't answer, but she had no fear. She knew what was going to happen and said, "Yes. I just moved in."

"I like this. Do you have much of a yard?"

"No, but I'm not here for the yard."

"What do you do?" he asked.

"A little of this and some of that," she said.

"You know, you haven't answered one of my questions all night."

"That's what I thought you wanted. Anonymity."

"Well, it's nice to know something about the woman you take to bed."

Now she grinned. "Is that what you expect?"

He smiled back. "And you?"

She reached down, grasped the bottom of her T-shirt, and lifted, pulling it over her head. She tossed it to the floor, out of the way. She then unzipped her skirt and let it fall away so that she was standing in front of him wearing only panties that were made of the lightest, flimsiest cloth. She might as well have been naked.

He studied her very carefully and said, "Nice. Very nice. Now what?"

She moved past him, opened a door and turned on a light. She pointed at the stairs and said, "This way. Down here to the playroom."

He said, "I'll follow you. I want to watch."

She walked down the stairs, into the lower level, sparsely furnished room. The floor was hardwood, a laminate actually, but it cleaned easily. A vinyl couch, a chair and a lamp and a secretary completed the decor with the exception of the flat panel TV on the far wall. It was hooked to a DVD recorder and into a stereo system. This was a setup for her, if she wanted to play for a while. Tonight she didn't feel like it.

"What are we going to do down here?" he asked.

She kept her back to him, opened a drawer on the secretary, pulled out a small caliber pistol and pointed it at his face. She watched him react, first smiling in disbelief and then in growing horror as he began to understand that she was actually going to shoot him.

Without a word, she pulled the trigger, the shot muffled and nearly impossible to hear outside because of the caliber of the weapon and the insulation in her walls. Besides, she was in the basement, which deadened the sound even more.

The man staggered and fell to his knees, but hadn't lost consciousness. Blood dripped from a spot above his right eyebrow and Miller knew that the bullet had been deflected slightly by the bone of his skull. That was the problem with the small-caliber bullets. Bone was sometimes tough enough to stop them or deflect them.

She aimed again, at his eye, and fired. He fell back as if his bones had suddenly melted.

Johnson said, "I never did find out that man's name. I have a list of three possibles. Men who disappeared about that time and who fit the basic description, but I don't know which one he was, or if he was even one of those three. This is just guesswork on my part."

"You've shared all this with the police?" asked Goldberg.

"Not yet. We'll need some proof."

CHAPTER THIRTEEN

When Sarah Hartwell finally woke up late in the afternoon, she was alone in the hospital, confused, sore and afraid. She wasn't completely sure what had happened or how she had wound up in the hospital, wrapped in white with an IV stuck in her arm. She turned her head slightly and saw the window. Night was beginning to fall, but she didn't know what night it was or how long she had been asleep.

The door opened and a man she didn't recognize entered. He seemed to believe that she was still unconscious because he moved quietly and didn't look directly at her. He just slipped into a chair and sat, looking out the window.

A moment later a nurse entered the room, walked to the bed and looked down. "So you are awake?"

Hartwell began to speak, but her mouth was dry and her tongue seemed swollen. It wouldn't obey her so she just nodded.

"Well, I'll get the doctor in here shortly, but first I would imagine you'd like something to drink. We have some water, and I'll let you have some of that, but I don't want you drinking too much right away."

The nurse turned, spotted the man and asked, "Are you a member of the family?"

"Captain Mitchell. Police."

"Well, you're just going to have to wait outside until the doctor gets in here."

"I think I'll just wait here, quietly, if you don't mind," said Mitchell, firmly.

"No," said the nurse, just as firmly. "You'll wait in the hall. Don't make me call security."

Mitchell looked as if he was going to respond and then smiled. He said, "Ms. Hartwell, I'll be back to ask you a couple of questions about Linda Miller and Tom Johnson, if you feel up to it." He then left the room.

The nurse summoned the doctor, who entered, looked at her carefully, looked deep into her eyes, probed around a couple of the bruises and wounds, listened to her breathing and then said, "How are you feeling?"

"Sore."

"Well, I would guess so."

The nurse said, unnecessarily, as if Hartwell had not heard Mitchell, "There's a policeman out there wanting to talk to you. You feel up to it?"

She nodded.

The nurse opened the door and waved. Mitchell returned and the doctor said, "She's going to be a little weak and she's going to tire easily. This might not be the best time to ask questions, but you can take five or ten minutes."

Mitchell stepped close to the bed and asked, "Are you feeling like doing this?"

She nodded, though she barely moved her head.

"Okay. Just tell me, briefly, what happened. We'll fill in all the details later, when you're feeling better. Right now I just want to know the basics."

The nurse, still in the room, gave her another little bit of water. Hartwell swallowed, closed her eyes for so long that both the nurse and Mitchell thought she might have gone back to sleep. Finally, she said, "Linda invited us to dinner."

"So you went to her house?"

"Yes."

"And you had dinner?"

"Yes. She didn't eat much."

"You think that is significant?"

"Yes."

"Why?"

"Because of what she was."

"What was she?"

Hartwell closed her eyes again but this time her forehead wrinkled, as if she was deep in thought rather than asleep. When she opened her eyes, she said, "I don't know."

"Okay. What happened next?"

"I don't know."

"And then?"

"I don't remember. I just remember having dinner. I remember an argument. I don't remember anything else."

"You were having dinner. Miller didn't eat much. Then something must have happened. What was it?"

Hartwell looked confused and then said, "I don't know."

The nurse interrupted then and said, "I think this has gone on long enough. She needs to rest. She answered your questions."

Mitchell looked at the nurse and then at Hartwell. "She didn't tell me much of anything."

"That's not my problem or hers. She needs to rest and you'll have to leave."

Mitchell looked as if he was going to protest, and then simply nodded. "Yes. Ms. Hartwell, I'll be back later to talk with you, if that is all right."

She didn't answer or nod. She just stared up at him as if he was speaking some foreign language.

Mitchell lowered her voice and asked the nurse, "Is she going to be all right?"

"Of course. The injuries are not life threatening. She'll just need a little time to heal."

Through half-closed eyes, Hartwell watched as Mitchell opened the door and then disappeared. When he was gone, she turned her head slightly so that she could see the window. It was now dark outside. From the bed, she could see a wing of the hospital with its lights running up an exterior corner, bathing the wall in brightness. She wondered about that and if it was a good idea. It might make it difficult for some of the patients to get back to sleep.

The nurse moved into her line of vision and said, "You'll probably sleep for a while. If you need anything, just push the button."

Hartwell nodded but didn't say anything.

"You get your rest." The nurse then turned and walked out the door, leaving Hartwell in the semi-darkness with no sounds except the quiet buzzing of the machines behind her.

Night was when they came out strong, she thought. Night is when they could get to her if they wanted. But now, she didn't think they would care. She had no real secret to expose because no one would believe her.

CHAPTER FOURTEEN

Thomas Johnson sat in his cell, looking out into the corridor and up at the color television that he couldn't hear because he had not put on the earphones. He sat staring at the swirling colors and dancing patterns, not at all interested in the drama that was being played out. Nothing on television could compare to what he was feeling or the drama he was living.

It was funny how life's decisions moved you in one direction instead of another. Had he not been interested in illegal immigration, had the INS not turned into a Keystone Cops operation that didn't seem to know what it was doing, had there not been so many people flooding across the borders, or landing on aircraft, or just slipping through the cracks, he wouldn't have been interested and he wouldn't be sitting in jail. He would be sitting at home, probably with the same show on television and not worrying about the next twenty-four hours.

Johnson had always wanted to be a writer. Not necessarily a journalist or a novelist, but a writer, able to tackle whatever happened to interest him. He could move from topic to topic at his own whim, but he often watched the news and read the magazines, finding in those stories something that moved him. The INS, because of the situation, now interested him, and he wondered how easy it was to penetrate the borders and how easy it would be for him to find some of those people.

So, he had worked the story slowly, carefully and come up with Linda Miller, a seemingly nice lady with money who apparently shouldn't be in the United States. It had been a chance meeting that led to his discussion of his story with her or her story with him, depending on how you looked at it. She had been reluctant, which Johnson had understood, but he had pressed her for information.

Given the circumstances, he wondered why she hadn't just killed him, and an instant later he knew. Police investigation would lead from him to her, even if they didn't suspect she was the killer and that was something she could not tolerate. She avoided anything that could bring her to the attention of the authorities because they would ask questions.

He had known her about a month when he visited her for the first time at her home. She had invited him over for drinks and then they would circulate through the city as she pointed out the sites that impressed her.

She met him at the door, dressed in a very short skirt and a very tight top. It was clear as she turned to lead him deeper into the house that she wore neither a bra nor panties. She stopped once in the hallway, grinned at him and then continued on.

They reached the great room and she waved him into it. "I thought we'd sit in here for a while, and then I'd begin to make dinner. I thought something simple. Steak and baked potato?"

"That would be fine," said Johnson.

She walked over to the stereo, selected a couple of CDs and then bent at the waist to put them into the changer. If he had any doubt about her intentions, she had now removed it. Clearly she wasn't wearing panties and just as clearly, she wanted him to know it. She hadn't taken long to make sure that he knew.

Johnson had to admit that her skin was flawless and her legs both long and slender. She was using her attributes to their fullest at the moment, and he didn't understand why.

When the music started, she straightened and turned slowly. She stood still, near the stereo. She let him watch her as she crossed the room and then sat down opposite him, her knees slightly parted and the lights arranged as if to illuminate her legs.

"So," she said, "what would you like to know?"

"Tell me about your background."

Later he would learn that much she said to him, except that she had entered the United States through Canada, had been a lie. She hadn't been born in Scotland as she said that night, she hadn't been educated in England as she claimed then and she hadn't lived in Italy or Australia, although she might have visited both countries. Johnson thought that she was about twenty-eight or nine, but he would later learn that he was wrong about that too. But later she would bring out documents, suggesting a personal connection to some of what she was saying, and letting him see a story that was more fascinating than someone sneaking into the United States from Canada on a fake passport.

She spent the time talking, displaying herself, thrusting out her chest, though it wasn't all that obvious. It became more evident that she wasn't wearing a bra as her nipples stood out against the thin material of her tight shirt.

She crossed her legs, letting the skirt ride higher and then uncrossed them, just in case he hadn't noticed. She smiled at him, pretending that she was innocent, but putting on a show that would have aroused the dead.

Johnson, because of Sarah Hartwell who was again his girlfriend and because of the obvious display, tried to avoid the invitation. He wanted to gather information and not engage in sex games.

Finally, she said, "Just what do you plan to do with this story when you finish?"

"Sell it to a magazine and make some money."

"Is there a lot of money writing for magazines?"

"Not on a freelance basis. I might make four or five hundred dollars, maybe as much as a thousand or two."

"Sounds somewhat risky."

"Well, it can be. You have to work very carefully and not burn any bridges. And, you're at the whim of the public and the editors. There might be something in your article they don't like, so they reject it and buy a similar one. Or, two or three writers might be working on the same story so they just buy what they believe to be the best."

"Uh-huh. Maybe you should look for something a little more stable."

Johnson laughed and said, "You're not the first one to suggest that. Sarah has said that on more than one occasion. I sometimes think about it too."

She leaned forward, elbows on her knees. "Well, I might be able to help."

"I'm afraid I don't know exactly what you mean here," said Johnson.

Miller grinned, showing her perfect teeth, and leaned back, slowly crossing her legs. She watched his eyes dip and knew that he was looking at her, just as she had planned. She said, "You're a writer. What do you know about vampires?"

Johnson couldn't help but laugh. Given the show she had been putting on, it was the last question he had expected. He said, "Not much money in vampires unless you write a book about them. A work of fiction."

"Have you ever done any research into the beginnings of the legend?"

Johnson shook his head but said, "I know the basics about them. I know that contrary to the legend, they can go out in sunlight but they can't change form in the daylight. I know that it isn't garlic but garlic flowers that bother them. I've often thought it odd that they recoil at a cross but not the Star of David, for example. I guess I have always been aware of the inconsistencies in the various vampire myths."

"While I was in Europe, I did some studying about them. Learned some interesting details that might make for a good article. I could share the information with you."

"You mean write an article together?" asked Johnson.

"Oh, no, nothing like that. But I have all this information that I thought might be interesting to a writer."

"Sure," said Johnson. "I have very diverse interests."

Miller got to her feet and said, "You wait here and I'll go get the stuff. We can look at it before we eat, and you can decide if it is interesting enough for an article."

She walked out of the room slowly and then disappeared down a hallway. Johnson wondered then if this was a scheme to buy him off. When sex didn't work, she decided on a monetary bribe. She knew better than to offer him money outright, but she could help him earn it. She would be the conduit that funneled the cash into his pocket. He wouldn't follow up on the immigration story but would go off on another tangent, one that she directed.

She returned a few minutes later carrying a white "banker's" box. She set it on the floor, at Johnson's feet, untied the strings and opened it.

"I had some of my stuff shipped in once I had a place to live. This was one of the boxes that came."

She pulled a large book that had black pages and was held together with string from the box and opened it. She said, "You know of Vlad the Impaler?"

"Yes. A despot who enjoyed impaling his victims. I think once, because some Turks refused to removed their hats, he had those hats nailed to their heads."

"Fez, not hat, but yes. Though there are those who consider him a hero for what he did for his region. It's all a matter of perspective."

"And his legend has grown into that of the vampire," said Johnson.

"Yes, but he wasn't a vampire. He was a terrible human who liked to watch the death struggles of others as he ate his lunch. Great entertainment for a meal."

"You're not going to tell me that you believe in vampires, are you?"

"Of course not. I'm going to tell you about something else that is just as strange, but might have caused this legend of the vampire to grow." She handed him the photo album.

Johnson opened it and saw a photograph of an old, crumbling castle set on a bluff. The forest had grown up to the stone walls, hiding part of the facade. Although the sun was shining and the trees lower down the hill were bright green, those closer to the castle had taken on a grayish cast, almost as if to match the dark stone. The castle, sticking up on top of the hill, and the little sky visible above it, seemed to be from a black and white photograph rather than color. It was a distinctively odd effect, looking as if it was a picture made from two different photographs taken from exactly the same angle and the same time and then skillfully Photoshopped.

"That," she said, "was once the ancestral home. Oh, it's been out of the family for a couple of centuries at least, but my grandfather . . . or great-grandfather or great-great-grandfather, or whatever, once lived there."

"In Transylvania?" asked Johnson. He couldn't keep the amusement out of his voice.

"Romania, actually," she said.

Johnson turned the page and there was an old newspaper clipping. Not a microfilm copy, but the actual clipping. Handwritten under it was a date from the eighteenth century. He scanned it, seeing that it was a story of murder and an attack on the castle.

Miller pointed at it and said, "Rumors, stories, untruths circulated in the village that my family was stealing children in the night and using their blood for our own evil purposes. We needed their blood to survive according to them, and we weren't careful about hiding the fact."

She reached over and turned the page. There was another newspaper article. This one mentioned Elizabeth Bathory, who had been killed about two hundred years before the castle was attacked. Bathory believed that bathing in the blood of young girls would keep her youthful. Sometime around 1611, the bodies of more than fifty girls were found buried beneath her castle and rumors of vampirism and occultism had begun to circulate. She was later walled up in a room in the castle as her punishment for murdering so many.

"See," she said. "People of that time were so superstitious, so ignorant, that they believed in vampires and werewolves and thought these creatures roamed the night."

Johnson wasn't sure what to say, so just agreed, saying, "Yes, they were."

"So, when children began to disappear, the people thought that those in the castle were responsible because that was what had happened in the past. They thought they were taking and eating the children as a way to protect their own youth."

She turned to face him. "My family had been blessed with genes that made us all look youthful. You couldn't tell if a person was fifty or sixty because they all looked to be thirty. We don't really age superficially like the rest of the population so that the people thought we were demons or witches or worse."

That should have been his first clue. She talked about the rest of the population as if she was not part of it. They were somehow set apart and because of that, were labeled as witches or demons.

"And they attacked the castle?"

"Yes. Killing about a dozen of the servants and two of the guards. My family escaped out the tunnels built under the walls for the purpose."

She grinned and added, "All castles have an escape hatch in case the worst happened. Almost all the family got out through the escape hatch."

"And then?" asked Johnson.

"We had lost some of our wealth when the castle was attacked, but that wasn't the only place where treasure was stored. And there were relatives scattered around Eastern Europe. It was just a small matter of getting to the treasure and to the relatives. In today's world, that treasure would have been about a billion U.S. dollars, I think."

"What form did it take?"

Now Miller smiled for the first time in several minutes. Her voice had been low, sad, almost as if she was reliving a painful memory, but now it was brighter, higher. "Oh, we had some gold and silver coins, some of them from ancient Rome, other coins minted by various governments, and artifacts of gold and silver and covered with jewels. The value of the gold coins, to collectors, is sometimes more than a hundred times the value of the gold itself. What might be a twenty-dollar gold piece will sell to a collector for ten or twenty thousand dollars."

"Your family fortune is built on that sort of wealth?" asked Johnson, thinking that this would be an interesting story in and of itself. How did one sell coins that were worth so much? And, did you have to feed them into the market carefully so that you didn't bring down the value of the coin? Who would buy those sorts of coins and how did they authenticate them?

It was a fascinating story. A family who had managed to save gold and silver coins from the times of the Romans in the same way that Americans now saved pennies, dimes and quarters. Throw them into a jar and a thousand years, two thousand years later you had an expensive collectible. What an interesting way to build a family fortune.

"Now it is," said Miller. "Before it was built on land and farming and protecting the peasants. They shared their food with us and we saw that they were protected from raiders and vandals and thieves. We administered the area, collected the taxes and everyone was happy."

Johnson wasn't really hearing her words. He was looking, with fascination, at the scrapbook, but he did say, "Yeah, it was a wonderful system in which that woman, whatever her name was, felt that she could bathe in the blood of young girls. That tells you something about their thinking."

But he was looking beyond all that, seeing a family history, laid out with documents that would be of interest to any number of magazines. This scrapbook provided a glimpse into the past and the ways that people thought then and how some of the superstitions and beliefs had grown and spread throughout Europe.

"We, my family, left Eastern Europe, and moved to France and England."

"My family came from Germany and Scotland," said Johnson, idly.

"If you're interested in family," said Miller, "then I have the book for you. It's a family history that was printed in the late eighteenth century. I have what might be the only copy of it in existence."

She dug through the box and came up with a bulky book about nine inches wide, twelve inches long and maybe three inches thick. The edges of the paper were touched with gold and the binding was thick and dark and heavy.

"This book has to be worth twenty, thirty thousand," said Johnson.

"More, if people knew it existed."

"This is really fascinating."

Miller pushed herself off the couch, leaving the box at Johnson's feet. She said, "Why don't you read some of that and I'll get dinner started."

Johnson nodded but didn't say anything. He had forgotten all about her provocative dress, or lack thereof, had forgotten the views of her body she had provided and seemed unaware that she was practically throwing herself at him. Instead, he wanted to read through the book. He knew that there was a story in it, possibly a big one. He just didn't know how big. What he didn't understand was why she was telling him all of this.

CHAPTER FIFTEEN

Johnson opened the book carefully, almost as if he was about to perform surgery on the brain of a friend. The book looked heavy and rugged, but it was also ancient and maybe a little bit delicate. Paper, leather, ink and glue often did not age well, and it would be very easy to damage a book that might be thought of as priceless. So, he handled it with care, opening the cover slowly so he didn't harm it.

The first page was printed with an ornate typeface that made the *S* look like a lowercase *F* and a few of the letters that were nearly unrecognizable. The words had the funny spellings of Middle English, and the punctuation and capitalization had no standards at all. The book looked as if it had been written by a first-grade student who didn't pay much attention to the rules of grammar.

He turned the page and found a drawing that seemed to show the castle he had seen in the photograph, though it was newer and surrounded by farmers' fields rather than forest. It was the castle as it must have looked shortly after the major construction was completed.

He found the first chapter of the story and began to read, unconsciously translating the bizarre English into something that he could recognize.

In the year of our Lord, 1123, we, the Baron of Moldavia, Wife, Son and two Daughters, came into the region with the Blessings of the

Prince, and with a Grant for lands that reached from the Statis River to the Hillum Ridge and to include the Rheinland Forest and the Balfour Plains. We came with a Company of Soldiers for protection from Bandits and Gypsies and the Demons that haunted the forests and streams along our route and that looked to harm Travelers such as Ourselves.

We found a hill where there was wood for fires, stone for building and water for drinking that flowed from a rock into a large, clear pool. Our camp that first night was filled with trepidation because we knew not what to expect. We knew only the stories that had come from the area for centuries and feared that many of them would be true. But the morning dawned clear and fresh and we found nothing amiss in our camp. All were well if not completely rested.

Scouting parties of our Soldiers were sent out and they brought in men to help build the castle and they brought in food to be served to those working with us. Soldiers circled the camp at night, scaring away beasts and the Demons, keeping us safe. We were secure, though at night there were many strange noises from the forest that frightened the peasants and kept our Soldiers awake.

The first sections of the castle were completed in a month while the weather was still warm and pleasant and we moved into the new quarters. Next was the erection of the Barracks for the Soldiers and the Stable for the horses. When those were completed, the walls were strengthened, and then raised, and finally the castle was protected from assault by a log palisade. Quarters for the servants were finished, also made of wood, some of them outside the wall to protect the fields from Bandits and Beasts. By Winter, all had moved into the castle.

The peasants began to move from their huts and erected new dwellings closer to the walls. They believed that we would protect them and if an enemy appeared, they would be able to hide inside our walls. We did nothing to discourage them.

Everyone now felt safe. During the Summer, two Maidens had walked into the forest looking for berries but they had never returned.

Searchers failed to find them. They had vanished from our camp as completely as if they had ascended into Heaven bodily. We never found a trace of them.

Our first Winter was very tough. Food was scarce and game seemed to avoid our forest. Hunters were gone for days and often returned with little meat. Ranging farther and farther from our walls, they had better luck, but the length of the journeys made the hunt difficult for the men and frightening for the women.

We were very lucky. Only a single party of hunters failed to return. There were four men in it, all very young. They might have become lost in a snowstorm. We never learned what happened to them.

As soon as the weather permitted, the peasants began to work the fields. Construction on the castle continued with stone replacing the wood. Hunters roamed the forest and found the game plentiful now that the weather had warmed.

In the middle of the Summer, a strange beast was observed in the forest and hunters were dispatched to kill it. There were many descriptions of it, telling us that it was nearly seven feet tall, covered in dark hair and walking on two legs. It roared in the night and killed some of the cattle, ripping them apart.

Another girl disappeared. She was in her fifteenth year and she was not seen again. Some suspected the beast, but it always left something behind. It never approached any of the peasants or Soldiers and was only seen in the distance in the daylight. Some believed it had taken the girl as a wife because we found no Mortal Remains. Some believed she was a sacrifice demanded by the beast. After she vanished, the beast was not seen again that year.

The castle was finished and more Soldiers were recruited. The peasants planted their fields and all looked well for the coming Winter. There would be food for all. There would be wood for warmth.

All through the Winter, people disappeared. They went out to hunt, to gather wood, to search for others, and always someone failed to return. No Mortal Remains left behind.

Rumors began to spread that the Family was responsible. We were killing those who disappeared. We were drinking the blood. We were eating the bodies to hide the evidence. We told them there were Demons in the forest and we all had to be careful.

The disappearance of a young maiden in the early Spring sealed our fate. Though they feared the Demons and Witches, we lived in the castle among them. They came in the night with their farming implements, torches and hate. We were lucky to escape through the tunnel.

He stopped reading and glanced up at the light-colored wall and took a deep breath. The book read as if someone was setting up an alibi, though Johnson didn't know why anyone would do that in a private book. This was a book of which there would be a single copy and the likelihood that anyone other than family members would see it was small.

He just thought about what he had read. It was a peek into the life of a noble family nearly a thousand years earlier.

CHAPTER SIXTEEN

Mitchell waited until morning before he returned to the murder house, as he thought of it. The yellow police line tape that had barricaded most of the yard and barred the way of sightseers and trespassers had been removed. There was a yellow notice stuck to the front door, sealing the house, but Mitchell ignored it, using the key for the lock that he had gotten from the police property room that morning.

When he pushed open the door, he got a whiff of decay from the blood that had pooled in the great room. The odor was offensive, unpleasant and seemed warm. That warmth was from the lack of air conditioning. It had been turned off at some point and no one had turned it back on.

He walked along the entry and stopped, looking into the great room. The carpet was stained with blood. Miller's body had been outlined, partially in her own blood and then with tape in case investigators needed to make measurements. Pictures of the crime scene, in full, living color, had been taken and could be used for some measurements, but the outline would help confirm the accuracy of those measurements.

Mitchell stepped into the kitchen and then over to the breakfast nook and sat down. He looked first into the great room and when no inspiration hit, out the windows, down, into the woods behind the house. Plenty of space to hide things in those woods with trees to mark the spot, if Miller had been inclined to hide anything outside the house and needed a way to mark the spot. Mitchell had no reason to suspect that she had.

Finally, he stood up and walked over to the refrigerator and opened the door. There wasn't much in it other than a covered pitcher of tomato juice, a wedge of cheese and a jar of pickles. In the freezer he found a roast, four T-bone steaks and a sirloin. The ice trays were not filled, there was no ice cream or other deserts, and no frozen dinners. Just the meat. Odd, but then Mitchell didn't know if she entertained much, if she ate out most of the time, or if she just hadn't gotten to the store in the days before she was killed.

He closed the refrigerator and wandered back through the hallway to the master bedroom. There was a mattress and box spring, a single table on the far side of the bed and a dresser. There were no decorations on the walls and no curtains or blinds on the windows, though no one could have seen into the room without a ladder.

He opened the dresser drawers but found nothing in them. He looked into the closet and found it empty. That struck him as strange because she had to have clothes. She'd lived in the place for more than a year but it looked as if she was just moving in and hadn't had time to unpack her clothes . . .

. . . or she was moving out.

Maybe she had found another place to live. Maybe she hadn't finished the transition. It puzzled him as he walked into the bathroom and found almost nothing. Not toilet paper, toothpaste, towels or soap. The medicine cabinet was empty and there was no evidence that she had ever used the sink. The dust in it had to be weeks old if not more.

The other bedrooms and bathroom were equally empty without sign of much use. In one of the closets he found two skirts, a blouse, a pair of blue jeans and one shoe. Just one and he found no mate for it anywhere else.

Downstairs was a little different. He found evidence that this was the room she used the most. The furniture was old and stained, as was the floor, but the stains were small, almost invisible, and looked as if she had tried to clean them at some point. The room was neat and relatively clean. Light came from two rather large windows, each with blinds, shades and curtains, giving the impression that Miller was afraid that someone would look in. This in stark contrast to the lack of window coverings on the floor above.

He moved along one wall that had been covered with a dark wood veneer paneling. It looked rich and expensive, but it was paneling, which seemed out of character. Idly he tapped at it and found that it hid something. There was certainly a wall behind it, but there wasn't the solid sound that suggested it backed up against the outside, concrete wall.

He pressed at various points as he walked along and felt a give in one small section of the paneling. First he examined it carefully, but saw nothing. He closed his eyes and ran his fingers over it, letting the sensations build the picture for him. He felt a slight bump and pushed on it. Something gave and he opened his eyes.

There was a crack in the wall near the corner and he walked closer, seeing that there was a door there. Pushing on it, he found there was a small, dark room that might have been four feet wide and about fifteen feet long. A narrow but long workspace concealed behind a false wall and something that the police on the scene on the night of the murder had failed to find. Not that he blamed them. It was well concealed and wouldn't have been visible to them. They wouldn't have made the same careful examination that he was making because they had found the killer, standing with the smoking gun in his hand, telling them that he had, in fact, killed her. There had been no reason for the police to make a careful search of the house.

He began to reach in, to use his hand to search for a light switch, but then stopped. If she had gone to the trouble of making the false wall then she just might have set some sort of a booby trap for anyone who found it. Reaching into and then rubbing the wall where he expected to find a light switch, where he and everyone he knew had been conditioned to find it, was the perfect place to set some kind of a trap.

He took a step back, out of the doorway, and decided he would get his flashlight out of the car. He'd look around carefully because he walked into that room. He didn't like the feel of it, and he didn't like the feel of the house. There was something definitely wrong, and it was something more than the transient nature of everything that he had seen.

Finally, with his flashlight, Mitchell looked into the long, thin room. The walls were painted a dark color. Not black, but more of a chocolate or dark brown. There was tile on the floor, but it was a dark gray. It was not a continuation of the flooring in the rest of the room.

Using his flashlight, he looked at the light switch but still didn't touch it. There was something about it that frightened him. If anyone had asked, Mitchell wouldn't have been able to explain it. There was just something wrong with it.

Finally, he used his plastic ballpoint pen and flipped the switch, but the light didn't come on. He flipped it up and down a couple of times, but nothing happened. So, maybe he was right, or maybe the light had simply burned out.

He knelt on the floor and swept his flashlight from right to left, moving it deeper into the dark room. He found nothing of interest, just a counter and a cupboard at the far end, though he could tell nothing about them from where he stood.

Finally, he stepped back out of the dark room, and walked to one of the chairs. Realizing that he would be contaminating the crime scene, though it had already been processed, he sat down.

There was something unsettling about that room, the way it was hidden, the burned-out light, and this whole setup. He didn't like it at all but couldn't explain why.

Finally, he pushed himself from the chair and began another tour of the house, looking at everything carefully, attempting to find additional hidden rooms or passages. Back in the walk-in closet in the master bedroom was a carpet-covered trap door that opened on the hidden room on the floor below. Mitchell thought of it as nothing more than an escape hatch. If Miller had been trapped in the bedroom, no matter how that happened, there was a way for her to get out without having to break the bedroom windows or leave the house. He had seen a similar arrangement in the house of a friend long ago.

Having found that, Mitchell returned to the lower level and walked to the hidden room. Again using his flashlight, he entered it and slowly, carefully walked to the far end. He found a handle on the counter and grabbed it, lifting. Inside was a metallic escape ladder leading down to what he assumed would be another hidden room or maybe some kind of tunnel.

This whole thing reminded him of stories he read about medieval castles with hidden passages, panic rooms and escape tunnels for the privileged. The walls here were made of concrete instead of stone and the ladder down was aluminum rather than wood. There was a light switch near the top and Mitchell was sure that it would illuminate the tunnel, but remembering the other switch, he didn't touch it.

He hesitated, afraid of booby traps. Someone who went to the trouble of building an escape hatch would have some sort of protection around it. Then he thought about the situation. Someone using it would probably be afraid and not thinking in terms of traps. She would want to get out as fast as possible and probably figured that the trap at the light switch, if there was one there, would slow her down more than it would any pursuit.

He took out his cell phone and touched one of the buttons to light the dial and the screen. He pushed two, which dialed the station for him.

"Captain Mitchell's office," said a voice.

"Yeah, Sadoff, this is Mitchell. I'm still at Miller's place. I'll be another hour or so."

"Sure, Cap. You found something?"

"Don't know yet, but she has an escape tunnel. It's on the lower level, hidden, but I'll leave the door open. There's also a trap door in her closet that leads directly down into it. If anyone should follow me, tell them not to use the light switch. I think it might be a trap."

"Christ, Cap, what you got there?"

"I have a very strange lady who has an escape hatch, and I don't know what it means."

"How long you going to be gone?" Sadoff asked, forgetting what he had been told.

"Another hour or so. Anything pressing?"

"Just that Johnson. He is making noise about getting the body burned again. Cremated."

"Yeah, well, that's not our problem."

"Yes, sir. You going to interview him again? His attorney has been calling."

"Yeah, I'm going to want to talk to him. I can't seem to figure this thing out. I don't know why he would have shot her the way he did."

"If we had all the answers, we'd be out of business."

"That we would," said Mitchell. "Okay. I'll see you in about an hour."

"Sure thing."

Mitchell touched a button and disconnected. He put the phone into his pocket and then looked down into the tunnel one more time. There was no reason for him to hesitate. He had told the office where he was, and how long he would be gone. If anything happened, in two or three hours, there would be an officer out to investigate and he would know where Mitchell had gone inside the house. There was very little danger.

He climbed up on the edge of the cabinet and touched the top rung of the ladder. He slipped forward, putting more weight on the rung, ready for it to break, but it held fast. He turned slightly and then began to back down the ladder, testing each rung and waiting for a booby trap to spring. The skin at the base of his neck tingled and he felt slightly cold. There was no reason for his feelings, other than he felt that he was waiting for the other shoe to drop.

He reached the bottom of the tunnel and used his flashlight. The tunnel turned to the right gradually, and led down slightly to a wall about twenty feet away. There was a hint of a door there and Mitchell walked to it.

The tunnel was not something hacked into the ground by an amateur with a pickax and shovel. It was well engineered, with concrete walls, floor and ceiling. There were hints of bracing behind the concrete so there was little chance that it would collapse. Miller had spent some money on the tunnel. Mitchell wondered how she had explained it to the contractor.

He reached the door and looked at it carefully. If there was going to be a trap, it might be here, but he found no sign of anything. It looked like a regular door, solid core with heavy metal on it. Not something you would find on a vault, but a heavy door that would prevent anyone from crashing through it with ease. It was well sealed all around to prevent any tiny creatures from getting in.

There was a heavy bolt that Mitchell threw manually. He twisted the deadbolt lock and then turned the knob. He pulled gently and the door swung open on whisper quiet hinges. Beyond him was another short tunnel with daylight filtering in.

He was outside the house now and under the backyard.

He walked down the last few feet of the tunnel, saw a large bush and pushed aside some of the branches. He was halfway down a hill, looking into a wooded ravine. He knew that he was behind Miller's house. He walked out into the forest and looked back up the slope. He could see the roofline of Miller's house and little more.

The tunnel entrance was well concealed behind the bush and had he not known it was there, he wouldn't have been able to find it. The only clue was a bit of a path, running down the hill into the bottom of the ravine, but the path was so light that it would have been easy to miss or thought of as a game trail. It suggested that she had used the escape tunnel at some point, and not just for an escape. It had been used for something else.

Mitchell stood there for a moment, wondering, and then ducked back behind the bush. He would climb back into the house and then he would return to the office. He wanted some answers about this strange woman and he knew who to ask.

CHAPTER SEVENTEEN

Thomas Johnson, wearing an orange jumpsuit, sat in the small room that had no windows and no one-way glass, but did have a small, metallic table bolted to the floor and two rather uncomfortable chairs, also bolted to the floor. The floor was tile and the walls were of painted cinder block. It was a functional room, provided by the jail so that attorneys could talk with their clients without fear of interruption. Some attorneys believed the rooms were wired for sound so that private conversations could be recorded, but they were not. Jail officials did not want to be responsible for an important case being overturned on a technicality that let a guilty man or woman go free. They played by the rules.

The door was opened by a guard who allowed Goldberg to enter. She was dressed in a short skirt, a long jacket and a light blouse. She set her briefcase on the table, opened it and took out her pad.

"Okay, let's get started," she said.

"Have they destroyed the body? Have they cremated it yet?" asked Johnson without preamble.

"No. They are looking for family so that someone can claim it and pay the funeral expenses. If they don't find someone, the body will be buried in potter's field."

"No, no, no. That's not good enough. It has to be burned. Otherwise all this is for nothing."

"The city is not going to pick up the expenses for a cremation."

"I'll pay for it," said Johnson slightly hysterically. "I'll be glad to pay for it."

"I don't think that's the point," said Goldberg. "This insistence on destroying the body leads some to believe that you are attempting to destroy evidence."

"What possible good would that do me? It's not as if they had nothing else. What do they think? They'll find drug use? So what? They can't prosecute her now."

"Tom, I just think this is a point that you need to drop given your circumstances."

"There is good reason for this, but you just don't want to hear it."

"Anything that will help with the defense is something that I want to hear."

"Okay," said Johnson, leaning back in his chair. "I'll tell you a little story, and you then tell me if we shouldn't get the body burned."

Goldberg flipped open her legal pad and uncapped her fountain pen. "Shoot," she said.

"In those weeks after she showed me the family album and had me over to the house, I spent quite a bit of time with her. I always tried to keep it professional, but she sometimes had other things in mind. She would push the envelope, dressing in skimpy little outfits and sort of displaying her body for me. I knew what she was doing and I tried to ignore it."

"Tried?"

"Did," said Johnson.

"Okay, did."

"We fell into a pattern then. I would show up about dusk and she would be dressed, or nearly dressed, always on display. Sometimes she wanted to go out to clubs, in search of men who were just a little more receptive to her than I was. She would pick the club and she would drive. She insisted on that and I didn't really care. Gone are the days when a man has to do the driving while the woman rides along quietly. Gone are the days when the man made all the decisions and the woman went along."

"You were dating her?"

"Not really," said Johnson. "I was with her. Sort of as a wing-man."

"I don't think I get it," said Goldberg.

"I didn't either, at first. She needed someone with her. Sort of an assistant."

"I still don't get it. Why would you do something like that if it wasn't to . . . get into her pants?"

"There was something fascinating about her. Something that suggested there would be a good story for me. A old royal family who had lost the throne but who had retained the wealth. Something old world about it and I wanted to know more."

"And what was in it for her?" asked Goldberg.

"I think she saw me as the scapegoat. I think she was trying to cover her tracks with someone she thought of as slightly on the stupid side. She needed help with her camouflage and she believed I could provide that help. I think she thought she was running this and that at some point, if necessary, she would eliminate me and disappear."

Goldberg shrugged, not sure that she understood, or that she really cared.

"So . . . ?"

He grinned and then said, "Miller liked the loud clubs that were dark and jammed with people. If a club didn't have enough people, she would insist we move on. She would keep moving until she found what she often called her prime hunting ground. Then she would break free from me and circulate on her own."

"This is all well and good," said Goldberg, "but it really doesn't take us anywhere."

"But it does, and you'll see. When we're done, you'll have the defense all lined up."

"Sure."

"Anyway," said Johnson, "She would circulate, and I would sit at the bar, drinking beer. I'd watch the people dance, and sometimes I'd dance, but that wasn't the point. I was there as an escape hatch. Linda always had an escape plan. Not the same as a scapegoat, but a way to get away in the short term."

"Which means?"

"If some man attached himself to her and she decided he wasn't right, she'd come back to me and usually that would be the end of it. The man, angry, would back off rather than get into the middle of something domestic. I think some of these men were married and out playing around for the night. She steered clear of anything like that."

"She had scruples?"

Johnson grinned. "Oh, no. That they were married didn't bother her. No, it was the fuss that would be raised later, if the man didn't come home on time or at a reasonable hour. She didn't want the authorities to begin a search. Attached men, and women, would cause searches."

Goldberg stopped writing and looked up. "Didn't come home? You want to explain that?"

"Thought that might catch your attention," said Johnson. "You see, she was hunting, just as I told you. She was looking for prey. She wanted a loner at the lower end of the food chain so to speak. She wanted someone who could disappear without raising much of a stink. Kind of like the man who kills prostitutes. It's not that their deaths mean less to society, but that they are transient. If they disappear, everyone just figures they moved onto another town or state. The search for them is less than enthusiastic, if there is even a search. Sometimes people don't even know if they're gone. They're the disposable of our society. They come and go and no one really notices them."

"What was she doing? Robbing them?"

Johnson said, "Let me finish. So we'd, about once a week, go out clubbing, but she was always careful not to strike up any sort of relation with the regulars. She wanted each time to seem like the first so that people wouldn't notice her. She was careful not to hit the same club too often or to be too much of a standout. She was someone you might notice that night but who you wouldn't recognize the next time because she wasn't spectacular."

He grinned and said, "Sort of the anti–Paris Hilton."

Johnson stopped talking and asked, "Could I get something to drink?"

Goldberg got up, walked to the door and signaled the guard. He came back a moment later with a couple of Cokes and then locked them in again. He had been induced with a promise of a free drink for himself and Goldberg thought he was looking at her a little too closely, as if he had something else on his mind. She didn't mind exploiting that for a Coke.

Goldberg set the Coke on the table and said, "You know, you're dragging this out."

"Yes," said Johnson. "I'm not very proud of this next part, but I had the story of the century in my hand. I had book and movie deals and the last of the struggle to live well. I didn't understand, at first, what she was doing, but with her history, with her family history, and what I learned, I knew this was the big one. I had to have evidence because, otherwise, no one would believe it. This was only interesting if it was true."

"Just tell me."

"Okay. So, she would find someone in the club. Mostly she

found men, but that didn't really matter. She would cut them out of the crowd and then come on to them. She would tell them the most outrageous things, moving into their fantasy world. Find someone interested in leather, then that was what she was. Find someone wanting to hook up with the housewife prostitute, then that was what she was. She had a way of learning the kink, which meant that the prey also had something to hide and that he, or she, was a little bit secretive."

"You keep saying 'prey.' "

"Yes, because that was what they were. She would separate them from the pack and lead them over to the bar where they would buy her drinks. She tried not to pay and if she did, then she used cash to eliminate any record. She would sit near me so that I could watch her in action. She was very good at it."

"At what?"

"Leaning in and talking to them, just loud enough so that I could eavesdrop. I could hear her work her magic."

He stopped, took a drink and then set the can on the table, looking idly at the ring made by condensation.

"One man, a big guy with light hair and really big hands, sat there, staring at her as if he couldn't believe his luck. He wasn't a brute, he wasn't the best-looking man in the room, but she had sort of selected him. They sat while she finally learned that he liked to tie up his woman. She grinned at that and said that she thought she would never find anyone like that. She just loved restraint. It meant that the man had to keep her interested and that he had to work on her pleasure.

"The guy sat there, almost with his tongue hanging out. He asked about pictures and she said that it was no fun unless there were pictures. He asked about really short skirts and tiny tops and she said that she preferred to do that without panties. Made it more exciting."

"I think you might be giving me more information than I

care to have here," said Goldberg.

"The point is that she was feeding a line to him, to keep him excited about her. She was telling him exactly what she believed he wanted to hear, to lure him in."

"And then?"

"She looked over at me, grinned broadly and said to the man that she wanted to take him home. She had everything they needed including a digital camera so that they could make color prints of the night's activities. Without another word to me, she and the man left."

"So, what happened?"

"Now, you must remember that I didn't see this. I didn't know it at the time either. I just thought she was a real kink and had it not been for the story, for some of the documents she had, and what was going on now, I would have punched out. I wouldn't have had anything to do with her."

"Understood. What happened?" asked Goldberg, no longer writing anything down.

"From what she said, and from what I was able to piece together," said Johnson, "she drove them to her house, convincing him to leave his car behind because they could get it later. They went in, and she took him downstairs, to what she called 'the playroom.' There was nothing special about it, other than it was downstairs and was sparsely furnished. She hinted that the toys they would need were hidden because that wasn't the sort of stuff you wanted to leave lying out for anyone to see."

"Of course," said Goldberg.

"Once he was downstairs and relaxed, or I guess excited about the activities about to begin, but not fearful, she left the room for a moment. When she came back, according to what I have learned, she was naked. In her hand, she carried a long-bladed knife, sharp on both edges of the blade, which I guess makes it a dagger. She walked up to the man, who was sitting on the couch and who apparently didn't see the weapon. She knelt on the couch, facing to the rear with her knees on either side of his thighs and looked down at him. As he leaned forward to kiss her breast, she slashed him across the throat, deeply. He thrashed, his hips thrusting forward, against her, but she held onto the back of the couch. With one hand, he reached up to his throat and she leaned forward, her lips against the wound. He tried to talk but couldn't and in seconds, with his blood flowing, lost consciousness."

"Shit," said Goldberg. "I don't believe any of this." But she was pale, shaken and had trouble forming the words.

"There is evidence for those who wish to look," said Johnson. "You can document parts of the story. The man's car was impounded, for example. He is listed as missing and there has been no activity in his banking, checking or credit accounts since the night he went away with Miller. Of course there is nothing to connect him to her."

"So he didn't disappear without making a bit of a ripple," said Goldberg.

"No, but he did disappear and there was nothing to link him back to Miller. Friends told police that he had been going to the club and a couple of people remembered seeing him there and remember him with a girl. The descriptions fit about fifty different women so there was nothing that led back to Miller even though one of the descriptions did fit her pretty well. No one remembered him leaving with anyone, and it was two days before anyone missed him."

"So, your defense, or part of it, is that Miller was what? A serial killer who thinks she's a vampire?"

Johnson was about to deny that but then rocked back in his chair. He nodded and said, "Yeah. I think, under even the strictest of definitions, she was a serial killer."

"You know for a fact that she killed this guy?"

"Oh, there is no doubt about it. He's dead and she killed him."

"You saw the body?"

"No. She told me."

Goldberg felt faint but not because of the strange story. It was because she was sure that Johnson was trying to set up an insanity defense while lying to her about it.

She said, "Why would she tell you that? Why did she trust you so much?"

"Because I knew so many things about her already and hadn't gone to the police."

"That she told you. Did you verify any of it?"

"That was part of what I was doing, verifying her family history."

"And, he's not the only one she has killed?"

"Nope. I know of others. Mostly they were prey, but when anyone threatened her existence, or to expose her, then she could be ruthless."

Goldberg took a deep breath, took a sip of her Coke and then said, "Well, the sixty-four thousand dollar question is this. If you knew what she was, knew that she killed people, then why didn't you go to the police?"

"Yeah," said Johnson. "That is the question."

Of course the real question was why Miller was telling him anything at all.

CHAPTER EIGHTEEN

Rachael Goldberg was not a happy woman. She had just listened to her client, and more importantly her friend, tell her that he had been acting as the bird dog for a serial killer. Or rather, he was alleging that he had been the bird dog for a serial killer. If he was attempting to suggest some sort of self-defense, then that would never fly. He hadn't been in immediate danger and there was an obvious avenue of retreat when he shot Miller. And the other circumstances just added to the list of crimes he had committed. He could be charged in some of the murders because he apparently knew what she was doing and he was actively helping her to do it.

She left the jail, walked quickly to her car and then climbed in. She sat there for a moment, looking out at the trees standing along the river, at the skyline of the city, at the dark clouds building to the west that suggested a rapidly approaching thunderstorm.

That, to her, seemed appropriate, given what she had just heard. A nice touch of the gothic to go along with tales of a woman hunting men to kill them. A woman who had sneaked into the country, who had a family that could be traced to Eastern Europe, with counts and barons and other royalty who had somehow survived into the twenty-first century. A family who had been accused in the old country of stealing children and eating them.

"Oh, crap," she said, suddenly understanding and then

wondering why she hadn't seen it before. Johnson was really talking about a vampire, but he was trying to disguise it in the language he used. He had been the "familiar" for it. He had been the one who helped protect the identity. That was where he was going with his bloody tales. Not self-defense. Insanity. He believed Miller to be a vampire and had killed her because she was not human. She was undead.

And then she had to grin. An interesting defense. How could he have killed a person who was already dead? The law specified a human being but the undead were no longer human. There were theories that the vampires had never really been human.

Of course, it would never work because she would have to prove that vampires existed, that they were undead and therefore no longer human, and that Miller was, in fact, a vampire. And she couldn't do any of that. Even if it were true, she couldn't prove it in court.

It did pose an interesting question though. She had not seen the autopsy report and hadn't considered it to be of much importance because she knew that Johnson had shot Miller. Hell, he never denied that he killed her. He just said that he hadn't killed a human.

But then, if Miller was not human, or rather, if Johnson sincerely believed that she was not human, then didn't that suggest something about his state of mind and didn't that mean he couldn't recognize that his act was wrong? In fact, didn't that mean that he believed he was obligated to kill Miller, and if he truly believed that, then didn't he just meet the requirement for a legal verdict of insanity?

She sat there for a moment longer and thought about it. Then she opened her briefcase and took out a clean pad. She began to scribble her notes on it, realizing that she would need statements from everyone who had heard Johnson claim he hadn't killed a human, from psychologists who would test him, from friends who might have heard him talk about vampires. Hell, she might want to check his computer to find out if he had accessed any sites relating to vampires.

And that book he had described. Or the box of papers that Miller had showed him. That would be important because it could link all this together. It wouldn't prove that Miller was a vampire but it would prove, or help to prove, that Johnson thought she was a vampire and that was really the point.

And, there might be some family for her to contact. Maybe help trace some of Miller's movements in the last couple of years. Miller was the, what, eighth most common last name in the United States. She'd need more that just that. Of course, the box of documents would help.

Finally, she ran out of ideas, put the pad back into her briefcase and started the engine. She drove back to the office, on the fourth floor of a bank building, and took the elevator up. This was a prestigious law firm with richly paneled walls, a receptionist sitting behind a large, curved desk and quiet hallways that led to the offices of the attorneys, with a small conference room to the right and a large one to the left. Hidden in the rear was a break room, a cafeteria where the clerks, secretaries, and paralegals could congregate and eat. The lawyers, and especially the partners, never set foot in the break room where the peons met.

Goldberg walked into her office, looked at the messages arranged on her desk, out the window at the sparkling of the city at twilight just before the rain hit, and then opened her briefcase. She took out the pad with her notes on it and left her office, walking down the thickly carpeted hall to that of one of the senior partners.

C. Richard Howell was an older man, in his mid-fifties, with graying hair and an expanding waistline. He exercised, tried to eat sensibly, but nothing seemed to stop the march of time and his growing girth. He was a neatly dressed man who didn't spend a fortune on clothes, but who did not buy off the rack. He had a distinguished air about him, yet would scream at the television when a newscaster or commentator said something that he found disgusting when he thought no one was around to see him. He was a kind man who worried about the ills of the world, tried to do what he could to correct some of them and charged his wealthy clients as much as he could so that he was able to do pro bono work for those who could not afford him.

Goldberg stopped at his open door and tapped on the frame. When Howell looked up, she asked, "Are you real busy?"

He grinned, showing white teeth that were capped. "I'm always busy, but not real busy at the moment. Why don't you come in and sit down?"

Goldberg walked to one of the visitor's chairs that sat in front of the massive desk. Behind Howell was a slightly different view of the city. A meandering segment of the river was visible, as were two of the tallest buildings. To her right were floor to ceiling book shelves that held no volumes on the law and to her left were the framed pictures of the great and near great, of certificates and awards, and, of course, Howell's diplomas suggesting his excellent training in the law.

Goldberg sat down, crossed her legs and set her notepad on her lap. She said, "I have caught a tough one here. Thomas Johnson, charged with murder . . ."

"Just how in the hell did we get into that?" asked Howell, not so much in anger or annoyance as in surprise.

"I know him personally and when he was arrested, he asked for my help. I drove over to the police station to see what I could do for him there. I didn't realize where it was going to go until I met with him."

Howell rocked back in his chair and laced his fingers behind his head. He said, "I really wish that we had avoided that one. It's going to be messy."

"Yes," agreed Goldberg. "More than you know. I've got a problem here and thought I would get your opinions on it."

"Okay. Shoot."

Goldberg hesitated, studied her notes and then said, "There just is no easy way to get into this. It's clear from the evidence, and Johnson's own words, that he killed Linda Miller."

She grinned and said, "It is a case where he was caught with the smoking gun in his hand, standing over the body. The hypothetical you get in law school but the case that no one sees in real life."

"So we begin making noises about a plea agreement, get the best deal we can and call it a day."

"Well, sir . . ."

Howell grinned and said, "Now I know we're in trouble. You aren't normally so formal."

"This is going to be a bad one. Johnson claims he's not guilty because he didn't kill a human being and the charges do specify that he killed Linda Miller, a human being."

"That's crap," said Howell without thinking.

"Yes, sir, but he seems to be of the opinion that Miller was not human and in fact, suggested that she was, well . . ." Goldberg fell silent.

"She was?" prompted Howell.

"She was a vampire."

"Oh crap," said Howell.

"Precisely," said Goldberg. "But, if he truly believes that, then isn't his sanity in question? And, if he truly believes that, and he believes that he had to kill her because she was a vampire, then isn't his capacity to distinguish between right and wrong compromised, and isn't that, basically, the legal definition of insanity?"

Howell rocked forward, dropped his hands to his desk, and looked at Goldberg. He said, "I don't like this vampire thing. It smacks of afternoon matinees, and it smacks of superstition and it smacks of desperation. It is not a strategy that this firm would back in any way. It is sensationalistic and not worthy of us or an attorney who works here. In fact, I'm surprised that you would come to me with this sort of nonsense. I really don't want our firm to get a reputation as one that goes for the technicality regardless of the facts. This would be a very hard sell, not only for the court, but for our public image. A vampire."

"Is public image what we're after?" asked Goldberg.

"Rachael, that is not a fair question and you know it. The image problem is one that faces all attorneys. We're viewed as a bunch of smart-alecks who will do anything to get our clients off when we should be viewed as protectors of the law. You're going to introduce a technicality in which the murderer gets a couple of years in a nice hospital before being released into the world again because he can't distinguish right from wrong. He believes he killed a vampire. Just smart lawyer tricks."

"But if he actually believes . . ."

"Is irrelevant here. I don't care what he believes because that isn't important. When we begin to present a case that he thought this woman was a vampire we're going to look like a bunch of shysters. Good God, Rachael, what are you thinking?"

He slammed a hand down on his desk. "No," he shouted, "this is ridiculous. He thinks she was a vampire. This is not the nineteenth century and this is just too far out. No. We just won't do it."

Goldberg was surprised by the emotion. She'd never seen Howell angry, happy, sad or anything else. He was always calm, without emotion, at least in front of the underlings or at least he tried to be.

She said, "We can't just drop the case now."

"Of course we can. You're not a criminal attorney and you're not comfortable in the courtroom. Your client will just have to find someone else to handle his case. We'll find a criminal attorney and get him or her up to speed on this."

Howell had calmed himself, slightly embarrassed by his outburst.

"But he's my friend. He's counting on me," said Goldberg.

"That is not sufficient justification for taking on this loser case." Howell took a deep breath and again attempted to control his anger. "We do not have the time or resources to properly defend this man."

"But we have a strategy that our client is legitimately delusional, couldn't tell right from wrong and should be hospitalized rather than incarcerated," said Goldberg. "It doesn't matter what he believes."

"Haven't you been listening," asked Howell. "This is not a case that this firm will try. It is not one that we want to have our good name attached to. It is a loser all the way around. For everyone."

Goldberg said, "Johnson has some money. He might take some time paying the bill but he will pay it. We'll get our fee."

"That is not the issue and you know it. You are sitting here, telling me calmly and rationally, that you plan to defend the case by suggesting the client didn't kill a human but killed a vampire."

The anger and his attempt to control it was evident on his face. He said, "You don't see the bigger picture here. This is not a case that this firm will try. That is the end of this discussion."

Goldberg stood up then and said, "I'll try it on my own time and won't mention the firm."

"And you think that will work? You don't believe that the name of the firm will come into it?"

"I suppose it will."

"Then we understand one another?"

Goldberg nodded. She understood that she was about to lose her job. She turned and left the office.

CHAPTER NINETEEN

Tom Johnson didn't like the orange jumpsuit that he had to wear. The bright color bothered him, but he could understand the rationale behind it. No one would wear such a bright jumpsuit unless required to do so, and that meant that only the prisoners of the jail would be wearing them. It made it simple for the jailers to spot them in a crowd, or across the yard, or in the hallways or outside the walls, if the prisoner managed to get that far. The color seemed appropriate, and it made sense given those circumstances.

No, Johnson didn't like the jumpsuit because it was made of rough cloth and not all that well made. The zipper was long and often jammed and was cold when the jumpsuit was first put on. There were no pockets, and the legs were too long, but no one on the jail staff seemed to care about any of those concerns. The whole thing was a pain in the ass and there was nothing Johnson could do about it except wear the ill-fitting garment and pretend that he didn't care at all.

So, when he was escorted to the conference room to meet a visitor, he wasn't in a particularly good mood. When the guard opened the door and he saw police captain Steve Mitchell sitting there wearing a light blue shirt and old, faded jeans, he grew even more annoyed. And, when he spotted the can of Coke sitting on the table for Mitchell's benefit, but nothing for him, he became downright irritated.

As Johnson entered, Mitchell surprised him by asking,

"Would you care for a soft drink?"

"Coke," said Johnson.

Mitchell ordered the guard, "Get Mr. Johnson a Coke, will you please?"

There was a momentary look of resentment on the guard's face, but he said, "Yes, sir."

Then Mitchell said nothing until the guard returned with Johnson's Coke. Finally, he said, "I have a couple of questions for you."

"I am represented by an attorney," said Johnson. "She should be here for any questioning."

"I'm not thinking of this as an official interrogation, Tom," said Mitchell conversationally, "May I call you Tom?"

Johnson bowed his head slightly as if to say, "It doesn't really matter."

"Tom, I have some questions for you, and we can talk off the record if it will make you feel more comfortable."

"Since I have already requested my attorney, this interrogation is illegal."

Mitchell took a swallow of his Coke and said, "I'm not the enemy here. I'm interested only in the truth. You have to know that we've got you cold on this. Prosecution of the case is going to be a routine and simple matter. Your only hope is that we agree on mitigating circumstances. This is just a conversation between the two of us so that I might learn a little more about what happened that night."

Johnson said nothing.

"First, why did you do it? I'd like to hear about how you came to be in that room and why you shot Miller once in the head with a large-caliber handgun."

Johnson ignored the question. Instead, he asked, "Have you burned the body?"

"Well, there's an interesting response. Why would you want

us to burn the body?"

Johnson took a pull at the Coke. He set the can down carefully and then said, without much conviction, "Following her religious convictions."

"Yes, and what is her religion?"

"Some Eastern European philosophy."

"Well, that's just not going to do it. Not without some instruction from the family, not to mention that the body is evidence in this case. We can't cremate her until after the trial has ended anyway."

"You don't understand," said Johnson, suddenly sounding like a little kid.

"Why don't you fill me in then. Why should the body be cremated?"

"I told you."

"Yes, and that doesn't do it. We need to finish the autopsy and collect the evidence."

"I forgot about the autopsy," said Johnson. "That buys some time."

"Interesting comment," said Mitchell. He took out a cigarette pack and held it out to Johnson, who shook his head. Mitchell then put the cigarettes away without taking one himself. He was trying to make Johnson comfortable. He was trying to make Johnson think of him as a friend rather than as a police officer.

"When was she autopsied?"

"Yesterday, I think."

"And the pathologist cut her open, removing organs?" asked Johnson. "Separated the organs from the body?"

"I'm not sure that I like the direction of this conversation," said Mitchell.

"Please. I have to know."

"As far as I know it was a standard autopsy."

"Were the organs returned to the chest cavity? The brain put back in the skull?"

"Other than for small samples taken for tox screens, blood and tissue samples and the preparation of slides, I believe that is the case," said Mitchell.

Johnson visibly relaxed. "I hadn't thought about the autopsy. That might do it. The damage inflicted in the autopsy might be enough."

"You care to tell me what you're thinking about?" asked Mitchell.

Instead, Johnson picked up his Coke and drank deeply. He set the can down and then calmly said, "I really should have my attorney present for questioning."

"I'm not happy with your attitude."

"Captain," said Johnson, "I'm sorry, but everything I know suggests that you are not here as my friend. You are engaged in a homicide investigation. Your interrogation techniques are superb but I recognize them."

"Well," said Mitchell, grinning, "if you hadn't been standing over the body with the smoking gun in your hand, you'd be right. However, this isn't a whodunit, nor do we have to assemble any more evidence against you. We have the eyewitnesses who saw you standing over the body, heard your comments at the crime scene, your prints on the gun, and the blood spatter on your clothes that tell us you were standing near Miller when she was shot. All we need to do is go to trial so nothing you say to me is going to damage your defense. We have all we need now. You're going to stay in the slammer for a very long time regardless of what you say to me here today. So, why'd you shoot Linda Miller?"

"Self-defense."

"Well, I'm afraid that isn't going to fly, Tom. You had the weapon and she didn't. You had an avenue of retreat and didn't use it. Self-defense as a legal strategy here is just not going to work for you in this case."

"I'm not convinced that I should take legal advice from you," said Johnson.

"Well, I won't argue that," said Mitchell, grinning. "Still . . ."

"She had killed before," said Johnson.

Mitchell nodded and said, "See? That's what I mean. That might help you with your plea if we can substantiate those sorts of things. Now, why do you think she killed before?"

"I think that if you search her house carefully," said Johnson, "you'll find the evidence."

"I have found evidence of blood from a number of individuals in her house, but that doesn't lead me to evidence that she's killed before. It only tells me that people have splashed blood around that house and not that any of the bloodletting was fatal. Too little of it left."

Johnson raised his eyebrows in surprise. "You've been to her house?"

"Of course. Standard investigative technique. Even if it wasn't the crime scene, we would still have searched her residence since she was the victim here. Now, why do you say she's killed before?"

"This puts me in a very precarious legal position," said Johnson. "I can supply information but that might involve additional criminal charges . . ."

"You have committed other crimes?" asked Mitchell.

Johnson knew in that moment he had already said too much. No one, not Mitchell, not the police, not the DA, knew that he knew of Miller's crimes. He could point them in the right direction, but to do so would compromise his own position, suggesting that he knew of criminal activity that he hadn't reported to the police, the FBI or any official agency and that could make him an accessory to those crimes. Suddenly he understood why defense attorneys told their clients not to talk to the police. He tripped himself up with what he thought of as an innocuous statement.

Johnson spoke slowly then. He said, "I would think that a look into the missing person files would be of some use. I would think that you could find some clues there."

"You have names?"

Johnson considered his answer before speaking. Finally, he said, "I have gone through the disappearances in the last couple of years, from before the time that Miller arrived in town. I have put together a list of names of those who have vanished and who have not returned or who have not resurfaced in some way. I eliminated some names because the person was too old or too young or didn't frequent the club scene. That is where Miller did her hunting."

"Hunting?"

And even though he knew he was telling Mitchell too much, he was lost in the tale and he forgot where he was or who was doing the questioning. He was now telling another part of the story that had become so important to him.

"She wanted young men because she thought the blood had more energy. She thought that youth translated into energy and that the blood of those older than forty wasn't very good. It wasn't as satisfying as that from younger people. Young men were best but young women were fine."

Mitchell sat quietly, listening. He shook his head once or twice, as if he didn't believe what he was hearing, but now that he had Johnson talking, he didn't interrupt.

"She thought the clubs made the best hunting grounds, but she wasn't going to ignore a gift if one came her way."

"Gift?"

"An easy mark. Easy prey. She told me once that she met a man in the grocery store. He was buying a dozen TV dinners, and those prepackaged vegetables. The sort of thing that you put in the oven and thirty minutes later you had a meal. She figured that he lived alone because he obviously didn't cook, and he wasn't buying anything that took time to prepare. He wasn't buying anything that a wife or live-in girlfriend would want to eat."

"What did she do?"

"Approached, smiled and asked if he was free for dinner. Then she tried to learn a little about his family, or the lack of family. If there was no family, no real close friends, if he didn't have a job that suggested responsibility, then she would take a chance."

"And then?"

"You understand that I know very little from firsthand observation. I'm repeating stories that I have been told and that I was unable to verify."

"Tom, I told you we were off the record. I'm just looking for the truth and not to convict you of additional crimes. But, if you can clear some of those crimes from our books, it would be of a help to me."

"And I really should have my attorney here so that I don't get myself into more trouble."

"Okay, we've both sung our song. Tell me what I need to know to move forward."

"The grocery store victim, I think, was Gene Blair, a construction worker who had been in town for only a few weeks. Lived in a cheap hotel that had some kitchen facilities. Living cheap and saving money and then just disappeared."

"Miller killed him?"

"That is my understanding."

"You know that I can check this out."

Johnson grinned broadly. "I would hope so. You find that a Gene Blair is missing, then you have part of the story. It also seems to me that if you have found any blood in her house, then you might be able to do a DNA analysis and learn who some of that blood belonged to."

"You have any other names?"

"Yes, but there is something that I want in return."

Mitchell laughed and said, "I can't make any deals."

"This one you can."

"Okay. If it is in my power to grant, I will do so, if you remember that there isn't much that I can do for you other than tell the judge that you have been cooperative."

"Have Miller cremated as soon as possible. The autopsy bought some time but might not have done enough damage."

Mitchell wasn't sure how to react. He started to grin but stopped. He hesitated long enough to take a pull at the Coke and then carefully set the can down.

Finally, he said, "Just why would I do that?"

"Doesn't cost you anything and it makes me a very co-operative individual."

"But I don't need your cooperation," said Mitchell. "You're here, in the slam, and you aren't going to get out any time soon, as far as I can see."

"It also makes sure that there are no other murders around here."

Mitchell shook his head. "Sorry. I don't get that."

"How many murders do you have, on average, in this city, not counting the drug dealers gunning each other down and not counting the domestic violence that turns nasty? How many unsolved cases do you have?"

Mitchell shrugged. "You take out the turf wars and the drugs, then the number drops quite a bit. Sometimes I think we ought to arm the drug pushers and let them fight it out and arrest whoever is left standing, but I dare not say that to anyone publicly. Anyway, take out those elements, and there aren't all that many murders."

"And I'll bet Miller accounts for half of them, though you don't know that yet."

"So you want me to burn the body so that we have no hope of ever clearing those."

"Keep a DNA sample. Keep tissue samples. But burn the body and do it soon."

"I'll consider it," said Mitchell, "if you can give me one good reason to do it. Just one."

Now Johnson fell silent. He sipped at his Coke as he thought about it. He knew that Mitchell would never believe the real reason. Mitchell, like everyone else, was firmly grounded in the science of the twenty-first century. He wasn't going to be swayed by arguments that smacked of medieval superstition. He would laugh, probably out loud, and might even promise to do it, but in the end wouldn't. There was nothing to fear from a human body, to his way of thinking.

But Johnson had thought the question through and he knew what might work. He asked, "Remember the Ebola scares a couple of years ago? Remember how the transmittal of the virus was through the blood products and bodily fluids and it wasn't all that difficult to become contaminated?"

"Yeah. I remember."

"Well, Miller has been contaminated by a similar disease, one that isn't recognized outside of a couple of top-secret labs here and isn't talked about much in the press. No real sensational aspects to it so that nobody is really talking about it. The only way to ensure that this disease doesn't spread is to burn the body."

Mitchell took another pull at his Coke. "Isn't it already too late? The medical examiner has been digging around in the body for a couple of hours."

"It's never too late," said Johnson.

"If this is a top-secret project, how do you know about it?"

132

asked Mitchell.

"The labs are top secret, but the information is not. You can find it on the Internet. Transmittal of the disease is difficult, but it happens. Burn the body and there is no longer a risk of contamination."

Mitchell nodded. "All right. I'll look into it. Just as long as you remain cooperative.

Johnson slumped in his chair, looking as if he had just been relieved of a huge burden. He felt as if a weight had been removed from his chest and he could breathe again.

"Thanks," he said. "Thanks."

CHAPTER TWENTY

Police captain Stephen Mitchell, who was rarely called Steve anymore, couldn't believe that he was going to carry out the promise he had made to a murder suspect. There was no reason for him to do it because there was really no way for Johnson to learn that his request had not been granted. It would be easy enough for Mitchell to pretend that he had cremated the body of murder victim Linda Miller. No one would know the difference if he set it up properly. The medical examiner, a mortuary, and a mortician would all cooperate with him.

Then again, there was no reason to find out how difficult it would be to carry out Johnson's instructions. Rather than use the telephone, Mitchell decided to drive over to talk to the medical examiner in person. Mitchell believed that some things needed to be done in person, face to face, rather than over the phone or through email or text messages or Twitter. It was not a belief shared by many in the twenty-first century.

He found Blanchard in his office, which was small, tucked in a corner and piled high with books, papers, journals, reports, computer disks, CDs, awards, photographs and twenty-two small state flags, indicating, according to what Blanchard told those who asked, trips to medical conventions in those states, but reflected instead sexual conquests, or he sometimes claimed. The desk was an antique rolltop that looked as if it was two hundred years old but that had slots for additional CDs built in. There was an unmistakable odor of alcohol in the air, but of the medicinal and not drinking kind.

Blanchard didn't look up when Mitchell entered. He seemed to be reading something from a small flat-panel tucked into a corner of the massive rolltop.

"Good afternoon, Doctor," said Mitchell by way of announcement.

Blanchard sat for a few seconds as if he hadn't heard and then turned. "Yes, Captain?"

"Got a strange question for you. Or maybe a strange request. I'm not sure which."

Blanchard touched the mouse and the screen went dark. He turned in his chair, leaned an elbow on the desk and said, "I get a lot of strange requests here."

"Have you completed the autopsy and lab work on Linda Miller yet?"

"You mean the murder victim that came in a couple of days ago?"

"That would be the one."

"Well, unless you have a question or suggestion about something that we haven't done, or you want a specific toxin screen completed that might require specific tissue samples, brain tissue, for example, then yes, I have completed my work and await only police authority to release the body to the mortuary. Of course, I expect the body to be held until the completion of the trial. That's standard."

"Then you would have no objection to cremation?" said Mitchell.

Blanchard grimaced and scratched at his ear. "Personally, no, I have no objection, though, as you know, that would destroy any evidence that we might have missed and eliminates the possibility of another autopsy, if someone should suggest that we missed something on the first. But, as I say, we generally hold onto the body until after the trial."

Mitchell rubbed his face and said, "But, it's not like we don't have a case against the killer already. I don't know what else we could learn about her, except that she was on drugs or something."

Blanchard asked innocently, "You think that might have some relevance?"

"No," said Mitchell. "I was just saying that we're not in need of fiber evidence to tie the killer to the victim or anything of that nature. We know who committed the crime and we have him in custody. The case, for us, is virtually over. But the killer wants the body cremated."

"I'm always somewhat reticent to destroy our evidence, but then, the mortuary would embalm her and bury her so there is a degradation of the evidential value of the victim, once we release it."

"If you have finished your work," said Mitchell, "then I think we should arrange for the body to be moved."

"There is one thing that I found interesting," said Blanchard. "Well, actually, there was more than one, but the most unusual was that, for a young woman, her bones seemed to be old. I looked at that closely, and if I had only a skeleton to examine, I would have told you that she had to be in her eighties or nineties. You might say that she had old bones."

"There a reason for that?"

"Degenerative disease," said Blanchard. "She wasn't getting enough citrus or calcium in her diet. She also seemed to have a blood disorder but I haven't identified it in the literature as of yet. I'm not sure exactly what it was, but her blood was not normal."

"So she was sick," said Mitchell.

"Nothing that would have been outwardly noticeable, at least when she died, but the cumulative effect would have eventually been fatal. Maybe in five years or so."

"Treatment?"

Blanchard shrugged. "If we could identify the problems, then there might be a regimen of treatment. For the bone disease, just additional calcium might have reversed the course, at least in a young woman. There are a number of treatments available to reverse the calcium loss. I don't know what to do about the blood problems since I didn't take time to identify the specific pathologies. I confess that I've never seen anything like them."

"Is this something that needs further study?"

"Well, if I was a researcher rather than a pathologist and I had the time, there are some interesting avenues to explore, but frankly, I just don't have the time. If people would stop killing each other, and themselves, I might be able to do something to pursue these irregularities." He grinned as he said this, as if the thought had just occurred to him.

"You have samples?"

"Oh, yes, I have samples. There are some things that I do want to explore, and if Miller was unique, I would be remiss if I allowed everything to be destroyed. My only problem is storage, but I'll work that out."

Mitchell took a deep breath and then leaned back in the chair. He looked out the door into the morgue area with its stainless steel tables and its refrigerator units. It was a chilly room, made that way by air conditioning, but it was a cold-looking room. Too much steel and white enamel. He didn't like being in the morgue.

Finally, he said, "Then I'll arrange for a mortuary to pick up the body."

"Given me another day," said Blanchard. "If you're going to cremate it, then I'll want to make sure that I have everything that I need. In fact, I'll make all the arrangements myself." Although he thought about it, he said nothing about getting a clearance to release the body from the district attorney. He just kept his mouth shut.

Mitchell got to his feet. He looked down at Blanchard and wondered why he had even done this. He owed Johnson nothing and there was no way Johnson would know if the body had been destroyed. It was just something he said that he would do if possible, which at the time had been a lie, and yet here he was, checking into it. It was as if something that Johnson had said scared him enough to learn a little more.

Of course, he didn't realize how this simple act of kindness would complicate the case in the following weeks.

CHAPTER TWENTY-ONE

Sarah Hartwell came awake slowly, unsure of where she was or how she had gotten there. She noticed that she was thirsty, her mouth dry. Then she noticed a dull ache centered in her lower back, and then various pains throughout her body. She felt as if she had fallen down a flight of concrete stairs.

When she opened her eyes, her vision was blurred so that she had the impression of light grays that faded into areas of charcoal or brightened into areas of flat white. There was a square of darkness punctuated with small, bright points and gradually she realized that she was looking out a window into a world at night. She thought it was still the night she had been injured.

Slowly the world began to focus and Hartwell could hear the buzzes, chirps and pops of the medical monitoring equipment around her. She tried to move her arm but it was held down. She turned her head and saw the IV bags and the tubes.

A moment later a nurse entered and Hartwell remembered that she was in the hospital. She had been awake before and slowly those memories flooded into her mind. She had talked to the police once or twice and it was now several days later.

The nurse walked over, looked down and said, "You're awake again."

Hartwell nodded and said, "Water."

The nurse picked up a cup, looked in it and then put the cap back on. She bent the straw and let Hartwell drink from it once or twice. Then she asked, "How are you feeling?"

"Hungry."

"Well, you haven't eaten much in the last few days. Just that stuff hanging beside the bed. I'll see what we can do. Maybe some Jell-O."

"Tom? How's Tom?"

"Tom would be?"

"My friend. He was there."

"Tom, I believe, is just fine."

Hartwell closed her eyes in relief and then asked, "How long have I been here?"

"Well, we had to take you into surgery to repair some of the damage so you've been out of it for a couple of days. The police have been in and out wanting to talk to you again."

"I could talk to them now."

"Maybe it would be best to wait until you've had a little more rest."

"Could you put the back up so that I'm not lying flat?"

The nurse reached for the control and took it in her left hand. She said, "Let me know when you're comfortable."

Slowly the back came up and Hartwell felt herself slip slightly in the bed. She felt dizzy for an instant and said, "That's good."

There was a quiet tap on the door and then it swung open slightly. A short, stocky man in a rumbled suit looked in and asked, "Mind if I come in?"

Before the nurse could chase him away, Hartwell said, "I could use some company."

The man came to the side of the bed and looked down. "How are you feeling?"

"Tired. Hungry. Sore."

The man reached into the inside pocket of his suit and pulled his wallet out, opening it to reveal his badge. "I'm Sergeant Novotny. If you are up to it, I'd like to ask a few questions about the other night."

Hartwell nodded. "Yes. I think I would like to have the company."

The nurse looked at Novotny with anger and said, "She has been badly injured. She has been in surgery. She has already talked to the police."

"I'll try not to tire her too much," said Novotny, "but there are some questions that need to be asked and answered."

The nurse retreated to the door and said, "I'm sure the doctor will be in shortly." With that, she left.

Novotny took a small, palm-sized recorder from his pocket, pushed a button and said, "Sergeant Novotny with Sarah Hartwell. Do you mind if I record?"

"No. I don't mind."

Novotny stopped the tape, rewound it and listened to it, making sure that her voice was audible and that the recorder was working properly. Satisfied, he pushed the record button and said, "Interrogation held in Hartwell's hospital room and begins at seven forty-two in the evening. Now, in your own words, tell me what happened during the murder."

"I'm not convinced there was a murder," said Hartwell, slowly, quietly, as if reviewing her answer carefully before she gave it.

"I'm just wanting to get your perspective of the events that led up to the death of Linda Miller."

"She's really dead?"

"Yes."

"You're sure?"

"Yes. But I think that I should be asking the questions here. I want to know what happened."

"Linda Miller attacked me." She spoke.

Novotny glanced right and left and then grabbed a light, metallic chair. He dragged it over and sat down. "I think I need a little more information."

Hartwell tried to remember what she had told the other policeman. The one she saw that first night. The memory of the interview was hazy, obscured by the fog created by her injury, and seemed a little distant, as if it had happened twenty years earlier and not just a day or two ago.

Finally, she said, "Linda Miller was a sick woman. She believed that she needed blood to survive and she killed to get it."

"That really doesn't tell me much. I need details." Novotny smiled as he said it. He had, of course, just complicated the investigation, first by interviewing Hartwell while she was still in the hospital, then by getting the new information about the attack, and finally with his comment about Hartwell's answers.

"Tom had been working with her . . ."

"An accomplice?"

Hartwell's brain seemed to tumble. She wasn't tracking well and realized that she was in no shape to answer police questions. She could cause more damage than she knew with on ill-advised comments.

She said slowly, as if thinking about each word, "No. I think he thought of himself as a journalist chasing a story. He told me that she had an interesting background. Something about Eastern Europe and being related to Hungarian or Romanian royalty. She had documents and books that were hundreds of years old."

"So he was what? Researching her background?"

The question seemed tame enough. She said, "He thought he would write a book about it. Give the history of her family."

"But it didn't work out?"

Hartwell stopped and reached for the cup of water. She took a drink and then set it down. "She was using him to help her."

"Meaning what?"

"I don't know exactly. I know that they went out some nights, but he rarely followed her home. She picked up men, and sometimes women, and took them home. Tom wasn't allowed to go home with her on those nights."

"What was she doing?"

"I don't know, exactly. Toward the end there, Tom started getting suspicious. He began tracking the missing person reports and found that a couple of the people who had been with Miller had disappeared shortly after they met her."

"Meaning?"

"Tom wasn't sure."

"Ms. Hartwell, Tom is already in deep trouble for killing Miller. If there are extenuating circumstances, that can only help him out."

"Tom was careful about what he said. He didn't confide everything in me. He seemed to think she might be engaged in some kind of illegal activity."

"Then he should have called the police."

Hartwell wasn't up to an argument. She closed her eyes for a moment and then said, "And tell them what? Some people might have disappeared? He thought she was doing something illegal?"

"We could have confirmed it. Might have saved everyone a great deal of trouble."

"He said that he had no evidence of anything illegal, only some suspicions. He also thought that she might be delusional, which would account for her activities, but there was nothing illegal in that."

"We're getting off on a tangent here," said Novotny, "and I don't have a lot of time right now."

Hartwell closed her eyes for a moment and then said, "What do you want to know?"

"What happened that night?"

Hartwell was quiet for a moment. She stared at the window and could see that it was getting late in the day. That disoriented her slightly. It had been night when she had been attacked and she had slept. It should have been daylight, not evening.

Hesitantly, as if afraid of the words, she said, "We went to Miller's house for dinner. She had invited the both of us."

"And you thought nothing of it?"

Hartwell tore her eyes away from the scene outside her hospital room and looked at Novotny. "Why shouldn't she?"

"I don't know."

"She invited us both. I think it was to finalize her control over Tom."

"Meaning?"

Hartwell took a deep breath, as if extremely tired. She exhaled slowly and said, "I don't know. She wanted to prove to Tom that she was in charge of everything. This was going to prove it to him."

"Go on."

"Well, we arrived and went into the living room. Miller sat down in one of the chairs and pointed at the couch. I sat down at one end and Tom on the other. There was a coffee table that had stuff all over it. Magazines, books, some of them looking old, and an ornate dagger. Long hilt with jewels on it. I thought they were rhinestones."

"And?"

"We talked. Linda was talking about her childhood in some Eastern European country. Sounded like she had lived in a castle or something. Tom was listening to her carefully but he wasn't taking notes."

Novotny shifted around, looking bored with the whole thing. After all, they knew who the killer was.

"We talked and then Linda said that we should go into dinner. She told Tom to bring the dagger, which made no sense to me. He left it on the table."

"And then?"

"I don't know. I don't really remember much. I remember walking toward the dining room and there was a flash of bright light. Bright white light and I didn't understand that. I felt a sharp pain at the back of my head. The next thing I knew, the next thing I remember, I was in here."

"You're sure he didn't pick up the dagger?"

"He left it on the table."

There was a tap on the door and it swung inward. The doctor entered, looked first at Novotny and then turned his attention to Hartwell. "How are you feeling?" he asked.

"Tired. Thirsty."

"I would expect both and maybe a little hunger too. Who's your friend?"

Novotny stood up and said, "I was just leaving. I'll be back if I think of anything else."

The doctor noticed the look on Hartwell's face and said, "Check with the nurses station before you come visiting. She's been through a lot and we need her to get her rest."

Novotny looked at the doctor like he was speaking a foreign language and then left.

Novotny found Captain Mitchell sitting at his desk, his feet propped up on the top and staring out the small, rectangular window at the clouds barely visible over the building across the street. He was eating a hardboiled egg, the shell on his desk along with salt and pepper.

Mitchell waved at the empty chair but didn't speak. He just chewed his egg.

"Talked to the Hartwell woman."

Mitchell swallowed and asked, "She say anything?"

"Gave me a little more than we had. Remembered some of

the discussion after she and Johnson arrived and said that she remembered getting hit in the back of the head. She seemed to be suggesting that the murder was in self-defense, or more accurately, Johnson defending her, though she didn't say that specifically. She was very careful in what she said."

"So Johnson is going for an affirmative defense. To save Hartwell he had to shoot Miller."

Novotny shrugged. "I don't know for sure. She wasn't sure what happened, but she seemed to be thinking in that direction."

Mitchell finished his egg, swallowed and then asked, "What did she say, exactly?"

"That's just it," said Novotny, "nothing that really meant anything. I think, as we talked, she began to get suspicious of what I wanted and her answers became less complete. She was thinking about it and didn't want to say anything that would hurt Johnson."

Mitchell took a deep breath, leaned forward and pushed the eggshells off his desk and into this hand. He dropped them into the wastebasket before he said, "There were three people in that house. One is dead, one in jail and the third in the hospital. She can tell us what we need to know."

"Of course," said Novotny. "I'll talk to her again. But after she has a chance to think about it and after Johnson's attorney gets to her, we're going to have a tough time getting anything out of her that will be useful."

"Then you better get her statement on the record before the attorney gets to her."

It wasn't anything that Novotny needed to hear. He'd already figured it out for himself.

CHAPTER TWENTY-TWO

William C. Blanchard sat in his tiny but brightly lit office in the morgue, having shoved aside the blizzard of papers that had drifted across his tiny desk and threatened to spill to the floor. He sat in a high-backed chair that allowed him to recline so that his feet were propped up and he could use a wireless keyboard on his lap. The arms of the chair were wide and covered in leather, the right of which worked as an oversized mouse pad for his wireless mouse. He found that he would not have to move his body at all, only his hands and fingers were connected to the Internet for his research.

It was the kind of research that Blanchard enjoyed. He had a mystery to solve and had the tools at his fingertips to do it. The pictures from the autopsy, captured digitally, had been loaded into the computer so that he could assess them for review. His notes had been captured electronically and converted using a voice recognition program that understood the medical terms he used so that it didn't come up with inventive spelling that sometimes fooled everyone. He could decipher it by the context in which the bizarre words appeared.

He tried to keep from becoming too excited by what he had seen. The dead woman, Linda Miller, was such a deviation from normal that he wondered if he was seeing some form of a mutation or if he was looking at another species of primate, as different from humans as the chimpanzee was from the gorilla. There were tests to be done, but it was possible that Miller represented something that was not really human.

The first thing he wanted to do was learn if any other, similar specimens had been described in the medical literature. Given his job, he had access to databases that were not part of the public Internet. He could access medical libraries around the world and look for anything that remotely resembled what he had seen at the autopsy.

He watched the information parade across the screen. Thousands of words about every deviation from the normal human structure that had ever been observed and recorded. Conditions that were very common to those that had been mentioned only a single time. There were tiny, perfectly formed humans and giants that rivaled anything thought of in Hollywood. There were people with six fingers on a hand and six toes on each foot, people with small heads and large eyes and people who had no eyes. There were people who looked like animals and people covered with thick, black hair. People who couldn't go out in the sun and people who couldn't tolerate thin air. There were people who looked more simian than human and there were all the variations of the normal person.

Everything he wanted to know he could find on the Internet, in the restricted files of universities, in the online medical services that required monthly fees, and in the literature of the medical journals. Every human condition was outlined, examined, explained and detailed. Except the one he wanted to find and that made him feel much better.

Then, in an obscure German medical book that had been published before World War I, he found a description of a body that had washed up near Berlin. A young man, certainly no more than thirty, who had apparently been mauled by some large predator such as a bear or a wolf, was found half submerged. He was missing an arm and part of his skull had been smashed. Either wound would have been fatal.

Blanchard read the article carefully, cursing his poor German but thankful for parents that had insisted he take a foreign language in high school, which meant he took the same one in college.

He noted that the skull was thicker than normal, that the heart and lungs seemed to be enlarged, and there were internal organs that seemed to have no counterpart in a normal human. The purpose of the organs wasn't discussed and there was no real description of them, yet Blanchard recognized the illustrations of them. He had seen similar organs in the body of Linda Miller when he opened her up.

The journal only carried drawings, made at the time of the autopsy and while they were detailed and exact, they weren't quite the same thing as photographs. Blanchard studied them carefully onscreen, highlighting and enlarging portions of them. Finished, he printed out a copy of the article, studied the illustrations and then printed each one out separately.

With those in hand, he returned to the morgue so that he could compare what he had with Linda Miller. He believed now that he had found another example of her strange body type meaning that she was not unique and that there were both male and female representatives. It meant to him that he would be the first to describe, in the scientific literature, this new adaptation to humanity and that he would get the credit for discovering it.

He examined the body carefully. He hadn't performed a regular autopsy because he had recognized early on that this was something special. With Mitchell standing there, he had to work carefully. Mitchell wasn't a rookie who could be fooled by a lot of jargon and who wouldn't pay attention because he hadn't seen an autopsy before. Mitchell knew the ropes.

The shot to the head had been the saving grace. It was obvious that the wound was fatal and once he had said it was the cause of death, Mitchell had been happy. He wanted a report, but he didn't need to hang around the morgue while Blanchard cut up the body.

And that question about cremation had been helpful. Blanchard would use it as his excuse. When the police and the DA began to talk about the body, Blanchard would say that it had been cremated on police orders.

He stared down at the dead woman and could have sworn that the body had healed itself slightly. The head wound didn't seem as livid as it had once been. It wasn't as pronounced, nor quite as large.

The edges of the wounds in the chest and down to the abdomen were a little less as defined. Blanchard grinned to himself, wondering what that meant. He'd never seen anything quite like it in all his years as a pathologist. It was just one more thing that made Miller different from all the other bodies that he'd seen pass through the morgue.

There was a sound behind him and the door opened. The man who entered looked as if he should work in a mortuary. He was tall and very thin, nearly gaunt and looked as if he was on the verge of disintegration. He had thin white hair that looked as if it had never seen a comb. His chest was sunken and his arms long, ending with thin fingers that almost looked like tentacles.

"You got a pickup for us."

Blanchard covered Miller's body and said, "Yes. You have the special instructions?"

The man reached around and pulled a folded sheet of paper from a rear pocket. He opened it slowly and then nodded. "Yeah. I got them."

"Okay," said Blanchard. "Here's the deal, I don't want to hear about this again. I don't want you talking to your friends or your girlfriend or your mother about this. I want you to forget this just as soon as the body is transported. For that I'll give you an extra hundred dollars. All you have to do is forget that you ever did this."

"This illegal?" asked the man.

"Do you care?"

"I don't want to go to the slam is all."

"You make the delivery. You have your instructions. You are not versed in the law. You did what you were told. You won't go to jail."

"You give me a hand?"

Blanchard sighed because they rarely asked for help, but this time Blanchard was asking for special treatment. He said, "Just bring in the gurney."

The man walked back out into the hall and returned. He pushed the gurney up to the shelf pulled from the locker door, and set the wheel locks. He then opened the black plastic body bag that was set there so that they could put the woman into it.

The man reached up under the shoulders of the dead woman. Blanchard grabbed her ankles and together they slid her onto the gurney and into the body bag. As they did, the sheet pulled free and the man stared down, first at the woman's breasts and then at her pubic area. Even the large wounds, now loosely stitched together, didn't seem to shock him. He was more interested in the cheap thrill.

Blanchard was going to say something and then didn't. He didn't want to offend the man because he needed his silence. Instead, he just zipped up the body bag without comment.

"I will meet you there," said Blanchard. "You have the address?"

"Yeah, I got it."

"And you weren't here and you never saw this body."

"For a hundred bucks, I'd set it on fire."

"Then get going," said Blanchard.

As soon as the man had wheeled Miller out of the morgue, Blanchard turned off the lights. He had prepared for this, meaning that in the last several hours, he had prepared. This was the chance of a lifetime and he wasn't going to share that discovery with anyone. He might find himself in trouble, but it would be minimal compared to the fame he would find. His name would be up there with Darwin and Leakey and Galileo. He would be one of the pioneers of the century.

He pulled into his driveway and then into the garage. He leaped from the car but left the garage door open. He ran around the side of the house, now glad that his wife had left him five years earlier. She wouldn't be around to ask annoying questions and to tell him what he was doing wrong. When his name appeared in the newspapers and there were invitations to speak at major conventions, appearances on television, she would be there, telling him that she was sorry. He'd just laugh at her then, knowing that she was more interested in the fame and the money.

Oh, yes, there would be money. Trucks of it. Mints of it. It would seem that he had permission to print the stuff. The Noble Prize paid nearly a million and that would just be the beginning of it.

He unlocked the door and opened it. He hurried downstairs, into his basement lab that was now a small-scale morgue. He had a used autopsy table, he had bright lights, he had cameras both film and digital, including DVD. Everything would be documented for the world. No one would be able to question his results or his conclusions because he would have everything that he needed.

The outside labs needed for the DNA sequencing and analysis would do the work, assuming that it was for the state. He could call on labs around the country to verify his work. There would be no questions.

He heard a car engine and hurried back up the stairs. He looked out the window, sure that it would be the man from the funeral home and afraid that it would be a friend dropping in unannounced.

The driver backed into his driveway and got out of the car. As he did, Blanchard opened the side door to the house and said, "Over here."

The man looked around, confused, spotted Blanchard and then nodded. "Gotcha."

Together they opened the rear of the car and took out the body bag. The driveway and detached garage were set to block the view of most of the neighbors. Pine trees and bushes blocked the view of everyone else, except those directly across the street. Blanchard didn't think they were home.

They carried the body into the house and then down the stairs, into an area that had the chill of an arctic night. They set it on the autopsy table.

The man said, "Don't see many of these in your average American home."

Blanchard had to grin. "We remodeled the morgue and were replacing the tables. I had one of them brought here."

"Doin' a little freelancing?"

Blanchard was startled by the question. The man hadn't seemed bright enough to tell night from day but now had asked a fairly astute question.

Blanchard said, "I just thought it might come in handy. I don't know why I did it, but it didn't cost anything. Just a little time and the help of a friend with a truck."

"There was talk of money," said the man.

"Wait here and I'll get it for you."

"No, man. I don't want to wait here. I'll wait for you upstairs. Outside, if you don't mind."

Blanchard waved him at the stairs. "I'll be up in just a moment."

When the man disappeared, Blanchard entered another room and went to the small safe that held important documents like the deed for the house and some extra cash for emergencies. Blanchard took out a couple of hundred dollars and then walked back upstairs.

As he climbed them, he noticed it getting warmer and warmer and heard the air conditioning running. Suddenly he thought about his electric bill and wondered what it was going to cost him to keep the basement area cool enough. And then he thought, who cares, the money from the Nobel Prize was enough to keep penguins cool.

Outside, standing near the screen door with the back door closed to keep the heat out and the cool in, Blanchard handed the money over to the man. As he did, he said, "You were never here and you know nothing about this."

The man stood mute.

"Listen, if this goes bad, I will say nothing about you to anyone. The only way for you to get into trouble is talk about this. Keep to yourself, and you're in the clear."

The man took the money, looked as if he wanted to say something, but then just turned and walked back to his car. He started it, rolled to the street and then turned toward town.

Blanchard watched him go and then reached for the screen. He'd seen no one on the street, no one near his house and no one watching. He believed that he was in the clear, at least for the moment.

CHAPTER TWENTY-THREE

Rachael Goldberg sat at her desk, or what she believed would be her desk for only a short period of time, and read through the notes she had taken in her conversations with Tom Johnson. She read them all carefully and realized that if Johnson believed all that he had said, he was, by legal definition, insane. If he was making up the story, then he was handing the prosecution proof of premeditation. It could see him in jail for the rest of his life without the possibility of parole, if not something worse.

Hartwell was the key. It all depended on what she remembered and how she presented that information to the prosecutor. Handled improperly, anything she said would harm Johnson. Handled right and there might be a case for justifiable homicide.

When the desk telephone rang, it startled her. She took a moment to get her breathing back under control and then picked up the receiver.

"Rachael Goldberg."

"Good afternoon. Have I caught you at a bad time?"

"No," she said, trying to place the voice. A deep, gravelly voice that she had heard before.

"You sound out of breath."

"Phone surprised me. Everyone calls on the cell."

"What a world. Used to be that only the wealthy could afford a private telephone line. The rest of us had party lines and were at the mercy of our neighbors to be polite enough not to tie up the lines all the time and not to eavesdrop on our conversations. Now children have cell phones."

Goldberg didn't know what to make of the philosophizing. She knew that this wasn't a client. They'd know better than to waste billable minutes on general conversation. They'd know to get right to the point and get the attorney off the phone as quickly as possible because even the telephone conversations were billed. That was, of course, if she ever placed the voice.

"Listen, I think we'd better talk about Tom Johnson."

And in that moment she knew that she was talking to the prosecutor assigned to the case. Not a rookie who had just joined the district attorney's office, but one of the old hands. Paul Brisco. Goldberg had met him once or twice at conferences. She remembered a short man, balding, with bright blue eyes, facial hair but she couldn't remember if it was a moustache or beard, and huge hands. They looked like rubber gloves filled with water.

She pulled a new pad forward, cradled the phone against her shoulder, and said, "What can I do for you, Mister Brisco?"

"I'd like to dispose of this Johnson matter right away. We have him cold and I'm sure you know it. Let's put this to bed now and everyone can go home happy."

She didn't like the sound of that. She wished that she had one of the senior partners in the room with her. She wished that she had talked to Johnson about the possibility of a plea. She was operating without a net and knew that she was teetering on the brink of disaster.

"What did you have in mind?"

"Second degree and twenty-five years with a possibility of parole at fifteen."

Goldberg didn't bother to write that down. Instead, she asked, "Why so generous?"

"I want to get this taken care of. I've got some complicated cases coming up and you have to know you can't win this." He laughed. "I mean, standing over the body with the gun in his hand. It's like something out of a bad movie. Even Marsha Clark could win this one."

"You know that I have to run this by my client. I can't make any decision without talking to him."

"Go right ahead. But from what I hear from the police, he's not denying he fired the fatal shot."

"I'd like to know exactly what the police have turned up in their investigation before I begin to jump at any offers."

There was a hesitation at the other end of the line. "Well, you can wait around and demand your rights, but this offer does have an expiration date."

To Goldberg this sounded like a used car salesman telling the potential buyer that he couldn't guarantee the price very long. Prices were going to go up and this was a good deal. Act now or lose it.

"Again, I couldn't accept anything without talking to my client and you know that. I have to go see him and that's going to take hours . . . especially if the jailers decide to stick strictly to the rules."

"I'll leave this offer on the table for twenty-four hours," said Brisco. "You call me back and we'll deal. If I don't hear from you, I'll assume the answer is no."

Goldberg nodded, realizing that Brisco couldn't see the gesture. She said, "I'll let you know, one way or the other."

"Good talking to you," said Brisco, and having said all that he wanted to say, he hung up.

Goldberg leaned back in her chair and then spun to the right so that she could look out the window. On the street below were people walking along, swarming actually, as they searched for something to eat or some place to drink. In the far distance thunder heads were building but Goldberg knew it wouldn't rain. The atmosphere didn't seem right for it. Not enough humidity or something.

Finally, she turned back to her desk and wondered if she should go talk to Howell. He'd told her to dump the case, and now she could tell him that the prosecutor wanted to settle. She knew that Howell would tell her to cut her losses and take the deal. At trial, Johnson could find himself facing the death penalty or life in prison without parole. This was a gift from the gods and she'd be a fool for not taking it.

But that made her wonder what had happened. Why would the prosecutor offer to settle? He could go for broke and would have a good chance of winning it all. Of course, even if the jury came back in the penalty phase and suggested twenty-five years to life, he still won.

The deal didn't feel right to her. She pulled out her cell phone and dialed the police station. When the desk sergeant answered, she asked for Captain Mitchell. She was told he wasn't available, but if she would leave a number he would get back to her. She gave them both the office number and her cell.

Three minutes later, her cell rang.

"Goldberg," she said.

"You wanted to talk to me?"

"Yes, Captain Mitchell. I just got the strangest telephone call from the prosecutor. I thought I would talk to you before I advised my client to accept his kind offer."

"I'm afraid that I have nothing to do with that," said Mitchell. "That's strictly the bailiwick of the prosecutor. Your questions should be addressed to him."

Goldberg ignored that and said, "I was just wondering why he was so generous to me. Why would he want to offer a deal if the case is as strong as you say it is?"

"You'll have to discuss it with him."

"You know that the law requires that all evidence relative to the case must be turned over to the defense."

There was a laugh at the other end and Mitchell said, "Not by me and not by the police. My job is to gather evidence and provide it to the prosecution. Not to do the work for the defense."

Now Goldberg laughed. "Captain, we were getting along so well. You talk to my client without benefit of counsel, you continue to investigate this crime by talking to Sarah Hartwell and snooping around Miller's house and then you won't answer a simple question for me."

"Let me ask you one. Who cleaned out Miller's house?"

"I don't follow you, Captain."

"Miller's house. It looked as if she was either just moving in or that she was moving out. Hardly anything in there at all, yet our boy Johnson talked of one box that held old family documents. That seems to be missing, as do her clothes, any pictures of her, furniture except the basics, food, any evidence that she actually lived in the house."

Goldberg rocked back in her chair, which squeaked once. She looked up at the ceiling, as if seeking divine guidance, and said, "I haven't been to the house."

"Then ask your boy . . . things are missing from there, and I'd like to know where they went."

"Tom said that she had no family, and he seemed to be her only friend here."

"Someone was in there, and someone removed them. Some of it could be beneficial, if we can get our hands on it. Corroboration, you might say."

"I'll do my best, Captain."

"Let me know when you have something."

"I plan to attempt to get bail set for Tom. He's of no danger to the community, he's not going to run and we can talk about self-defense in this case. Mitigating circumstances."

There was a pause at the other end of the phone line. "I'm not overly opposed to that," said Mitchell.

"Captain, when we met that first night, you would not bend at all. You followed procedure, and you made it clear that you had Tom cold. What's changed?"

"We have him cold. He shot Miller in the head . . . but, there are indications that it was not a premeditated murder."

Goldberg wasn't sure what she should say. Finally, "Would you mention this to the prosecutor?"

"I don't run his office nor do I work for him. Anything I would say would be considered inappropriate."

"I don't believe that," said Goldberg. "He would listen to you, and we could get Tom out of jail, at least for a few weeks."

"And that does what for me?"

So, this was becoming a bargaining session. Mitchell wanted something from Tom, and Goldberg knew what it was. Mitchell wanted access to Tom and what he knew about Miller. Something had come up in the investigation that had caught Mitchell's attention, and he thought Tom could provide the insight he needed.

Goldberg said, "You can't interview my client without me present. However, I would tell him that you had been not helpful, but at least not opposed to bail."

There was a chuckle at the other end. Mitchell said, "I think we understand each other."

Chapter Twenty-Four

Goldberg had been surprised at how quickly the bail hearing had been arranged, how quickly she had managed to get the money posted and then how quickly she had managed to get Tom Johnson out of jail. She stood at the bottom of a wide flight of stairs, outside in the late afternoon sun, and watched as Johnson walked out into the fresh air. He stopped at the top of the steps, almost as if he had been inside for years rather than days and was taking his first breaths of freedom.

"I'm down here, Tom," she called.

He raised a hand to shade his eyes, spotted her and then hurried down to her.

"I can't tell you how grateful I am," he said.

"Well, don't get too grateful. You're only out on bail, and we have a lot to do so that you don't go back in. Not to mention the money I've spent on your behalf."

"I'm glad to be out."

"What're you going to do now?"

Johnson squinted in the bright light, looked down the street, as if searching for a taxi and said, almost as an aside, "I think I'll go over to the morgue."

Goldberg, who had expected him to thank her for getting him out, who had expected him to ask about Sarah Hartwell and maybe for a ride to the hospital, who might even had asked to be taken to a fast food place for a hamburger or fried chicken, instead wanted to go to the morgue. It was about the strangest thing she had ever heard coming from the mouth of a human being.

"Tom, maybe there is some better way to spend your time out of jail."

He looked at her as if she had spoken a foreign language and said, "No. This is something that I must do right now."

He started to walk toward the street and then stopped. He turned and looked back at her. "Do you know where it is?"

"That question doesn't come up often in my line of work."

"I suppose I could look it up in the phone book . . . or on the Internet."

"Tom, maybe the best thing for you to do is go home and get some rest. Take it easy."

He shook his head in disbelief. "I told you, I told the police, the body had to be cremated. I'm just going to take care of that now."

"You won't get in and the police won't allow it. You'll just get your bail revoked and then where will you be?"

That stopped him for a moment, and then he grinned. "I'll be polite and just gather some information."

Goldberg was going to let him go and if he got into trouble, try to get him out of it, and then she thought again. Howell had told her to accept the plea, and she hadn't even mentioned it to Johnson yet. She had been told that the firm would not be a party to what it considered "lawyer tricks" and she had ignored that. If something more happened and she was connected to it, she knew that she would lose her job. And yet, she began to walk down the rest of the steps to join him on the sidewalk. She was going with him to the morgue.

It looked as if Johnson and Goldberg would never get beyond the reception area of the morgue. It wasn't exactly what they had expected when they walked into the building. It looked as if it belonged in a huge corporate office and not a state facility that dealt with the recently deceased who were usually dead by some kind of violence. The carpet was plush, clean and light blue. The receptionist's desk was large, dark wood that came up to their shoulders. The receptionist was nearly hidden on the other side of the desk. She wore a headset that looked like a Bluetooth connection to a cell phone.

She looked up, smiled and said, "May I help you?"

Johnson smiled back. "We're here to check on Linda Miller?"

"Are you family?"

Goldberg answered first. "No."

"You have police authorization?"

"No."

Still grinning, she said, "Then there is nothing I can do to help you."

Johnson took a step closer so that he could look down at her. She seemed to be a frail woman, almost a girl, with long hair bleached light, a narrow face and dark eyes. She was a nice-looking girl who didn't seem to be very bright.

"We just need to examine the body for only a few moments. We'll be gone before you even know we were here."

The woman took the tiny ear piece off and set it carefully on her desk. And although it looked as if she was about to help, she said, "Dr. Blanchard is quite explicit in his instructions. He leaves me no room to maneuver. He said that if you are not relatives and have no authorization, then I can't let you back in to examine a body. Changes to this policy, or exceptions to it, must be approved by Dr. Blanchard."

"Then it's easy," said Johnson. "Just call Dr. Blanchard and let me speak with him."

"Dr. Blanchard is out for the day."

Johnson leaned on the desk and glanced back at Goldberg. Then to the woman, he said, "Is Miller still here?"

"I'm not allowed to provide any information about anyone who might or might not be here. Dr. Blanchard is the point of contact on that."

"Where is he?"

"I'm sure that I wouldn't know," she said. "He left for the day and I don't know when he'll be back."

"And only he or a police authorization will allow me to examine the body."

"If it's still here," she said.

"Thank you," said Johnson. His voice was calm, without a hint of sarcasm. Although she hadn't been helpful, she had done her job and Johnson appreciated that fact.

To Goldberg he said, "Let's go find Captain Mitchell. Maybe he'll give me an authorization."

They left the icy cold of the morgue and walked into the blast furnace heat of the late afternoon. The sun was still high and there was no breeze. Johnson felt as if he couldn't breathe.

CHAPTER TWENTY-FIVE

Dr. William Blanchard was literally phoning it in. He called the office, talked with the receptionist and two of his attendants, but he did not go into work. Others were taking care of business for him as he pleaded a bad summer cold, and while he understand that his patients wouldn't care, since they were already dead, it was his living colleagues he worried about. They certainly could catch the cold.

If he had one. A bad summer cold was a good excuse for him to stay home, in his makeshift lab and morgue, and study the remains of Linda Miller. He had locked the doors upstairs and closed the blinds down in the basement where he was. He had made sure that no one would walk in on him and, satisfied with the arrangements, had turned on all the lights and turned up the air conditioner. It was as cold as a meat locker and that was just the way he wanted it.

Miller was lying on the autopsy table naked. There were long incisions in her chest to her pubic bone and there was another around her skull. Blanchard had taken dozens of pictures, documenting everything strange about her body. He was preparing to take another look at the internal structure.

Then he noticed something odd. The bullet hole that had smashed into her forward seemed to be smaller than it had been. The edges had bruised and darkened, as had the area around her eyes. It looked to Blanchard as if healing had begun, as it would around a bullet hole that had not been fatal. The reaction he was seeing suggested healing and he knew that was impossible because she was dead and even if the bullet hadn't killed her, the autopsy would have. You can't cut open a body and have the subject survive.

That meant that Blanchard was mistaken about the healing. He leaned forward to examine the wound carefully, probed it with his fingers and then straightened. He moved to the computer, brought up his preliminary photographs and concentrated on the wound to her head.

Given the markings, given the scale he used to measure, and given the lighting, it still looked as if the wound had begun to heal. He zoomed in on the wound and could see that it was more ragged, larger, with bone fragments easily visible. There was no sign of bruising, and there was no blackening around the eyes. It was a different wound than that he was seeing now.

Blanchard rocked back in his beat-up office chair and said out loud, "What the hell?"

Finally, he stood and walked back to the body on the autopsy table. He looked at the wound and knew that he was right. It was healing. She was dead, but the wound was getting better. Something in her body, something in her metabolism, something about her genetic makeup was strong enough to overcome this wound and begin the healing process. It was clearly something that continued after death, and if he could discover what it was, if he could isolate it and reproduce it, the Nobel Prize for Medicine would be his, and the wealth generated by the discovery would be enormous. He would be up there with Jonas Salk and Louis Pasteur. His fame would be as enduring as theirs.

He couldn't take his eyes off her forehead but knew there were things he had to do. Finally, he turned and looked at the Y-shaped incision of the autopsy. It was a rough cut, not the precise incision that a surgeon would have made, and here too was evidence of healing.

He reached out to probe carefully along the incision and then wondered about the strange internal organs that he had seen. Once he had seen that internal structure, he had done no additional cutting. He wanted to make sure that he had each organ mapped. He wanted color photography of the chest and abdomen. He had wanted to be sure that those who looked at his notes, his papers and his photographs would see the same thing he had and know that this was not a human being.

Now he tried to peel back part of the incision, surprised by the resistance he encountered. It was almost as if he was tearing flesh that had begun to knit. He was destroying the healing process by pulling at the edge of the autopsy incision.

He reached up and repositioned the light so that it was shining right down on her chest. He looked into the chest cavity and saw that the internal organs had no sign of damage. Where he had made his preliminary cuts, there was only scar tissue. Where he had severed the attachments to the body, the organs had begun to reattach themselves to the various body systems.

"Regeneration," he said out loud, but knew that it wasn't really regeneration. There was some other process at work here, but he didn't know what it might be.

Suddenly he wondered just how far the process would go. Here was a woman with a strange body, with internal organs he couldn't identify, whose genetic makeup seemed to be as different from human as human was from the chimpanzee, and who was able to heal herself, at least partially, after death. Surely, as he had been taught, brain damage would set in quickly once the heart stopped and after just minutes, according to everything he knew, it would be irreversible. So how far would the process continue before it stopped?

Given that, he closed the chest, but rather than using the big, sloppy stitches meant just to hold the tissue together, he began to repair the incisions carefully, including the muscles and sublayer tissues.

Finished with that, he looked at the skull, repaired that as best he could, picked the bone fragments that he could see from the brain, and then attempted to bandage that wound. He knew that this would not limit his work on describing the new species. He had the photographic record that he needed for that.

Now the question was if cold hindered or enhanced the healing process. Should he put her back into the coldest environment, where he had stored the body between sessions, or should he leave her out, in the fresh, warmer air? Which would be the best? He just didn't know. The assumption would be for the warmer environment, but that was for a badly injured human and not for the . . . what, creature . . . that was in front of him.

With nothing else to do with the body, he decided to begin the preliminary work on his scientific paper. He would have to pull the references from the various databases so that he could cite them in his paper. It was a long, laborious task that was usually given to a graduate student or assistant, but Blanchard didn't want anyone to know what he was doing. Hell, he couldn't allow anyone to know what he was doing.

Once he thought he heard something and looked back at Miller. She was still lying on the autopsy table and hadn't moved. The noise was probably just normal noise but Blanchard realized he was getting jumpy. It wasn't the body because he had been around the dead all his adult life. It was something else and he didn't know what it was.

Goldberg was surprised to learn that Mitchell was still in the office and even more surprised that he would meet with them. Goldberg didn't like the idea of meeting with Mitchell, but Johnson had insisted, and she couldn't think of any way of getting out of it. Johnson had made it clear that he was going to talk to Mitchell, and Goldberg knew that as the attorney of record she would be remiss if she wasn't there to advise her client.

They were taken to Mitchell's office. Mitchell was sitting behind his desk, his feet propped up and his hands locked behind his head. When Goldberg and Johnson appeared, he nodded and said, "Have a seat."

When they had sat, Mitchell said, "I want you both to know that anything said in this room may be used against you in the trial. We are not off the record, and I will prepare a report about our conversation and provide it to the prosecutor. I'm not sure this is a good idea at this point."

Goldberg leaned forward slightly and said, "I told Tom that we should not be here and that talking with the police at this stage is probably counterproductive."

"Then we understand one another," said Mitchell.

He dropped his feet to the floor, leaned forward with both elbows on his desk and said, "Now, what can I do for you?"

"I want to see the body," said Johnson.

"No."

"Just like that?" asked Goldberg.

Before Mitchell could say a word, Johnson said, "There is no reason to withhold permission. You have no right to withhold permission."

"Actually, I'm well within my rights," said Mitchell. "You are not a relative. You are the accused killer. There is nothing on the body or about the body you need to see."

"I need to see that she is dead," said Johnson.

Mitchell looked at him and said, "No, she was not a vampire. She is not some kind of supernatural being. She was a young woman you shot in the head with a large caliber weapon killing her, if not instantly, then damned close."

Goldberg interrupted to say, "The defense has the right to

examine all the evidence gathered and that includes the body of the victim."

"Are you a pathologist?" asked Mitchell. "Do you have some special training that I don't know about? Are you competent to gather slides and review the complex and technical medical information available, or to properly interpret the results of those other examinations?"

Goldberg didn't answer the questions. Instead, she said, "Is there some reason you don't want me to see the body? Is it possible that she didn't die from the shot fired by my client?"

Mitchell took a deep breath and sat back, as if trying to distance himself from Goldberg and Johnson. He said, "There is no reason for you to see it. And she died from a single gunshot wound to the head. We'll get the autopsy report to you first thing in the morning."

"I just need to see the body," said Johnson. "Just for a moment. You don't know what to look for. I do. Just for a moment or two. What could that hurt?"

And Mitchell, for the life of him, couldn't answer that question. What would it hurt? The police and the coroner had photographed and recorded everything. They had pictures, tape, specimen slides and a hundred other types of evidence. Even without that, the case was open and shut. Johnson had been standing over her with the gun in his hand.

"I see no point in this," said Mitchell, and that seemed to be his final word on the subject. But then his face changed subtly, and he tensed, as if expecting the argument to begin again, but louder and more threatening.

He said, "If you have no objection to an escort, then I suppose there really is no harm."

"An escort is fine," said Goldberg without looking at Johnson. "When?"

Mitchell took his cell phone from his pocket and looked at

the time. "I have nothing scheduled this evening, and we should be able to get into the morgue if we hurry. Now?"

Goldberg was on her feet and said, "Of course."

Mitchell stood up and snagged his coat from the hook near the door. He put it on and then opened a drawer to retrieve his pistol. He checked to make sure it was on safe before putting it in the holster on the left side of his belt. He then waited for both Goldberg and Johnson to leave his office and closed the door as he followed them.

Mitchell drove them to the morgue in a police car that had door handles in the rear and no mesh cage between the front and back seats. The radio was out of the way and though there was a rack for a shotgun, there wasn't a weapon in it. Surprisingly, there was air conditioning and a radio that picked up the commercial broadcast band. Had they not gotten it in the police garage, neither Goldberg nor Johnson would have guessed that it was a police car.

At the morgue, there was a different receptionist. She was older, darker, and seemed to have an attitude of indifference. She smiled when they walked up to the desk and asked if she could help them.

Mitchell showed his badge and said, "We would like to see the body of Linda Miller."

The receptionist turned, typed for a moment and then said, "She'll be in Room Q, Freezer J. There will be an attendant there, and ask him to open the freezer. Please don't touch anything, and if you have questions, please ask them. Do you know the way?"

Mitchell said, "I've been here before."

They left the reception area and moved into an institutional area of brightly painted cinder block walls, gray tiled floors and overhead lighting that would have been sufficient to land aircraft. There were doors off each side, spaced about equidistant, some with signs and some with frosted glass windows, but most without.

Room Q didn't have much floor space. Across from the door were the freezers, stacked four high. They were stainless steel, with refrigerator handles and rubber seals. There was a little frame to hold a card with the name of the deceased on it.

An attendant met them at the door. He was tall, skinny, nearly bleached white so that it looked as if he never went out in the sun, but he had good muscle tone and deep brown eyes. He looked and smelled clean, as if he had just come on shift.

"You want?" he asked.

"Miller," said Mitchell.

They walked across the room and the attendant opened the freezer. He pulled the tray out but there was no body on it, just a wadded-up sheet that might have been used to cover the body.

The attendant didn't seem to be overly concerned. He said, "They must have released it to the funeral home."

"Wouldn't the receptionist have known that?" asked Mitchell. "Wouldn't it have been in the computer?"

"Might not have gotten the files updated," he said. "Not a big deal."

"Captain?" said Goldberg, asking what their next move should be.

Mitchell shrugged.

Johnson snorted once. It might have been a laugh or a sound of disgust. It might have been dismay. He said, "I knew she wouldn't be here. I just knew it. I warned you and I warned you but you wouldn't listen. And now she's gone. I just knew this would happen."

CHAPTER TWENTY-SIX

He hadn't been in jail very long, and he had been in a private cell with little or no contact with real criminals, but it seemed as if he had been gone for months. He opened the front door and expected a musty odor, but the air was sweet and fresh and not that of a house that had been closed for many weeks. He touched a light switch, and the lights came on just as they were supposed to do.

He walked to the master bedroom but everything was just as he left it. There was slightly more dust on the furniture, but Johnson rarely dusted anything so that was expected. He walked into the bathroom and his toothbrush and razor were where he had left them, the soap in the soap dish was dry but hadn't deteriorated or sprouted mold.

Johnson decided to take a quick shower to get the stink of the jail and the odor of the morgue off him. A sort of ritualistic washing to cleanse himself so that he could move back into normal society. He started the water to warm it and then stripped quickly. About the time he stepped under the spray, the telephone rang.

"Of course," he said, but didn't get out of the shower. He'd get the number off the caller-ID and call them back.

As he was soaping his head to wash his hair, he wondered how he would go about finding Miller. Clearly she couldn't afford to rejoin the club scene here, couldn't return to her house, and in fact, probably couldn't stay in the city. While the police wouldn't be looking for her, she had to know that he knew about her. There were others who knew her and would recognize her.

As he rinsed and stepped out of the shower, feeling cleaner and much better than he had in days, he wondered why he was still alive. If Miller had escaped the morgue, and he was sure that she had, he wondered why she hadn't tried to kill him. He was a real threat to her, especially now that her body was gone. That would lend credence to his story. People would begin to believe him because human bodies just don't get up and walk out of the morgue. She was in danger.

He dressed in clean clothes and walked into the kitchen. He opened the refrigerator and nothing in it had spoiled. There were sodas, a few cans of beer, eggs, cheese, potatoes and even some ham. He could make a very good omelet without much trouble when he got hungry.

Someone had picked up his mail and his newspapers and stacked them on the counter. He was sure that Goldberg had done it, or had someone do it. He flipped through the mail without much interest and then walked over to the caller-ID box with its tiny, flashing red light. He had twenty new calls on it.

The last, the one that had come while he was in the shower, was from someone he didn't know and a name he didn't recognize. William C. Blanchard had tried him.

Johnson walked to the rear window and looked out into the backyards of his neighbors. It was hot out and the heat had driven everyone inside. Sprinklers were splashing around some water in yards that looked as if the drought had started a decade earlier and the grass would never come back.

It was all so mundane, so ordinary and just about the same as he had left it in what seemed another year. He couldn't seem to grasp that he hadn't been gone very long, though it seemed that months had passed.

Finally, he opened a bottle of bourbon that had been in the pantry for more years than he could remember. He poured some over a couple of ice cubes, stirred it with a finger, and took a sip. He thought that it was smooth, that it had mellowed with the years he'd had it. No real burning of his throat.

Fortified, and now more relaxed than he had been in days, he picked up the telephone and dialed the number of William C. Blanchard.

The phone rang twice and then a voice said, "Mr. Johnson, thank you for returning my call."

Johnson was old enough to remember a time without universal caller-ID and for an instant was taken aback, but then remembered anyone could do that now.

"I'm afraid that you have the better of me, Mr. Blanchard."

"It's doctor, actually. I worked the autopsy of Linda Miller, and I have a couple of questions for you."

Johnson hesitated, took another swallow of his bourbon, afraid that this was some sort of trick. He had never heard of the coroner calling a witness like this.

"Yes?"

"Well, I wonder if you had ever observed anything unusual about her?"

"Unusual in what way?" asked Johnson.

"Anything at all?"

Johnson thought for a moment, realizing that this might be the place to plant the first seeds with the man who conducted the autopsy about what Miller was. Here was a chance, handled correctly, to begin to build his defense that Miller wasn't human. But Johnson just didn't know enough about Blanchard to make any sort of intelligent decision. He needed to talk to Goldberg.

And then he realized he didn't need to talk to her because he knew what she would say. She'd tell him that Blanchard was on the other side and anything he said to Blanchard would end up in court.

Yet here was a chance to discuss Miller with someone who had his hands in her body and who might have seen something strange in there. In fact, the telephone call and the question told Johnson that Blanchard had seen something strange.

"Mr. Johnson?"

"I'm trying to think of something that might be helpful to you," he said.

"You knew her a long time?"

"Around a year," said Johnson.

"What was her lifestyle like?"

"I'm afraid that I don't understand how this would be relevant for the autopsy. Lifestyle seems to be in another arena all together."

"Well, we try to learn what we can about the victim. Lifestyle can affect the autopsy. Smoking, for example, causes changes in the brain, lungs, arteries."

"Yes, but you'd observe those things at autopsy and would be able to say the . . ." he hesitated. He didn't want to say victim because of what that implied. "The person had been a smoker."

"Other things are more subtle," said Blanchard.

Johnson finished his bourbon and said, "I don't know what I can tell you that would be of value here. Maybe I should talk to my attorney."

"This is all just routine," said Blanchard, his voice sounding just a little desperate, as if it wasn't routine at all.

"Then maybe you can answer a question for me. Where's the body?"

There was a moment of silence at the other end of the phone after what might have been a sharp intake of breath. In a voice that wasn't very convincing, Blanchard said, "The body is right where it is supposed to be."

That decided it. "I'm sorry, but I don't believe you and I don't believe this is appropriate. Call my attorney to arrange a meeting."

"Just one question," said Blanchard.

Johnson hung up.

Though he hadn't thought much about it since he had shot Linda Miller, he decided it was time to review his notes on her life. He'd given some of information to Goldberg and had wanted to give more to the police but they didn't want to hear it, and Goldberg didn't want him saying anything about it to anyone, especially the police. Goldberg thought it produced a motive and the police thought it was an attempt to create a defense.

But the coroner's call had stirred his immediate interest in her. Now was the time to review that material to see if there was anything in it that could help him. Maybe hints about living relatives who might have the same affliction as Miller.

Johnson grinned at the word. *Affliction.* As if it was some kind of physical or mental disease. It was no more an affliction than breathing and eating were afflictions. These were facts of life.

Johnson got up and walked into his home office. It was on the first floor of his house and set off from the rest by French doors. The room was small and held a fine, old, ornate desk that Johnson had acquired at an estate sale. It didn't fit his decor and it really didn't fit in the room, but he liked having his computer, flat panel and printer on a desk that was more a part of the nineteenth century than it was the twenty-first.

Bookcases flanked the window, giving it a depth that it wouldn't normally have had. Through it he could see an expanse of lawn that needed mowing even though it was turning brown in the heat.

Johnson sat down at his desk and then opened a drawer where he kept the paper file on Miller. Most of the information had been scanned into the computer, but he did have a few documents. He liked the feel of them. He liked the odor and the texture and that he could lay them out, one next to the other, without them being reduced to fit the screen. Overall, it just seemed easier to review a pile of paper documents than it was to see them on a computer screen, even if there were two displays and various software that let him look at three or four files at once.

Miller had never really mentioned family, and in the time that Johnson had known her she hadn't met with or communicated with family. He had the impression that she was an orphan but many adults were in the same boat. Mothers and fathers had died, leaving their adult children as orphans. It was something that most people didn't think about.

There was no mention of siblings, but then, how could there be siblings, if Johnson was right about her. He supposed in the same way that there was a mother and a father and Miller had hinted at aunts or uncles or cousins in Europe, though she had never been specific.

And her name was no help. Miller was among the most common names in North America, like Smith, Johnson and now Gonzales and Garcia. Looking for a Miller was like looking for a John Smith. Too many to do any good.

So, he looked through the papers he had. Miller had loaned them to him, though he still wasn't sure why she had bothered. She knew her family history, much better than most Americans did. She could trace her family back a thousand years or more and could do it from documents at her house and not using the Internet.

That was the key, he realized. The documents in her house. These papers wouldn't be part of the police investigation because they had nothing to do with the crime. They would still be there, in the house, in the closet, in the boxes where he could get at them and study them carefully and slowly. The treasure trove was at her house.

He sat there and looked at his collected documents, at the pictures he had taken of other documents, and then at the scans he had loaded into his computer. The problem was he knew these documents and photographs well. He had studied them over and over, looking for some clue about Miller he had missed, and the only thing that he had really missed was how deadly she was. That had been the one thing that he had been unable to comprehend at the time.

Yes, he had been her wingman at the clubs. He had helped her find someone and helped her get him out of the club unseen, but he had never really known what she was doing. At least not then, and not until a day or so before he had shot her. He just hadn't understood what was going on because it was just too unbelievable. These things did not exist in the modern world, and in that moment he understood how they avoided detection.

In a world where science was the religion and no one accepted much without some sort of proof, Linda Miller had been protected by skepticism. Who would believe that an incredibly old woman was hunting the streets of American for victims so that she could use their blood to maintain her life? Why only blood and why only human blood? Why not animal blood? Why not cow blood? If that were the case, no one would ever notice.

And then, suddenly, he remembered reading or hearing about cattle mutilations and wondered if there was a connection. Could Miller have survived on animal blood? Or was it like a human who could survive on vegetables and grains without eating meat? Or was it something more?

Johnson had never considered any of this in the weeks that he had been studying Miller, and that had to be because he just hadn't believed everything she said, even when there was old documents to support it.

He needed more information, and he knew it was at her house. He'd just have to go get it. Once he had it, he could then begin a search for her family, or more likely, for others similar to her.

CHAPTER TWENTY-SEVEN

Rachael Goldberg didn't really know Paul Brisco, except by reputation as a prosecutor. She might have met him at any of the functions in the city that most lawyers attended, or she might have seen him at a political rally, but she didn't really know him. And when she asked the partners about him, they told her little, other than to settle the case or look for work elsewhere. It wasn't that they didn't want to defend murder cases, it was they didn't want to be associated with this particular murder case.

So Goldberg walked into the city building feeling a little apprehensive. That feeling didn't dissipate when she was escorted to Brisco's office on one of the upper floors. Through the windows, she could see the city spread out to the west, with the sun falling toward the horizon. She could see part of the river that wound its way through the city center and the tree-covered parks that dotted its banks.

Brisco was seated at his desk, in front of the window. It was a large desk and he was sitting in a large chair. Those chairs for his visitors were smaller, looking almost fragile. Goldberg knew it was a psychological trick to put her at a disadvantage, but knowing didn't make the feeling of inadequacy any less real.

As she sat down, Brisco asked, "What can I do for you, counselor?"

"You were the one who suggested that we get together."

Brisco shrugged, as if he had changed his mind.

181

Goldberg looked him in the eye and held her gaze steady. She knew that these negotiations weren't about evidence or guilt or innocence. It was about who held what cards and how those cards could be played for an advantage now and later at the trial. She had often heard that he who made the first offer lost, but if no one made an offer, then there was no negotiation.

When the silence seemed to become unbearable, she said, "I'm letting you know that I plan an affirmative defense. Johnson shot Miller to protect Sarah Hartwell."

"Well, that is your right, counselor, but I must tell you that I don't think it will fly. Not with what Johnson has told the police and what the evidence will show."

Goldberg, still clutching her briefcase as if it was some kind of talisman, said, "Statements made after a lengthy police interrogation. The jury will see that the police were overzealous in their interrogation of Johnson and that testimony will not be persuasive."

Brisco grinned and said, "We have the man standing over the body demanding that the body be burned immediately. We have him holding the gun. Hartwell was unconscious on the floor, and there is no evidence that Miller was about to attack her again or even that it was Miller who attacked her."

"Hartwell's testimony about that will fill in the gaps and it will show that Miller was the aggressor," said Goldberg.

"Do you have something in mind, counselor?"

Brisco had trapped her and in a not very clever way. She now had to bring up the plea deal or retreat. She said, "I just wanted to inform you of our defense strategy here."

As soon as she said that, she was horrified. The last thing she wanted to do was tell the prosecution what she planned as a strategy. She wanted him to make a plea offer, hoping to determine how strong he felt the case was, but Brisco didn't seem to want to deal anymore and that scared her. It meant

Vampyr?

that Brisco believed he could win easily and wanted nothing to do with a plea.

In fact, it seemed as if Brisco had initiated the meeting to learn more about her strategy than to negotiate in good faith. It seemed to be a trick to reveal what she knew and what she had in the way of evidence.

Surprisingly, Brisco said, "I don't think we'll try for the death penalty here given Johnson's history and lack of any criminal record. We're looking at life without parole."

"For self-defense?"

"We don't think it was self-defense," said Brisco. "We think we can make a case for premeditated murder. I don't think I can convince the jury that it is capital murder, but they might feel that way. I'm willing to take that off the table."

"The evidence clearly points to self-defense and the defense of Hartwell," said Goldberg.

Brisco leaned back in his chair and laced his fingers behind his head. He seemed to be looking down his nose at Goldberg.

"We'll see what the jury has to say," said Brisco. "I believe they will understand completely and if they do, then your client is in it deeply."

Goldberg started to say something and then stopped. She knew that Johnson had made a big deal out of Miller not being a human and therefore the law didn't apply to her. The charge was wrapped around the statement that Johnson had killed Linda Miller, a human being, and Johnson argued that she wasn't.

But to say that to Brisco or to even consider it for a courtroom was counterproductive. It wouldn't even lead to an insanity defense, which Goldberg was sure that Johnson had in mind. It was an interesting strategy, but it was one that was doomed from the very beginning. It was an argument over semantics that wouldn't work, even if by some incredible stretch

183

they were able to prove that Miller wasn't a human being.

So, instead, she said, "I guess we have nothing else to discuss."

"I leave the deal on the table for twenty-four hours. After that, I will go for the death penalty. You can keep your client off the gurney with tubes of lethal chemicals pumping into his veins. That's the best offer you'll get."

Goldberg stood up. "Then we have nothing to discuss."

Brisco dropped his elbows to the desk and grinned. He said, almost in a whisper, "Ask your client about the silver bullets."

Goldberg hesitated, not understanding the point, but said nothing. She didn't know what relevance silver bullets would have to the case.

While Goldberg was meeting with the prosecutor to determine his fate, Johnson was backing his car out of the garage. He backed into the street and saw a neighbor watering the plantings near his front door. Their eyes met for a moment and then the man looked away, as if he hadn't seen Johnson.

Johnson smiled to himself. After the trial, it would probably be worse. Everyone would think that he had gotten off by some clever lawyer trick and wouldn't understand that Miller wasn't human. They wouldn't believe that she ran through the city killing strangers, transients, those who had no roots and no ties and who probably wouldn't be missed. They would just think that Johnson was crazy and he would end up like O.J. trying to catch the "real" killers.

He drove the few blocks to Miller's house and then down the street slowly, looking at the place. The yellow police tape was still attached to a pillar near the door and to a shrub near the front porch. There was a bright yellow piece of paper attached to the front door but there was no sign of activity and no sign that the house was being watched. It had an unhappy, deserted look about it.

In fact, the whole street seemed deserted, though at that time of the day, or evening, he would have expected some of the neighbors to be outside. Maybe kids playing basketball, if kids still played basketball on the driveway rather than on the computer. He thought there might be someone mowing a lawn, or just walking for the exercise, but the street was as deserted as Miller's house.

Johnson was tempted to park in the driveway but decided there was no real reason to advertise his presence. Instead, he drove on to the next block and parked behind another car. He got out and walked back toward Miller's. Now he wished he had brought a dog so that he would look like he belonged there and was just out walking the dog on a nice, quiet evening on a nice, quiet street.

Trying to look as if he belonged, he walked up to Miller's door and rang the bell. He looked at the paper, which was a police warning that entry to the house was prohibited, but Johnson didn't care about that. He couldn't get into more trouble by entering the house. The murder charge was the heaviest, and he couldn't see anyone wanting to complicate the prosecution with a charge of breaking and entering. At least that was what he believed.

He reached down for the knob and was surprised that it turned. He pushed and the door opened. Apparently the last of the police in the house had failed to lock it when they left. One break for Johnson.

He stepped in and noticed that it was hot and smelled of shaved copper. He stood for a moment, looking into the room where he had shot Miller. The blood still stained the carpeting and the tape still outlined where she had fallen. Some of the furniture was now pushed aside, probably by the lab techs as they gathered their evidence.

He leaned back against the door and tried to ignore the odor and the heat. He slipped along the wall, almost as if he was on a thin ledge around a top floor of a building. He skirted the living room, and then hurried down the hall to the bedroom.

The bed was there but the drawers to the dressing table and the chest were open and empty, as if someone had taken every piece of clothing that Miller owned. Johnson didn't care about that. Clothing might yield some kind of forensic evidence, but nothing that would do him much good.

He opened a closet and found it as empty as Mother Hubbard's cupboard. No clothes. No shoes. No boxes containing the records of Miller's life. Just a square at the far end where there was a trapdoor.

He left the bedroom and tried the others. He found the furniture and other big items there. He found a television and a collection of CDs and DVDs but nothing of a personal nature. No family books, no scrapbooks and no papers. No band records or electric bills or credit card receipts. Nothing that would lead back to Miller. Just the debris of a woman that no one really knew. The sort of thing that could be easily replaced if there was a desire to replace it.

He gave up and made his way down to the basement, which really was more of a lower level finished to the same perfection as the rest of the house. He found the hidden door, but only because it was opened and he looked into it, finding the tunnel that led from the house. He even saw that the trapdoor he'd seen upstairs. So he knew where it led.

He returned to the main room and sat down in a vinyl chair. He looked at the ceiling and saw hooks screwed in for a lighting system that hadn't been installed. He saw that it was getting dark now and he would have to get out soon.

What he couldn't understand was where everything that was Linda Miller's had gone. Surely the police wouldn't have swept through and taken all her clothes. They might have taken some of the papers, though there was no reason for them to pack off everything. It wasn't as if they were trying to find her killer. He had been standing over the body.

But the police were certainly a possible answer for where everything had gone. Johnson just didn't think so. That left the neighbors, but he didn't think they would break in to steal her clothes and her papers and not take the TV or the stereo, or for that matter, the microwave or the food processor.

So, who had been here? Who would have taken everything that would suggest anything about Linda Miller? That he just couldn't understand, until, in a flash of insight that had somehow eluded him, he realized that Miller hadn't been alone. She might not have had family or friends in the town, but she would have them. She wasn't the last of her kind. There were others and somehow they had gotten here and cleaned up everything. They had taken away the evidence of what she was. They had gotten to the proof while he was still in jail, worrying about the body.

The question was how he would go about finding more of them. If he could find the colony, or nest, or village, then he would have the proof he needed. In fact, he would be able to save the human race, or maybe just members of it, from becoming food.

CHAPTER TWENTY-EIGHT

Captain Steven Mitchell sat in his dark office, the only light the glow from his flat panel. Outside, the sun had set and a thin overcast reflected the city lights but didn't let the stars shine through. It was a dreary night with a hint of rain, maybe storms, in the air, and that made the situation seem more ominous. A hint of the gothic that only needed the peasants out there with pitchforks and torches, hunting for the beast that was killing off the residents.

He was unhappy because he didn't know where Miller's body was. The morgue thought it might have been picked up by a mortuary, but there was no paperwork to show that. Mitchell had called those on the city list, but none of them had the body. If it wasn't in the morgue and it wasn't at a funeral home, then it was gone just as surely as if it had walked out the door.

He didn't believe that would cause any trouble at trial because they had the autopsy results, pictures of the body at Miller's house, and they could show that Miller had not been seen, had not used her credit cards, had not paid her bills from the day that she was shot. Still, losing the body was so stupid that he couldn't believe that it wasn't engineered.

And that was the key. Someone had to take the body, and who had motive for that? Johnson was the only person in all the world who benefited if Miller's body disappeared. He could say, or rather his lawyer could say, well, without a body there was a possibility that Miller still lived. Mitchell doubted that anyone on the jury would fall for that, but then, it only took one to hang the jury and create a mistrial.

Mitchell reached for the telephone and called the morgue. He got the night man who didn't know anything but did tell him that Blanchard wasn't there. Mitchell hadn't expected him to be but thought he would call just to make sure.

So he called Blanchard's house but got the answering machine. He sat back, staring at the phone, and then tried his cell. Blanchard was required to have it and was required to have it on at all times. As the medical examiner, he was on call twenty-four seven, and there was no excuse. True, he might delegate the examination to one of his subordinates, but he was required to answer his cell.

This bothered Mitchell. It smacked of dereliction of duty, but it was also strange. As long as Mitchell could remember, Blanchard had always answered his cell.

Mitchell pushed himself out of his chair, looked out the window, but saw no sign of the rain he was sure was coming. He walked into the squad room and saw the shift sergeant sitting at a desk, working on a report.

"I'm going out to see Blanchard. Cell will be on and I'll have the radio on."

"Anything special, Captain?"

"Nope. Just a couple of loose ends. I probably won't be back until morning."

As he drove out of the downtown, Mitchell realized that he had been to Blanchard's home once, for a New Year's Eve party. There had been lots of drinks, enough food to feed a battalion, music that was from a different era and everyone there was employed by the city in some capacity. Blanchard, it seemed, had no friends outside work, and few of those at the party could be called friends. They came for the free booze and food.

The house was a little shabbier than he remembered it. The

lawn needed cutting and it needed water. The paint was fading and in places it was peeling. Blanchard, apparently, never opted for vinyl siding. There was a detached garage that looked like something from the early twentieth century and had a door that opened to the side rather than up and over.

Mitchell pulled into the driveway. The house looked deserted, but the telltale signs of abandonment weren't there. No newspapers on the doorstep and no mail clogging the box. Just a lawn that should have been mowed a couple of days earlier.

Mitchell got out and walked to the front door. He rang the bell, heard it chime inside and waited. He could hear nothing to suggest that Blanchard was home and moving toward the door. He tried the bell again, and when that failed, he looked through the sidelights.

There was a light on in the back of the house, but he could see no movement inside. He stepped off the porch, looked in one of the big windows and saw an empty living room, meaning, simply, there was no one in it. There were several bookcases crammed full, a couch, chairs and a coffee table covered with magazines, papers and books.

He walked around to the side of the house. The garage door was closed but he could see a bright light on in the kitchen, which might have been the light he'd seen from the front. He stepped up on the small, concrete porch that led into the kitchen. He knocked on the door, but there was no answer and no movement inside. He reached down and twisted the knob, surprised when it turned. He pushed on the door and it opened.

There was the odor of fresh copper and Mitchell, without thinking about it, reached under his jacket for his pistol. He looked into the kitchen but saw nothing there. He glanced down the stairs, into the basement, and there was a light on down there, but Mitchell didn't want to get trapped with no way out. Instead, he stepped into the kitchen quickly and toward the wall so that he was not silhouetted in the doorway.

There was nothing of interest in the kitchen and he walked through it, his back against the wall. He hurried through the door, toward the right, glancing first there and then back to the left. The room was vacant. He cleared the rest of the upstairs in the same fashion, moving from room to room, checking closets, bathrooms and the laundry room. He was looking into anything that was large enough to hide a human.

As he began to return to the kitchen, he heard the screen door slam. He rushed back into the kitchen, looking out the window overlooking the driveway and a chest-high hedge. There was a flash of light brown there as someone or something pushed through and then disappeared.

Mitchell closed his eyes momentarily and rebuilt the scene. A person, possibly naked, certainly female, had run from the house. He had the impression of black hair. But he saw it, her, so quickly that he hadn't time to form much of an impression and certainly didn't recognize her. He would never be able to pick her out of a lineup.

Now it was time to go into the basement, which was where he should have gone first, given what had just happened. He should call for backup, but it was too late for that now. Besides, the shift sergeant knew where he was.

He walked down the stairs, his back to the wall, his feet at the front edge of each riser so that they wouldn't pop or creak, not that it mattered all that much now. He reached the basement floor and the odor of shaved copper was stronger, almost overpowering.

Most of the basement was open and unfinished. There was a wall at the far end that probably concealed the water heater, the furnace and maybe the electrical junction box. There was a single door to the left that closed off about half the basement. The bright light was coming from there.

Mitchell moved to the door and glanced inside. It was a home morgue complete with autopsy table. It looked just like those he had been in downtown, maybe a little older, as if assembled as used equipment is replaced.

Blanchard, naked, lay on the autopsy table, his hands at his sides. His chest had been ripped open in a huge, ragged "Y" shape that mimicked the incisions used by the coroner. His organs were piled beside the body and the top of his head had been removed. Someone had taken time to do this. Someone with a lot of hatred for Blanchard.

Mitchell stepped to the rear so that his back was to the wall. He held his pistol, almost forgotten, in his right hand. He scanned the room, saw that the computer terminal had been smashed, but the computer itself seemed to be intact. The file cabinet had been opened and files scattered, but there had been no effort to destroy them.

This now was a crime scene. It was clear that Blanchard was dead. You didn't need to be a coroner to know that if your organs were removed and stacked beside you, the chance for survival was zero.

Mitchell backed out of the room and then climbed the stairs. He left through the kitchen door and walked back to his car. He thought about using the police radio, but he didn't want to broadcast the crime so that everyone who had a police scanner or radio would hear. Instead, he used his cell phone to call it in. Then he sat in his car, the door open, and watched both of the doors to the house. He could easily see them from where he was.

Because the crime scene was secured and because the victim was clearly dead, the police arrived without sirens or flashing lights. They pulled up behind Mitchell's car and into the driveway. They got out and crowded around Mitchell, but no one made a move toward the house.

Mitchell got out of his car and said, "We have the coroner here, dead. Autopsied. The body is in the basement in his own private morgue. That has been ransacked. I saw someone flee to the east, through the hedge, but I didn't get a good look. I'm thinking five nine, five ten, dark hair, short, female and dressed in tan. That's a guess because my impression was that she was nude."

Two of the young cops turned and took a step or two toward the hedge.

There was a bark of laughter and Mitchell said, "You two just volunteered to check out the back of the house and the garage. I don't expect anything there, but be careful. This was a brutal murder, and it was someone who enjoyed the work. Careful and methodical. So watch yourselves."

"Yes, sir."

He pointed to another two cops and said, "You stay out here and keep the looky-lous away. We don't need them. The rest of you come with me. I'll want a careful search of the upstairs, and we'll want to secure the downstairs until the crime scene guys get here. Any of you know much about computers?"

One of the younger cops said, "I've had some courses."

"Blanchard has a computer downstairs. Take a look at it. I think the killer smashed the monitor, but I don't think she damaged the hard drive. Don't do anything to it, just see if it's still working."

"Yes, sir."

"Okay, let's go do this. Let me remind you that this is a particularly grotesque murder. If you've got a weak stomach, then secure the upstairs."

Mitchell began walking back to the kitchen door. For some reason, he believed this crime was tied to the Miller killing, and he knew that Johnson was out on bail. Maybe Johnson had killed Blanchard because he hadn't cremated the body and it was now lost somewhere in the jungle of bureaucratic nightmare. Maybe Johnson had done it. Or maybe he had Hartwell do it, and that would explain the woman running from the scene. If Hartwell was out of the hospital and up to murder.

All he knew at the moment was that it would be a long night and he wasn't looking forward to it.

CHAPTER TWENTY-NINE

Johnson knew that he was spending too much time in Miller's house, but he couldn't make himself leave. He was struck by the emptiness, meaning that almost everything of a personal nature was gone and he wondered if the police knew that. This would mean that she was still around, because a thief would have taken everything of value but not necessarily everything of a personal nature.

What he didn't know was if she had another base of operations and how he would find it. She couldn't return to the club scene here, because that was the first place he would look for her. She needed to find a new base in a new city.

So, there was no danger sitting in what had once been the basement of her house, watching the light fade and listening to the tiny sounds of the servos as they kicked in and out, running the machinery that would not be needed for a long time.

As he pushed himself out of the chair and started toward the stairs, he heard a sound, like the closing of a massive door. It came from under the house out somewhere in the backyard. He froze, closed his eyes in concentration and listened carefully.

Someone was coming, and Johnson knew who. He had shot her and tried to get the body destroyed, but the police and the coroner and even his own attorney wouldn't listen. Now she was back, and she was going to claim her house again, at least for a little while.

Johnson hurried to the steps and stopped. There was another

sound, this one closer, this one a little louder. He crept up the stairs, not wanting to make a sound because he knew that her hearing was better than his, and she would hear him moving about if he wasn't careful. He reached the top of the stairs and stopped again.

Then he walked to the front door, opened it and slipped out onto the porch. He kept the door open and listened, but the house was silent again. No lights appeared in the growing twilight, but Miller didn't need much to be able to see as well as if it was high noon on a cloudless day.

A voice, a muffled curse, came from the back of the house, probably the master bedroom. He recognized Miller's shout of annoyance as she found that everything was gone.

There was a crash as Miller tipped over the mirrored dresser, or that was what Johnson thought. It sounded like glass breaking.

He decided he didn't want to see her if she was in a rage. And he didn't want to see her because she would know that he had shot her. She would know that he tried to kill her and failed.

And he thought she would need food. He would be the perfect food for her because she could get her revenge and nourishment at the same time. She would kill him just as quickly as she could, if she knew he was there.

So, he closed the door and stepped off the porch onto the grass. He ducked low, under the window outside the formal dining room, just in case she was looking out, and then straightened up and ran back to his car. He knew running was foolish because anyone looking out the window would see him and know he was fleeing. A man dressed as he was wasn't jogging. He was running from something. He was running for a reason, and usually that reason would be something illegal.

The police had his pistol and they had his bullets. They had everything he needed now. They wouldn't listen, but then he could now prove that he hadn't murdered a human being because she was alive and on the loose.

As he reached his car, he grinned to himself. This was going to make an interesting trial, if it even went to trial now. All he had to do was somehow convince the police, the coroner and the judge that Linda Miller was still alive, or, at the very least, undead.

At his home, he was tempted to begin the celebration. True, he wished that Miller had remained dead and that he'd gotten the body destroyed, but with her moving around, he was going to be cleared of murder. It would even be difficult to accuse him of attempted murder because he was sure she would show no signs of the wounds he had inflicted.

But he was also confused by a couple of points. Where had her personal stuff gone, and why had she returned to that house? Surely she knew the police would look there for her first.

And then he laughed out loud. Of course the police wouldn't look for her there. They thought she was dead, and although Mitchell knew the body was missing, he would be checking with funeral homes and other morgues to see if it turned up there. They wouldn't stake out her house because they believed she was dead.

He walked into his office, sat in his chair and picked up his cell phone. He scrolled down the numbers, found the one he wanted and hit "Send."

"Rachael Goldberg."

Johnson, without thinking about it, blurted, "Linda Miller is alive. I saw her."

There was a moment of silence and then Goldberg said, "Tom?"

"Yes," he said excitedly. "Yes. I saw her. Linda Miller. I told you people to burn the body."

"Where did you see her?' asked Goldberg.

"At her house."

"What were you doing there?"

"I was trying to learn something more about her. I was trying to retrieve her personal papers. Say, did you know the place had been cleaned out?"

Goldberg ignored the question and said, "You actually saw her?"

Johnson hesitated and then said, "Well, I didn't actually see her, but I heard her. It had to be her. I recognized the voice but I had to get out."

"Tom, are you telling me that you broke into her house? That you searched it?"

The tone of voice, the skepticism, finally penetrated. Johnson took a deep breath and said, "I told you. I told everyone, that the body had to be burned, but you wouldn't listen. Then the body disappeared, and no one could find it. Now I tell you that Miller is again moving among the living, and you won't listen."

"Tom, listen to what you're saying. Miller was dead. She was autopsied. Now you want me to believe that she is alive?"

"Where's the body?" he asked.

"It'll turn up, and when it does, what will that do to your theory?"

"It won't turn up because she has . . . I don't know what the right word is here. Risen? Awakened? Returned? Whatever. She is back, and we'll have to find her and stop her again."

"Where are you now, Tom?"

"I'm home," he said. "I'm sitting in my office, with the records I have of Miller open on my desk, and I'm wondering when she is going to come for me."

"Why would she do that?" asked Goldberg.

"Because I know what she is, and I have acted on that. Now, if I can prove that she's alive and the same person, then she'll be exposed."

"But you said she wasn't a person."

"A figure of speech," said Johnson, waving a hand. "If I can prove that Linda Miller survived. We need to get Mitchell to meet us at Miller's house."

"How do you know she'll still be there?" asked Goldberg.

"Because, at the moment, she has no place else to go. She can't get to anything until the morning when the banks open."

"Won't she have credit cards?"

"Those leave records, and she can be followed. No, given what has happened, she has to tap into a new identity and get out of the city."

"Tom, listen to yourself. First she's coming to kill you, and now she's running for her life. All this and we know that she's dead. You shot her in the head."

"I shot her in the head," said Johnson, "but that didn't kill her. You need to burn the body. Destroy it."

"Tom," she said, sounding impatient. "Stay home. Get some rest. We'll talk tomorrow."

"Tomorrow will be too late," he said. "She'll get away and we'll have nothing. We have to meet."

"You stay right there and I'll be over. Don't move."

"Okay, but hurry."

CHAPTER THIRTY

Police captain Steve Mitchell stood just behind the technician where he could get a good look at the computer screen. He was looking at what had been on Blanchard's home computer. Whoever had broken in had smashed the monitor but not the CPU. The data were good and uncorrupted.

"Got some encrypted files here," said the technician. She was young, slender and brunette. She might have finished college within the last year. It didn't matter because she was good at what she did.

"Can you break through it?"

She turned and grinned. "Of course." She put her fingers on the keyboard, typed, backspaced, typed, deleted and then hit the "enter" key. Information began to scroll.

"These are the file names. There might be additional encryption on them but it won't be very sophisticated."

"Can you tell what he was working on last?"

"Of course," she said. She brought up the file. "Looks to be the writeup of an autopsy . . . no, notes about some kind of experiment, or something like that."

"Show me."

She touched a button and the file came up. It was in a PDF format with color pictures inserted. It looked as if it was a scientific paper.

Mitchell moved around and looked at it closely. With growing horror he realized what it was. Blanchard was describing, in the scientific sense, a new sentient being on Earth. He was, in effect, corroborating all that Johnson had said. Blanchard was making the case that Linda Miller, though closely related to humans, was in fact not human.

Mitchell took a deep breath and rubbed a hand across his lips. He could feel the sweat bead and begin to drip. It was almost as if he had run several miles and was now lightheaded. It was difficult to think and almost impossible to read.

The tech shot a glance over her shoulder, but if she noticed Mitchell's reaction, she said nothing about it. Instead, she asked, "You through with this page?"

Mitchell didn't say anything. He wasn't sure that he could speak. He didn't like what he was seeing, and then he realized that he didn't know if Blanchard had been accurate or not. Maybe he had slipped off his trolley and this was all science fiction.

"Let's see the next page."

It was more of the same. Information about Miller, now only the subject of the report, suggested that her organs were not quite right, or in the right places; that her blood seemed to be filled with the genetic material of a dozen others; and that she had some sort of regenerative capability that continued to heal even after the body seemed to be clearly and clinically dead.

He read a few more pages, but the report was evolving into a technical report filled with medical jargon. He didn't understand much of it.

Then came to a page holding several photographs of the body in graphic detail. It was clearly Linda Miller on the table, but something didn't look quite right about it. Mitchell leaned close and saw what it was.

"Oh, for Christ's sake," he said.

"What?" asked the technician.

"That dumb son of a bitch. That really stupid man," said Mitchell.

The research was not being conducted in the city morgue, but in the makeshift one that Blanchard had created in his basement. Just enough background detail was visible in one of the pictures so that Mitchell, having been in that morgue, recognized it.

"That dumb son of a bitch stole the body," said Mitchell. He touched the tech on her shoulder to get her attention. "Print this out for me. In color. Just one copy and then seal the file back up, and don't let anyone see it and don't tell anyone what we found. Understood?"

"Yes, sir."

"This is part of a criminal investigation . . ."

She interrupted to say, "I understand that. I understand that we need to keep this quiet for the moment. I will not say anything to anyone until you say I can."

"Okay," said Mitchell. "I just wanted to be sure that you understood this was slightly different than the regular case. That's all."

"Yes, sir."

Mitchell then asked, "Where's the printer?"

She pointed to a corner of the office, near a window and the coffee maker. "I'm networked into that one."

"Go ahead with the copy. I'll get it out of the printer."

Without another word, he walked over so that he would be the only one to get the print. As he waited for the machine to start, he looked down at the city where the lights were beginning to fade and the sun was coming up. He had been awake all night but hadn't realized how late it was.

As he watched a couple walk into a retro diner that was alight with neon and glowing with stainless steel, he suddenly realized that Blanchard had contaminated the case against Johnson.

True, there were police officers who had seen the body and technicians who had taken it to the morgue, but a smart defense attorney could argue that Miller was alive at that time. Yes, an autopsy would have made sure that Miller was dead, but the man who completed that autopsy was now dead, so he couldn't testify about the accuracy of his work, which wouldn't, normally, be a problem. But now the body was gone, and the man who took it seemed to have been Blanchard.

The printer clicked, cycled and began printing. Mitchell looked at the first sheet as it came out and saw that it was the article he wanted. He put the first sheet back and let the printer continue.

Now, that smart defense attorney would argue that Blanchard's autopsy couldn't be trusted because Blanchard clearly had an ulterior motive. Blanchard was preparing a scientific paper, and he hadn't actually collected the evidence that would be needed against Johnson.

"Oh, you stupid son of a bitch," said Mitchell again. And then he thought, "Where in the hell is the body?"

If Blanchard stole it, as seemed to be the case, then the body should have been at his house, in his basement morgue, but Mitchell hadn't seen it. All he had seen was Blanchard lying on his table looking like a frog in a high school biology class and just as dead.

He turned when the printer fell silent and picked up the sheets. It was a thick stack of paper, worthy of a scientific journal, but Mitchell wondered if it would ever be published now that the author was dead. He noticed a short bibliography at the end and thought that he would look up the reference when he had a chance. Now he needed to return to Blanchard's house.

He left the building and found his car parked on the street. Traffic was beginning to pick up and more of the parking spaces were occupied. A few more people were walking around, some looking like they were on their way to work and some on their way home from a night of clubbing. Mitchell wondered if he should put police into the clubs to look for Miller and then realized what a ridiculous idea that was. Miller was dead and he knew it. He'd seen the bullet hole in her head. He didn't know why the thought even crossed his mind.

He got in his car, let headquarters know that he was on his way back out to Blanchard's house and then pulled out into traffic. There were clouds building on the horizon that promised some relief from the heat later in the day, maybe by mid-afternoon. Maybe some rain to flush the humidity out of the air. If nothing else, the clouds would keep the sun from baking everything in the city and might even keep the temperature down.

When he arrived again, he saw that some of the cars were gone, but the coroner's wagon was parked in the driveway near the kitchen door. Mitchell thought it strange that the coroner's wagon would be at Blanchard's house now. Blanchard had been a young man, relatively speaking. He had no heart trouble, he wasn't overweight and he didn't smoke cigarettes with any regularity. He shouldn't be dead now, but he was. And it wasn't a very pretty death. Mitchell hoped he was dead before the carving started, but given the Gothic elements of this case, he suspected that Blanchard had felt the pain as the autopsy began and the terror as he realized that he wasn't going to get out of it alive.

Mitchell watched as they brought the body out and put it in the back of the wagon. Before the morgue attendants could get into it, Mitchell called out.

"Let's wait before you take him in."

One of the men, older with light-colored, receding hair, turned and said, "He's not going to get any fresher sitting here in the heat."

"Just hang around for a few minutes. There might be more business for you."

"You know something, Captain?"

"Just want to get a question or two answered so that you don't have to make another trip out here. Won't hurt for us to be sure before you go in."

Mitchell then pulled open the screen and entered. He let it slap closed behind him, felt the cold air of the air conditioner blow over him and then went down the stairs two at a time. He found two crime scene techs on their hands and knees examining a spot on the floor with some kind of black light or infrared light. They didn't hear him.

"What have you got there?"

"Looks like semen to me," said one pointing at the floor. "Not real fresh."

Mitchell felt his heart skip once and said, "You are telling me . . ."

"No, Captain," the tech interrupted. "I'm not telling you anything. Just that we have a stain on the floor that might be semen. That's all."

Mitchell felt sweat pop out on his forehead and under his arms. He felt warm, as if the air conditioning had broken and the humidity was seeping in somewhere. He felt slightly dizzy but only because the case was taking bizarre turns. He thought that Rod Serling was about to appear and tell him that he had just entered the "Twilight Zone."

He said, "I've got a problem for you. Blanchard might have stolen a body from the morgue. He seems to think that it wasn't a human body but some kind of genetic mutation or adaption or some such . . . shit. A body is missing, and I would assume that it is here, someplace."

One of the technicians stood up. He was a tall, slender man

who looked more academic than athletic. He pushed his glasses back up his nose with his middle finger and then took a swipe at the long black hair that had fallen over his forehead.

"It's not down here," he said. "We've been through the whole place once."

"Outside? The garage?"

"We haven't been up there but some of your officers have. They would have let us know if they had another body. Even if they found freshly turned earth in a grave-sized patch, I'm sure they would have told us. What was he doing?"

Mitchell waved a hand as if to wipe the thought away but said, "He had it in his mind he had found some new species. That's about all I know."

"There's nothing here, Captain."

"Well, let's keep this between us," said Mitchell, "at least until I can figure out a couple of things."

"You know us. We write our report about what we find. Here we had one body and that's it. We have no real evidence that anyone else has been killed here."

"No, I didn't say that. Blanchard took a body from the morgue. I don't know what he did with it."

"We just have the one," repeated the technician.

"Okay." Mitchell left the basement morgue and sat down on the basement steps. He leaned forward, his elbows on his knees, and looked at the tile floor.

Blanchard had violated any number of laws, and Blanchard had thrown the case against Johnson out the window. It was no longer a case with the killer caught with the smoking gun in his hand. It was now a complex legal proceeding with a missing body, a dead coroner, and a report that proved, in Blanchard's deluded mind at least, that Linda Miller hadn't been human just as Johnson had claimed all along. He just didn't know what else could go wrong, but he was about to find out.

CHAPTER THIRTY-ONE

Sarah Hartwell sat on the edge of the hospital bed and looked down at her shoes. She just didn't have the energy to tie them. She was afraid that if she leaned over she would pass out, and she couldn't get her foot up so that she could reach the laces. Maybe if she was sitting in a chair rather than on the high, off-the-floor bed.

She noticed that her clothes didn't seem to fit either. They were too big for her. The blouse looked as if it belonged to an older sister, and her jeans were so loose that she knew if she stood up, they would fall to her ankles. To her, it meant that she might not be ready to go home.

At least all the tubes had been pulled from her and the bandages had been reduced to bits of white. Her hair on one side was still short, having had no time to grow out, so she had a lopsided look.

She slid forward and began to stand up. When she didn't feel faint, when a curtain of black didn't begin to descend, she straightened, delighted to be standing on her own. She was able to step to the chair and to sit down without hurting herself or giving herself a headache.

As she was wondering if she should attempt to tie her shoes, there was a light knock at the door and Rachael Goldberg looked in. She smiled and said, "Can we talk?"

"Sure."

Goldberg stepped in and closed the door. She said, "Are you

going home soon?"

"Today. This afternoon. I just wanted to get out of the bed and to put on some clothes. This has been tiring."

If Goldberg picked up the irony, she didn't let it show. She moved to a straight-back chair that looked as if it had been old during the Truman administration. She sat down and said, "I need to know exactly what happened on the night that Tom shot Linda Miller."

"My memory is hazy on that," said Hartwell. "Brain trauma, said the doctor."

"Yes, but anything you can remember might help me defend Tom."

"We had a dinner set up with Linda. Tom picked me up, and we drove to her house. I remember it was a very hot afternoon, and the evening wasn't much cooler."

She grinned and said, "I was tempted to dress for the heat. As little as possible but in the end, I chickened out."

Goldberg stared at the other woman, not understanding what she meant and wondering why she would say something like that. It did nothing to help.

When Goldberg didn't respond, she said, "We walked to the front door and Linda opened it before we rang. She seemed excited about something. Maybe agitated would be a better word. She invited us in, and we all went into the living room."

Hartwell took a deep breath and said, "Linda kept looking at me. I wondered if I had grown horns. I didn't think of it as a sexual thing, just her staring at me for some reason. I remember it making me uncomfortable."

"You mean you thought she was a lesbian?"

"No, not at all. That thought never crossed my mind. She was just staring at me as she talked to Tom."

Goldberg leaned forward and said, "What were they talking about?"

"I couldn't follow it. She was saying something about her family and that they were ancient. She could trace her lines back thousands of years, which seemed odd to me. A couple of hundred maybe, but thousands?"

"So you just listened?"

"Yes. Then Miller stood up and said that she needed to prepare something for dinner. She walked into the kitchen. Tom stood up as if to follow her but then didn't. Suddenly, I felt as if my head had exploded. There was a painful flash of bright white, and I didn't know what was happening. I could hear voices, but I didn't know what they were saying. They were shouting, but I don't know what that was about, and then there was a loud bang that I guess would be a shot . . . or the shot. That is all I remember until I woke up in here."

Goldberg nodded but said, "That really doesn't tell me much of anything. Where did the gun come from?"

"I don't know. I don't think Tom brought it with him. I don't know if Miller had it or not. After she hit me, I really don't remember much."

"How do you know she hit you?" asked Goldberg.

Hartwell snapped her head up and stared. "What are you saying?"

"Just that you were hit from behind, so you don't know who hit you."

"It had to be her because Tom was in front of me. I was looking at him when I got hit." There was venom in her voice.

Goldberg held up a hand almost in surrender. She said, "I didn't mean anything here. I'm Tom's attorney, and I have to ask some hard questions."

Hartwell leaned back in the chair and took a deep breath. She then said, "Tom saved my life. I know this. She hit me and meant to kill me. I just don't know why. Has Tom said anything to you about that?"

Goldberg let her gaze slide away and said, "No. I don't think he knows what provoked the attack."

Now Hartwell laughed. "I think he thought she was a vampire. He was hinting about that to me, but I just didn't get it. I mean, I know there are, there were, people who believed they were vampires and then drank blood, but that was just their belief. They didn't need blood to survive. They could eat other food. They could go out in the sun. They didn't change into bats."

Goldberg started to say that vampires could go out in the sun, but then stopped. She didn't want to get into a philosophical argument about the habits of vampires.

There was a tap at the door, and it was pushed open. The doctor entered, looked at Goldberg and then at Hartwell and asked, "How are we feeling?"

"I'm fine. I would like to go home."

"Do you have someone who can drive you home?"

Hartwell looked at Goldberg, who shrugged. "I can get her home."

"That means getting her into the house and into bed." He saw the look on her face and held up a hand. "Okay. Onto the couch, but I don't want you doing anything more strenuous than calling for a pizza."

The doctor gave her a few more instructions, smiled and retreated.

"Thanks for the ride," said Hartwell. "I was going to call Tom."

"Tom is convinced that he saw Linda Miller alive. He wants to find her to prove he didn't kill her."

Hartwell smiled weakly and said, "I didn't see him kill anyone. All I know about that is what I read in the newspapers or the Internet."

Hartwell pushed herself up, stood wobbling for a moment

and then took a deep breath. "Made it."

Goldberg helped her gather her things, and then a nurse appeared with a wheelchair.

"I'm here to give you a ride downstairs."

Goldberg picked up the overnight bag that contained the rest of Hartwell's clothes, and they all left the room together. When they reached the front entrance, Goldberg went to retrieve her car, and a moment later the nurse was helping Hartwell into the passenger's side.

When the nurse closed the door, Goldberg said, "You'll have to give me directions."

"Just head west on First Avenue."

"Okay."

As they pulled out of the parking lot, Hartwell said, "I didn't want to talk in there. I know it's silly but I was just afraid that the cops might have bugged the place. I didn't want to say anything that would hurt Tom."

"And what would that have been?" Goldberg slowed for a stop sign, saw nothing coming, and in violation of the law, rolled on through. She turned onto First Avenue.

"Tom had the gun with him. He didn't know that I knew that. I also know that he had silver bullets made for it."

Goldberg gripped the wheel strongly and shot a glance at Hartwell. "Oh, come on . . ."

"He said that he had been studying the legends, and he knew that the bullets wouldn't kill her, but they would stop her. He said that if he shot her in the head it would take three or four days for her to regenerate."

Goldberg suddenly felt weak. Sick. This was premeditation. It was planning of a crime to take another's life. There was no way to explain the silver bullets and the talk of shooting someone in the head.

Unless it was insanity.

She slowed for traffic, was tempted to turn on the radio, and then decided against it. She needed to let Hartwell talk.

"Tom was worried about Miller. He said that she wasn't human. That she was something else. Some kind of intelligent creature that had evolved about the same time as humans but on a different branch of the tree. Sort of like us and the Neanderthals. Both intelligent, but different."

"He told you all this?"

"Yes, and he gave me some letters or papers or something that proved it, at least to him. I tried to follow his reasoning, but I got lost on one of the turns." She laughed. "There was something missing. Something that he wasn't telling me."

"Then why would he ask you to go with him to dinner at Miller's?"

"I think he was going to prove to me that Miller wasn't human, though I don't know how. You need to turn left at the next light, go three blocks and then turn right. It's the third house on the right."

"You still have that stuff?"

"Of course."

"I'd like to see it."

"Of course."

Goldberg made the turns and then pulled into the driveway of Hartwell's house. When Hartwell reached for the door handle, Goldberg said, "Hey, let me help."

Goldberg got out and hurried around to open the passenger's door. Hartwell held out a hand and Goldberg took it, pulling.

"I'm not really all that weak. I don't think I'll mow the lawn, but I can walk into the house without help."

"I'll carry your bag."

They walked to the front door. It needed painting and the flower gardens on either side needed weeding. The grass was long but turning brown in the late summer heat.

Hartwell pushed open the door and then stepped back. "I must have turned off the air when we went to Miller's. It's a little warm in there."

Hartwell then entered and hurried to the thermostat. She turned on the air and said, "It'll take a little while to cool off in here."

Goldberg entered and set the bag by the door. She said, "It's not that bad."

"Would you like something to drink. I have lemonade, tea, some Seven-Up and some Gatorade."

"No. I do need to see those papers that Tom gave you though."

Hartwell waved at the living room and said, "Have a seat and I'll go get them."

Goldberg wandered into the living room. The furniture was old and a little worn, but it was clean. No spots or burns. The carpet was as worn as the furniture but also as clean. The windows overlooked the front yard. A tree dominated one side, near the driveway. Across the street was a house with a gigantic RV parked in the driveway. It was an older model and looked as if it had been used for lots of travel but wasn't quite the eyesore it could have been.

Hartwell came back with a banker's box. She put it on the coffee table.

"You should have called. I could have carried it in."

"It wasn't all that heavy. Besides, I'm not fragile. Just a little weak from the stay in the hospital and from hospital food and from doing nothing but lying around all day."

"Well, it's getting cooler in here."

"The air works well. Have a seat and take a look."

Goldberg sat down on the couch, leaned forward and opened the box. She pulled a looseleaf binder out and opened it. The pages had been copied from something else. The writing was old, ornate and a little confusing. It was also the history of a species that had not been described by modern science and that for all intents and purposes didn't exist.

CHAPTER THIRTY-TWO

Captain Steven Mitchell sat staring at the flat panel monitor in his office and wondered just what in the hell Blanchard had been trying to do. This was a scientific paper, filled with medical terms and medical conditions and precise, though oftentimes gross, descriptions of pieces of Linda Miller's body. There were full-color photographs that looked as if they have been professionally taken, but that Mitchell knew Blanchard had done using a digital camera and his computer. It was a nearly complete paper that contained dozens of references to earlier, other published scientific papers and it described, to Mitchell's layman's mind, a new species of human. It described a creature that thrived at night but that could go out in the day, a creature that had incredible regenerative powers and a creature that had a thirst for human blood but would take that of a cow or a pig when necessary. What he was reading was the description of a vampire, though it wasn't the classic vampire because it hadn't been created by the bite of another. It was a creature that had evolved on Earth.

It was the most incredible document he had ever read because it was supposed to be believed, and it talked about a vampire in the sense that it was real and alive as opposed to legend and undead, and it was living in his city. Blanchard never used the term *vampire*, but that was what he was talking about. It was clear even though he hadn't used the word.

This document, handed to the defense, along with the disappearance of the body would create a reasonable doubt, and the man who shot Linda Miller in the head would walk. Johnson's claim that Miller was not human and therefore he was innocent could be reinforced by the document that Blanchard had created.

And Mitchell hadn't even thought about the social, scientific or historical considerations. He had thought about what it would mean if people began to truly believe that something like the vampire was alive.

Which led to the next questions. Who had killed Blanchard and why? It wasn't Johnson, because Blanchard was reinforcing his beliefs. It wasn't a former client because all Blanchard's clients were dead when he got to them. It could be a disgruntled family member who didn't like a particular ruling, but Mitchell couldn't think of a single case in which the coroner was targeted because someone didn't like a ruling.

Actually, and Mitchell hesitated to even think about it, the only person who benefited was Miller because her true nature would again be hidden from the world. And if Miller couldn't commit the crime because she was dead, then who did, and the only answer was there were others of her kind.

Mitchell actually laughed out loud, though the sound was high-pitched and strained. He couldn't believe that he could actually believe that there were vampires on the prowl. Even with Blanchard's alleged scientific paper, Mitchell couldn't believe there were vampires.

He turned away from the flat panel and looked out the window. Of course he would have to talk with Johnson, but that relationship was now clouded with threats of prosecution and attorneys. He couldn't just walk up to Johnson's front door and begin to ask questions now. The trial got in the way.

But there was a second murder now, and it was related to Miller in some way. If Johnson could help maybe he would. All he could do was ask. He didn't have to worry about tainting the case now. Blanchard had done that when he stole the body.

Mitchell was tired. He wanted to go home, but he also wanted the answers to his questions. He stood up, pulled his jacket off the back of his chair and headed for the door. He told the duty sergeant, "I'll have my cell on, and I'll be in my personal car. I'm on my way home, more or less."

The sergeant knew better than to ask what that meant exactly. Instead, she just said, "Yes, sir," and entered the time in the duty log.

On the way to Johnson's house, Mitchell concentrated on his driving. He found his way to Johnson's house and pulled into the driveway. As he got out of the car, he noticed that the grass was well worn and that the flowers under the windows had been smashed flat. A couple of bushes looked as if they had been trampled.

He stepped onto the porch and rang the bell. He heard movement inside and wondered where his cop sense had gone. He was standing directly in front of the door as if he was calling on a neighbor and not a man he had arrested for murder. He was asking to get shot, yet he knew he was in no danger. Johnson wouldn't shoot him because he wasn't a vampire. Mitchell believed that Johnson had shot Miller because he believed that she was one.

The door opened slightly and Johnson looked out. He made no move to let Mitchell in. He said, "I was about to call you."

"We need to talk."

"My attorney is not here."

"This is between you and me. We don't need attorneys," said Mitchell.

Johnson hesitated and then opened the door. "Come on in."

Mitchell noticed that it was a nice house. Clean, fresh, with furniture that looked as if no one had ever used it. They walked into the family room. Mitchell took the chair near the window where he could watch the front door.

"You were going to call me," said Mitchell.

Johnson, who stood near the fireplace, looked at the cop and then sat down in the closest chair.

"You're not going to believe me," he said. "I told you to burn the body but you wouldn't listen."

"Why don't you tell me what you know," said Mitchell.

"Okay. Miller was at her house last night. She came in through an escape tunnel she had built."

"You saw her?"

"No. I got out of there before then. I heard her, though. She was looking for clothes. I think someone cleaned out the personal stuff. I think she was not alone. There are more of them."

"More of what?" asked Mitchell.

"Whatever she was. Whatever she is."

"I'm going to tell you something that your attorney would learn through discovery anyway. Blanchard stole the body . . ."

"Blanchard?"

"Our medical examiner. He stole the body and wrote a scientific paper about a new species of intelligent creatures that look like us but are different enough that they fall outside the range of human."

Johnson grinned and almost laughed. "Told you she wasn't human."

"I thought it was an insanity dodge," said Mitchell. "I'm still not sure how this will play out. I would imagine that the vast majority of the scientific community will laugh at this, but Blanchard's paper does cite a number of references that, I think, suggest that others, scientists, have seen the same thing in the past."

Johnson sat quietly, but Mitchell saw that the color had

drained from his face. He said, "I didn't believe it. Really didn't believe it. I thought it was some kind of disease, but I knew that burning the body would keep the disease from spreading. I didn't think she could recover from an autopsy . . ."

"You seem to be filled with contradictions here," said Mitchell. "You spent all that time telling me that you hadn't killed a human being and all that time trying to get us to cremate her, and now you tell me you didn't really believe this?"

"I had been with her during her hunting. I knew that she was bringing people to her house. I knew that she thrived on the hunt and that she had some strange tastes."

Mitchell realized that he shouldn't be there. Johnson was talking about Miller and suggesting that she had killed any number of people. If he knew that, then he had committed another crime. He was, at best, concealing the crime and at worst, an accomplice. But he said none of this.

"Miller has got to run now," said Johnson. "She had other identities prepared just in case."

"You know them?"

"No. She was always very careful about that. It was her escape valve, and she wasn't going to compromise it. She arrived here with a suitcase and a credit card."

"Credit card," said Mitchell.

"Yeah. She has the credit cards prepared."

Mitchell was suddenly excited. He'd forgotten he had been there when they removed Miller's body, and he'd seen part of the autopsy of her. He had known she was dead, and now he was beginning to think in terms of a missing person. He was thinking in terms of trying to deduce the names on the credit cards, and as he thought about it, the more excited he became.

He stood up and said, "I've got to get over to Miller's house."

"There's nothing there. I told you that. Only the furniture and the drapes and the television."

"But did you look for trash? Did you look through the garbage? She might have left something there for us to find."

Johnson said, "No. I didn't do any of that. I was looking for the personal items that she'd had with her. I wanted to get my hands on them."

"So the trash might still be there, under the sink, in the pantry, in the garage. Stuff that everyone throws away but that might be able to give us a hint about where she would go."

"What about telephone calls?" asked Johnson.

"Sure. We can see if she called anyone . . . or if anyone called her frequently. Might tell us where to look."

Johnson laughed. "You know you just said us."

"Yes, but I was referring to my fellow officers and not civilians under indictment for murder."

"But how can I be a murderer if we are now going on a search for the victim?"

Mitchell stared at him for a moment. He didn't know when he had realized that Miller was not human and had probably survived, somehow, the shooting and the autopsy. It was incredible that he could get that far down a path that was so obviously wrong, and yet, he was about to search the allegedly dead woman's house for a clue about her hiding place.

"Can I go with you?" asked Johnson.

Mitchell's immediate reaction was to say no. But before he could speak that thought out loud, he had another. Johnson knew the woman . . . the creature . . . better than anyone. So he said, "Just to her house and you don't touch anything."

"Of course."

They left the house and Johnson locked the front door. He waited until Mitchell unlocked the passenger door of the car and then got in. He said, "This doesn't look much like a police car."

"It's mine," said Mitchell.

He backed out and turned up the street. He heard sirens then, several of them, and recognized them as those on fire trucks. There was one police siren mixed in. He thought that he could see smoke above the tops of some of the houses far away. "Something's on fire," he said.

They drove on with the sirens getting louder and the smoke drifting in the air. He pulled over to let a police car by and then pulled out again.

They turned onto Miller's street and saw the trucks parked around Miller's house. A police car was blocking the street about a quarter of the way to her house. Fire fighters were running toward the building. Flames were on the roof and climbing the front from a broken window there. The term was "fully engulfed." Mitchell knew the house would be a total loss, and now the fire fighters would work to keep other houses from catching fire and attempting to protect the surrounding yards.

As they pulled up to the police car, Mitchell rolled down his window and showed his badge to the patrolman. "Where's the incident commander?"

"Battalion chief near that yellow car."

"Thanks.

Johnson laughed. "She burned her house. Didn't want to leave anything behind."

"Yeah," said Mitchell, "but in today's world, you always leave something behind. We just have to find it."

CHAPTER THIRTY-THREE

As he stood near Miller's house, watching the flames as they shot a hundred feet into the sky, and as the fire fighters poured water into the broken windows trying to knock down those flames, Johnson's cell phone rang. He stepped back, away from the fire line and then turned so that he was facing away from the burning house.

"Hello."

He heard Goldberg say, "Tom, where are you?"

"Miller's house."

"Get away from there before you get yourself into more trouble."

Johnson laughed. "I'm here with Captain Mitchell . . ."

"What? Have you lost your mind?"

"Rachael, listen. First, he came to see me. I think he believes what I have been saying—"

She interrupted to say, "He'll believe anything to get you talking. You're going to bury yourself. I don't want you to say a word to him. And get away from Miller's house."

"It's on fire."

"What?"

"Her house is on fire, and I don't think they're going to be able to save anything."

"Tom, you need to get away from there and away from Mitchell. Nothing good can come of it."

"I don't have a way to get home," he said.

"You stay there. Don't leave. I'm on my way."

Johnson snapped his cell phone shut, and Mitchell turned toward him. "Who was that?"

"My lawyer. She's pissed that I'm here, and she's pissed that I'm here with you."

Mitchell grunted. "Well, it is a little bit of a strange situation."

There was a sudden, loud popping as if giant popcorn had begun to cook. Then there was a muffled crash and a rolling roar as flames shot two hundred feet into the air and then collapsed back in on themselves.

"Roof fell," said Mitchell.

"Rachael told me to stay here. She says that I shouldn't be talking to you."

"She's probably right. But then, how are you going to find Miller without my help?"

"Rachael has resources."

"Listen, Tom, here's the deal. You can pay for a private investigator and those guys are good. They'll probably be able to trace her, but it's going to take time and your money. Now, if you cooperate with me, I can bring to bear the resources of not only our department, but the state police and the FBI. I can get questions answered in an hour that might take you a week. So, we can cooperate, or we can each go off on our own direction."

"You know, I have heard from everyone that the police, in this situation, are not my friends. They're there to arrest someone for the crime. They'll lie to me, and they'll tell me that evidence has put me at the scene and they'll—"

Mitchell interrupted. "You said you were innocent of killing a human. I have all the evidence I need to put you in the slam. I got you standing over the body with the smoking gun in your hand. I can prove premeditation because it was your gun and you bought silver bullets for crying out loud. Silver bullets.

They're for werewolves."

"No, they have a terrible effect on vampires too. Makes it more difficult to regenerate. Doesn't stop them. Just makes it more difficult."

There was more noise from the house and then a blast of hot air. One of the walls collapsed and threw embers and sparks all over the neighborhood. There was an odor of burning wood that smelled like an autumn afternoon with football on the TV and the fireplace roaring.

"So," said Mitchell. "What's it going to be?"

Johnson wasn't sure what it should be. Mitchell was there to put him in jail, but he sounded as if he believed that Miller was alive and running. He seemed to want to track her, and Johnson could make that job easier.

"Look, if you're right, if you're innocent, it can't hurt to co-operate. If you're guilty, we've got you pegged three ways from Sunday, so it doesn't matter. The only thing you can do by not cooperating is to ensure your conviction and letting Miller get away."

Johnson shrugged and turned his attention to the fire. The flames were lower now and there was only one wall left standing. The firefighters were pouring water onto the hot spots and smoke and steam were rolling up, away from the fire.

Mitchell said, "I guess there won't be any trash to go through."

"I don't know why I should be surprised. She knew how to protect her identity."

"But she was telling you everything."

Johnson shrugged. "Not everything. She told me enough that I knew what she was. She was telling me that she could bring me to her way of life. They didn't know what the upper end was. There were members of the race who had lived more than a thousand years, and she could give me that secret."

224

"Did you believe her?"

"No. I think I know too much about genetics and how the body works. She couldn't transfer to me her longevity. She tried to convince me that there was a ritual that could be performed, and I think that might have worked, did work, in a less enlightened time. We just know too much for our own good."

"Maybe we should head back to the precinct," said Mitchell.

"My attorney said for me to wait here. She's coming here to pick me up."

"Your choice," said Mitchell, turning to go.

"I just meant we should wait for her, nothing else. I'm going to need your help on this."

Mitchell stopped walking and turned to watch the fire. It wasn't nearly as exciting as it had been when they arrived. Now it was mostly smoke with little flame. Little more than a bonfire that had gotten out of hand, temporarily.

Goldberg joined them just as the last of the patrol cars was moved so that the street was no longer blocked. There were still two fire trucks there, and water was still being pumped into what looked like the thoroughly drenched remains of Miller's house. Fire fighters were rolling up the now unused hoses and other equipment was being stored. The fire was out, the excitement was over, and even the reporters had tired of talking to neighbors who said little other than it had been a spectacular blaze.

Goldberg stood staring at Mitchell. It was as if she was trying to turn him into stone. She had a defense attorney's mistrust of the police, and she suspected that his new kindness toward Johnson was just a way to gather more incriminating evidence.

"There is nothing for us here," said Mitchell. "I think we should head back to the station."

Goldberg, thinking like a defense attorney, asked, "Why the

station? Why not Tom's house?"

"I have access to our computers there. I can't access them from his house."

"Why do we need them now? Shouldn't we sit down first and decide what our best course of action is?"

"We can do that at the station," said Mitchell.

"I'd be more comfortable somewhere other than at the station," said Goldberg.

Both of them turned and looked at Johnson who hadn't said a word during the exchange. He said, "I have the notes and papers at home, and I have what I scanned into the computer. It seems to me that it would be a logical place to start."

"With the added benefit," said Goldberg, "that the interview would be off the record."

"This isn't an interview," said Mitchell. "It is a search for information."

"Can I have that in writing?" asked Goldberg.

"Counselor," said Mitchell, "we will be at his house, and there will be no record of any interview. What possible good would a statement from me be, other than to create a legal document that we met and that could be used against your client? It seems to me that an off the record meeting should stay off the record."

"Rachael, I have no objection. But I do wish that we could get going. It's hot out here."

"Tom, you'll ride with me. I have some things to discuss with you before we have this sitdown with the police. If there are no objections."

Mitchell held up his hands in mock surrender. "I have none. I'll meet you there."

Johnson watched Mitchell return to his car. Once the police officer was in it, he turned to see what Goldberg had to say. She was staring at him, her eyes bright with anger.

"This is going to turn out bad," she said.

"He believes me. I think he saw Miller, but he doesn't want to admit it. Something has changed in the last day or two, but I don't know what."

"The coroner is dead and the body is still lost. I think that has a lot to do with it. They could move forward without the body because they had the evidence gathered from it, but the man who collected that evidence is now dead. The chain of custody is broken and that is going to mess up their case, so what do you do, you start talking to the lead cop."

"He believes me and he can help."

"I'm doing this under protest," she said.

"Let's just go meet him at my house and see what we can learn about Miller. What happens if we find her alive?"

"Clearly the charges will have to be reduced. Maybe criminal assault or attempted murder. Of course that might be a stretch, unless you feel the need to help the cops put you away."

They walked slowly over to the car. Johnson stood on the passenger side and let Goldberg unlock the doors. He opened his, but didn't get in. He wanted to give the interior a chance to cool off.

During the ride to his house, neither said much. Goldberg was still angry about the meeting with the police. Johnson was a strange client—sure that he was right, sure that he hadn't killed a human, and sure that they all would see his point. She was used to dealing with the thieves and the abusers and the deadbeat dads but in a civil rather than criminal way. She was not into murder or other heavy crimes, and her firm was careful which cases they took. They were still telling her to take any deal offered and to be done with this case. They had hinted that her work might be considered substandard, and her position with the firm was in jeopardy if she did not heed their sage advice.

Mitchell had parked in front of the house and sat in the car with the driver's door open, waiting. Goldberg pulled into the driveway but didn't get out right away.

To Johnson, she said, "Just be careful what you say, and if I tell you to shut up, then shut up."

"Okay."

As they all approached the front door, Mitchell said, "I think the first thing we need to do is come to some kind of an agreement here. I'm way out on a limb, and I don't want it sawed off."

As Johnson put the key into the lock, Goldberg said, "These sorts of communications, between suspects and the police, are highly irregular."

It was a dumb thing to say, but she was at a loss here. This meeting was something that she had never expected and didn't like.

"We're all here searching for the truth," said Mitchell. "And that's all I'm searching for."

Johnson pushed open the door and stepped back, waving the other two in. He said, "Let's go into the living room."

When they were seated, Mitchell said, "I saw her yesterday. I saw her running from the scene of a murder."

Goldberg said, "Are you sure?"

Mitchell looked at her and said, "Of course I'm sure. I just didn't want to believe it until I saw the fire."

"How did that change your mind?" asked Goldberg.

"There was no reason for that house to be on fire unless it was to destroy evidence. She set the fire and then took off."

CHAPTER THIRTY-FOUR

Linda Miller, looking dirty and tired and more than a little haggard, sat in one of the rear seats, next to a window, on the bus. She didn't like the vibrations. She didn't like the stench of diesel that bled into the passenger area. And she didn't like many of those on the bus around her. They were poor, dirty and unsophisticated. At least that was what she believed.

And, most important. She was hungry. Very hungry. She would have to find something to eat soon. Something with more sustenance than a rare steak.

She sat looking out the window and wondered how she had been so wrong about her choice of a friend. Johnson had seemed to be just what she needed to help her over the bumps that sometimes came up in a modern society. Someone she could slowly pull into her web with promises that she had no intention of keeping. Someone who didn't understand what was going on. Johnson had seen the potential of a book, but she knew it would never be written.

She had misjudged him completely. She hadn't expected the spine, the courage, the intelligence. She had led him down one path and then the next, but he hadn't followed as closely as she had thought he would.

It made no difference now. That was over and Miller was dead, or rather the police thought her dead, and that was the next best thing. Johnson would be tried for her murder, and he would be unable to convince anyone of the truth. That was the beauty of the situation. It was so unbelievable that no one would ever believe it. Johnson could tell the authorities whatever he wanted about her, but they wouldn't believe him.

The bus slowed and rolled to a stop on a gravel parking lot that looked like something out of the 1950s. The bus station was pushed into a corner of a truck stop. Nothing had been updated since Eisenhower had been president and someone had decided that the interstate highway would pass twenty miles south of here. The place was decaying, but the old metal sign, swinging in the late evening breeze and slowly rusting into oblivion, still announced the stop.

The driver stood up, turned and said, "Thirty-minute rest stop. You can get something to eat here. It's not fancy, but it tastes good and it's cheap."

As he disappeared out the door so that he would be first in line for food, Miller stood up. She stretched slightly, but her body was still sore. She could feel a delicate pull where the incisions had been and were not quite healed and hidden. She looked like the Frankenstein monster of so many bad horror films. Her hair covered the incision on her head that now was little more than a thin red line than it was an incision.

She joined the line of passengers, all seven of them, as they moved down the narrow aisle toward the door. One woman about Miller's size who carried an oversized purse hesitated and then joined the others. Miller moved closer to her.

She looked like a college student taking the bus back to campus. Not poor or dirty or unsophisticated. Just a college student who had to watch her money carefully.

Miller followed her out into the parking lot and then over to the truck stop café. They walked into a small, long room with a counter along one wall and booths along the other where windows looked out on a view of the parking lot, the highway and a cornfield.

The girl walked toward the restroom at the far end of the diner. Miller stayed right behind her and when the girl opened the door, Miller pushed in right behind her, fearing that it would be a single stall with nothing other than a dirty sink.

But unlike the rest of the place, the bathroom looked almost modern and was certainly clean. There were two stalls, each with solid doors on them. The floor was a light tile and two sinks were under two mirrors. There were paper towels in dispensers and a trash can that held a plastic liner and no trash.

The girl turned to look at Miller, who smiled. She said, "You were on the bus."

"Yes," said the girl.

"Where are you going?"

"Heading back to college. Going in a little early to get settled before my senior year."

Miller slipped closer to the girl who didn't seem to be worried about it. She was smiling and talking.

"I'm about through, and I think I've even got a job lined up already."

Miller struck her once on the side of the head and then kicked her in the belly as she fell. The girl landed on her butt and then rolled to her side. She didn't move and was unconscious.

Miller turned and locked the door and then opened one of the stalls. She pushed and pulled the girl up onto the toilet and then bent over her. She bit her once, on the wrist, where the blood vessels crossed the bone, and sucked deeply. She felt the blood warm her as she swallowed. It pooled and she felt a tingling throughout her body as if she had just finished most of the champagne in a magnum.

She rocked back on her heels and took a deep breath. She sounded like a little kid who was gulping his root beer. She leaned forward and drank again but then stopped. She hadn't taken enough to kill the girl. Just enough to make her feel faint and look anemic. To kill now might give a clue of where she was and the direction she ran. If anyone was looking for her, which she doubted.

Although killing her might be the thing to do, she decided against it. It would be hours before the girl recovered, and Miller knew she would be far away. She could get off down the road, take another bus and be lost in the crowd.

She stood up and straightened her clothes. She left the stall and picked up the bag, pulling some of the money out of the wallet and taking her ticket. If she got the chance, she could steal the girl's suitcase and would have new clothes. She would have a way to start over again.

She put the purse in the girl's lap and then closed the stall door. She unlocked the bathroom door and walked back out into the diner. No one looked at her. They were busy with their food and their personal conversations, and surprisingly, a number were talking on cell phones. Everyone had a cell phone and everyone used them in every situation.

She walked out to the bus and took a seat in the rear, near a window where she could watch the road and the countryside. In a few minutes the people began to straggle back to the bus. The driver came out and climbed into his seat without a look at the passengers. He started up, inched up to the two-lane blacktop, looked both ways and then pulled out onto the road.

Miller sighed in relief. She felt better than she had. Now she wouldn't have to feed for twenty-four hours and by that time, she would be in another city. She would have been able to establish a temporary base and begin to tap into her resources.

She hadn't wanted to burn her house and lose all that money, but there was nothing she could do about it. The insurance company would repay the bank for the loan but they wouldn't look for her very hard. If they couldn't find her, they could keep her share of the money and they could salvage some of their loss by clearing the property and selling the lot.

She settled back in the seat and was startled to see one of the older women standing over her. She had on a dark, worn cloth coat and a tweed skirt that looked as if it had come from the Victorian era. Her hair was short and an unnatural shade of red.

"Where's your friend?"

"Friend?"

The woman swayed with the motion of the bus and then dropped into the seat next to Miller. "That little blond girl. I saw the two of you go into the bathroom. I don't see her on the bus."

Miller wasn't sure what to do. She hadn't thought that anyone had been paying attention. She said, "I didn't know her. I just wanted to use the facility."

"I thought I saw you talking to her."

"No. I'm by myself."

The woman looked puzzled. She bit a lip and said, "I wonder if I should mention this to the driver. We seem to have lost a passenger."

The last thing that Miller wanted was for the bus driver to go back to search for the passenger. Miller was slightly confused now, but she knew it was the result of the trauma. She hadn't had time to get properly healed, or she would have known exactly what to do. Now, she had to think things through carefully.

Finally, she said, "I'm sure that he called out and told everyone it was time to leave."

"But if she was in the bathroom, she might not have heard."

"I'm sure the driver knocked on the door to make sure. He does this for a living."

"Well, I'm going to say something to him. It's the Christian thing to do."

"There will be another bus along," said Miller. "Besides, I'm sure she had her cell phone so she could call for help . . ."

And as she said that she realized another mistake. The girl could call the police and tell them she was attacked. Miller couldn't stand the scrutiny of a police investigation.

Had she not been weakened by the trauma and by hunger, she would never have let the girl live. She would have taken her in an area where there would be little chance of discovery and she would have disposed of the body. In fact, she would never have attacked the girl in the first place. She was not a proper target. She was a college student.

Miller could only feel the turmoil in her belly because of the mistake. To the woman, she said, "I'm sure everything is fine. We shouldn't bother the driver."

The woman stood up, held onto the back of one of the seats so that she wouldn't fall and then walked up toward the front. She leaned over and talked to the driver who shook his head but never took his eyes off the road. Finally, she returned to her seat and sat down.

Miller felt relief wash over her. But now she was going to have to leave the bus as quickly as she could. She needed to put distance between her and the girl she left at the diner. She hoped that the girl wouldn't be found for several hours. If she caught a break, it might be late at night before anyone found her. By then Miller would be lost in some city.

The bus slowed and pulled to the side of the road. Two men got on and moved toward the back. They looked at Miller and then walked even deeper into the bus. They dropped into the seats behind her and began to talk. In minutes she could hear the comments and suggestions. They were becoming bolder.

If the situation was different, Miller would have encouraged them. That was what made hunting so simple sometimes. The prey just threw themselves into the trap without knowing what was happening. But here, on this bus, she could do nothing about it.

Their scent was becoming overpowering. It was the odor of fresh meat. It triggered the Pavlovian reflex in her and made her realize that she would need plenty of food to recover. That doctor had done a great deal of damage. Had he been less careful, she might not have been able to recover. She had been lucky.

The bus slowed and turned and then sped up. The roar of the engines and the rhythm of the tires on the pavement filled the air so that she lost track of what the men were saying. She could still smell them, even over the stench of the partially burned diesel and the odors from the farm fields and manure piles.

They traveled through the afternoon, stopping here and there, but never in a place that Miller thought of as suitable. She wanted something more, needed something more than a small town or a truck stop. Of course, at a truck stop she might be able to con a trucker into giving her a ride that took her farther from the public arena.

About dusk they stopped on the outskirts of a city. Maybe 50,000 population, maybe a little more. This would be the place. She could disappear here and then move to somewhere that was better suited to her needs.

Miller got up and moved to the front of the bus, aware of the two men behind her. They were following her. She didn't know their intentions, but they didn't frighten her.

The bus driver opened the door, let the passengers out and then followed. He moved to the center of the bus and opened the cargo area. There wasn't much in the way of luggage in it. Miller stood, looking at the bags, trying to figure out which had belonged to the girl.

The driver looked up and said, "Which one is yours, lady?"

Miller saw one in bright colors. The others were dark, a

couple were drab and one looked as if it had been on the bus for fifty years.

The driver pulled it out and said, "Let me see your ticket."

Miller handed him the one she had taken from the girl. He matched it to the tag and then swung the bag around and dropped it at her feet.

"Thanks," said Miller. She picked it up and started walking into the terminal. She wasn't sure what her next move was going to be, but it probably involved a cab.

The two men, now both carrying luggage, entered and followed her to the telephones.

"You need a ride?" asked one.

He was a tall man with a thick chest and gigantic arms. Everything seemed to taper down to a narrow waist and spindly legs. He looked as if he had been assembled from mismatched parts. But his clothes were clean and his hair was neat. He did have tattoos on his forearms and part of one showed on his neck. Fifty years ago it would have marked him as living at the lower end of society, but today it said that he was a hip man who enjoyed a little bit of the wild side.

"I'm just going into town and looking for a room."

The other man, younger, smaller and not quite as clean, said, "We can help you out there, too."

Miller smiled at them. "You live together?"

"We have an apartment we use when we're in town," he said.

Miller didn't like the setup because these guys looked as if they fit into the society. They looked as if they had jobs. Maybe not careers, but they were employed. They might be married with things on the side, but that wasn't her concern at the moment. She needed somewhere to hide, if only for a day or two, and she needed food so that she could regain her strength. These guys were offering her both.

"Well," she said, "I was going to call for a cab, but if you have wheels, then I guess I could accept a ride." She smiled at them, suggesting something more than just a ride.

One of the men picked up her suitcase, or rather the one she had taken from the girl, and started for the glass doors at the rear of the terminal.

The car was an older model, but it had been expensive once. It looked as if it had been cared for. It would provide her with transportation when she was rested. It would give her a means to get even farther away before anyone even knew that she had been in the city.

She got into the front, on the passenger's side, showing a little more leg than necessary. She wanted them thinking about sex and not really thinking about how easy she had been to pick up. She didn't want to give them a clue about what was going to happen to them. She wanted them as dumb as the deer wandering through the forest that didn't know it was opening day of hunting season. She wanted them relaxed.

As she settled into the seat, she heard one say to the other, "I can't believe this."

No, she thought, *you won't believe this.*

CHAPTER THIRTY-FIVE

Captain Steven Mitchell sat at his desk, his back to the growing twilight outside his window. The flat panel glowed, showing him a list of assaults that had been committed in the last twelve hours in a fifty-mile radius. Ten years earlier such a list would have taken hours to compile, with two or three detectives putting in telephone calls to various jurisdictions. Mitchell had merely accessed one of the police databases, punched in the relevant information and in seconds the list was scrolling down his flat panel.

He didn't want anything that smacked of domestic violence, of armed robbery, or of gang-related attacks. He wanted stranger-on-stranger violence and could limit it even more by searching for those cases in which the aggressor was female.

He only had time for a quick nap in the afternoon, so he was tired, which might be why he missed it the first time. When nothing had appeared, he scrolled through the list again. A short list, and a disheartening one. Too many women were becoming as violent as men.

The woman had been found, unconscious, at a bus stop some fifty miles away. She had been beaten and had, according to the report, lost a lot of blood, but there was no evidence of that blood where she was found. She had been attacked somewhere else and dumped in a restaurant restroom.

Mitchell shook his head. Conventional thinking was getting in the way. No blood at the location meant an attack elsewhere

238

to the average cop, but Mitchell understood it. No blood at the scene meant the woman was attacked right there and the blood was sucked out of her. Whoever heard of beating someone in one location and then dumping the unconscious victim in a restroom at another?

He reached for the telephone and dialed a number from memory. When it was answered, he said, "Tom, I think I've found a trace of her."

"Where?"

"Listen, why don't I pick you up and we can drive down there."

"You know that my attorney won't like that."

"You don't have to keep saying that. The question is if you think it's a good idea."

"How long?" asked Johnson.

"Ten minutes."

"I'll be outside."

Mitchell cleared his screen and then grabbed his jacket. He walked out the door, but he didn't say a word to the shift sergeant who had his back to him. He walked downstairs and then out onto the street to retrieve his private car. This was not a time to take a police vehicle, even if it could be justified as police business.

Johnson was standing at the curb, waiting. When Mitchell swung over, Johnson opened the passenger door and climbed into the front seat.

"I was wondering if we shouldn't take Rachael with us on this," he said.

"There is no reason to get her involved. It might not pan out anyway. I just have a report of a woman attacked at a truck stop who has lost a lot of blood. Thought it might relate to Miller and it's not all that far from here."

"Why do you think Miller was involved?"

Kevin Randle

Mitchell slowed for a traffic light that then turned green and he accelerated. He slipped to the left and hit the on-ramp for the interstate. He stepped down hard, and the car shot forward, rocketing up the ramp. Mitchell, with a single glance over his shoulder, blended into the traffic easily.

"I think Miller because there was a severe beating, massive blood loss but no blood at the scene. What does that sound like to you?"

"Miller feeding. But the victim is still alive?"

"Yeah. I don't understand that either."

"How old is she?"

"Tom, I don't know anything else. I just read the report on-line and called you. I figured that we'd know all we needed in about an hour."

"Okay."

Mitchell fell silent and concentrated on the road. He came to the cross highway, took the exit ramp and found himself on an old, two-lane black top with farmers, fields on either side and only the occasional farmhouse. One of them looked new, modern and huge, suggesting that the farmer was doing well. Or had learned to work the subsidy programs.

They finally reached the truck stop and Mitchell noticed that it was also a bus stop. He pointed it out to Johnson and then pulled onto the gravel parking lot.

He got out and headed for the diner. A sheriff's deputy broke off from a crowd and intercepted him. He said, without worrying about small talk, "Diner's closed."

Mitchell smiled and said, "There seem to be a lot of people inside."

"Crime scene. You need to move along."

Mitchell pulled out his wallet and flashed his badge.

The deputy bent down, squinted and then said, "City badge. Don't mean nothing here."

"Who's your superior?"

"City badge don't mean nothing here," repeated the deputy.

Mitchell leaned close and in a quiet voice filled with ice said, "Didn't ask you about the city badge. I asked who your superior is. That's all I need from you."

The deputy stood frozen for a moment, as if figuring his odds and then said, "Sheriff is inside. He won't like being interrupted during an investigation."

Mitchell started for the door with Johnson behind him. The deputy said, "Hey. You can go in but not him."

"He's with me," said Mitchell.

"I don't care. He's not going in."

Mitchell said, "I'll have to mention to the sheriff that you have been less than helpful, and that we might have information that is relevant to the case. Now, how is that going to look?"

The deputy stood staring, his teeth clenched and his nostrils flared, but he didn't move to stop either Mitchell or Johnson. He just stood glaring at them and knowing that any move he made now would be wrong. He was sure that the sheriff would speak to him later.

Mitchell reached the door and pulled it open but didn't step inside. Instead, he stood, surveying the scene, looking at the placement of everything and everyone in the diner. Then, sure that he knew where the crime scene was in relation to the door, and where the crime scene technicians were and who the sheriff was and who the owner of the diner was, he stepped in.

"Closed," said the big man who looked as if he had swallowed a basketball or was about to give birth.

Mitchell held up his badge again but showed it to the man he believed to be the sheriff.

"What can I do for you, Captain?" the man asked. He was short and thin, wearing a white shirt with short sleeves but no tie. He wore blue jeans with a big belt buckle but rather than cowboy boots wore soft brown boots that might have been military. He was tanned and healthy and didn't really fit in at the diner, which was why Mitchell thought he was the sheriff.

"Actually," said Mitchell, "it's what we can do for you. Has the body been removed?"

"Not a body. Injured girl and she's gone on the ambulance about fifteen minutes ago. Should be fine after a little rest and some solid food. College girl who got hit in the head and who lost blood but damned if I know where."

Johnson leaned close to Mitchell and said, "I need to see the wounds."

"You got something to say," said the sheriff, "let us all in on it. Who're you, anyway?"

Mitchell said, "He's consulting with our department on a serial murder case."

"You think this is part of that? Girl's not dead. Just injured."

"Our suspect seems to have fled our jurisdiction, and we believe she made it out on a bus."

"She. Don't get many female serial killers," said the sheriff.

"Not many, but some," said Mitchell. "You have anything to go on?"

"Girl was found in the woman's john, sitting on the throne, unconscious. Been there a while. Owner . . ." The sheriff hitch-hiked a thumb over his shoulder, "Owner said that he thought she came in on the bus but wasn't sure."

Johnson said, "I need to talk to the girl."

"She's in the county hospital right now, but I don't think she'll be in any shape to talk to you. Took quite a slug to the head."

"You find anything here?" asked Mitchell.

"Not much of anything. Women been in and out of that room all day. Don't know what might be of importance. Crime scene is grabbing everything."

Mitchell rubbed his chin. "Then I guess we'll swing by the hospital."

"You learn anything there, you give me a call."

"Of course."

Mitchell turned and headed for the door with Johnson right behind him.

When there were in the car, Johnson said, "You didn't want to look at the crime scene?"

"There would be nothing there of value to us. What we need to see are the injuries to this girl and find out if they are consistent with those inflicted by Miller. If not, then we go on home and look at more police reports. If so, we see if we can guess her next move."

"That's easy," said Johnson. "She'll find someone to hole up with for a few days. Give her a chance to activate her new identity. If she can find someone to let her stay at his house or apartment, then there is no trail to her. She doesn't have to register, she doesn't need to use a credit card, she won't be seen by the general public. She won't be using a cell phone. She would be momentarily safe."

"And if she kills her host?"

Now Johnson laughed. "What do you mean *if? When* she kills her host, she has revitalized herself and given herself more time to get established in her new identity. If she is careful, she could be out of sight for a week or two."

"So we might be chasing a ghost."

"That's a very good way to put it, though I think I would have said apparition rather than ghost."

They drove in silence to the hospital. It was a small, brick building of two stories. The parking lot was small and there were few cars in it. The outward appearance was more of a rest home than a hospital.

Inside they were told that they couldn't see the patient

because they weren't family, but Mitchell flashed his badge. The nurse glanced at it and said, "She is in room five, and I think the doctor is in with her now."

They walked down the linoleum corridor that had light green walls. There was little noise. Just the low voices from a TV and a little music that sounded like it was pumped into the whole facility and came from a tape that was fifty years old.

The door to room five was open slightly and Mitchell looked in. The girl was lying on the bed, a sheet pulled up to her waist. There was a huge bandage around her head. For a moment Mitchell thought he was looking at Sarah Hartwell again. The girl has the same light hair and the same slender body. She could have been Hartwell's sister.

The doctor looked up and said, "Family?"

"Police."

"I'm not sure that she's ready for police."

Mitchell entered the room, smiled at the girl and said, "Just a couple of quick, simple questions and then I'm gone. Maybe for good."

The girl tried to smile.

"What's your name?" asked Mitchell.

"Cindy Jacobi."

"Your family been told you're here?"

"I haven't called them yet," she said.

"I can do that for you, if you'd like."

"No. If they get a call from the police, they'll flip out. If I call them, I can ease into this."

"Okay." Mitchell pointed at Johnson. "This is a colleague. Tom Johnson. He wants to look at the wounds."

"Is he a doctor?"

"No. Just an expert consultant we have. He needs to look at the injuries to see if they are consistent with a couple of other assaults." Mitchell looked at the doctor. "He'll need to see the wound on the arm."

"I can tell you it is a pair of punctures about two inches apart. Deep punctures that struck a vein so that she lost some blood. We've replaced that."

Mitchell turned to Johnson. "That good enough?"

"It'd be best if I could see them," he said.

The doctor shrugged and leaned over, pulling up the sleeve on Jacobi's gown. He snipped at the gauze and pulled it away.

Johnson moved closer, bent down and then looked up at Jacobi. He smiled and said, "Sorry. No match. Thank you."

"Cindy," said Mitchell, "What happened?"

"I don't know. There was this woman on the bus and she followed me into the ladies' room. I don't remember anything else until I was in here."

"Can you describe her?"

"She had short, light hair, and she looked like she had been sick. She was thin and pale. I thought there was a scar or an injury on her forehead, right at the hairline."

"Anything else?"

"Her clothes didn't seem to fit, but I thought it was because she had been sick." She closed her eyes as if answering the questions had sapped her strength.

Mitchell noticed that and said, "Thank you."

Without a word to the doctor, Mitchell grabbed at Johnson to pull him out into the hallway. Once there he asked, "No match?"

"That was for the girl's benefit. She doesn't need to know. Yeah, it was Miller."

"Description was off," said Mitchell.

"Dyed hair. And, she would be thin without having a chance to feed properly. Stolen clothes that don't fit quite right. And tooth marks that match. It was her," said Johnson.

"And we know she was on the bus. We will get the schedule

and see where it went."

"She wouldn't stay on it for long. She'd get off where she could catch a ride or find another way to travel. Or she'd go to ground."

"But we have a lead," said Mitchell. "We know where she was, what, twelve hours ago."

"In twelve hours she could be halfway around the world," said Johnson.

"Not today. Not with Homeland Security and everyone over eighteen having to show ID and with airlines checking and computers and everything else going on. She's still in the United States probably planning on how to get out."

"So she's hiding. All we have to do is find her hole."

"Yeah," said Mitchell, "that should be easy." He didn't mean it.

CHAPTER THIRTY-SIX

Rachael Goldberg wasn't sure why she had called the meeting, but she had. The DA on the case, Paul Brisco, had tried to discourage it, and she had taken that as a good sign. She believed that his case was weak and it was getting weaker by the hour. At least from her point of view it was.

Brisco stood up when she appeared at his door. He came around from behind his desk and held out a hand as if he was greeting a colleague he hadn't seen in a long time. He grinned broadly, showing his snowy, capped, perfect teeth.

"Rachael. It is good to see you. Would you care for a beverage?"

He turned, glanced at a clock and said, "It's late enough that we're not constrained as to the contents of that beverage. I have mix for nearly everything."

She set her briefcase down on the floor near a visitor's chair and said, "I would like something cold. Maybe a Coke or a Pepsi?"

"Certainly. Just a Pepsi?"

"Ice?"

"Of course."

Brisco poured the Pepsi into a glass and handed it to her. He waved at the couch and said, "Please. Have a seat."

Goldberg sat down and crossed her legs. She said, "My client has been working with the police."

"Okay. Let's get into this now. I have interviewed Hartwell,

247

and I'm satisfied that Johnson acted to protect her. That Miller would have killed her had Johnson not shot her. We're dropping the murder charges and will only charge him with assault and firing a weapon inside the city limits."

Goldberg actually laughed. Part of it was relief because she could now tell the partners that the case would not be going to trial, and they wouldn't have the stain of defending a murderer on their firm. And, because the charges were ridiculous. First, if Johnson was defending Hartwell, he wasn't guilty of assault and second, charging him with firing a gun in the city was just dumb. It looked almost as if it was a face-saving device.

She sipped her Pepsi and asked, "Why so generous? I thought you had this locked down."

"The evidence suggests that Hartwell was attacked and Johnson attempted to protect her. Hartwell will, of course, say this under oath and it corroborates what Johnson said the first night. We found nothing to suggest that Hartwell and Johnson talked after the incident, so it means that they didn't have time to compare stories. The police were there in minutes."

"And?"

"Johnson pleads to firing the weapon and to simple assault and we'll ask for time served and probation for three years."

Goldberg grinned, sipped her Pepsi as if she was considering the plea and then shook her head. "I don't think so."

"Shouldn't you ask your client before you make a decision like that?" asked Brisco reasonably. He walked to his desk and then leaned back on it so that he was looking down at Goldberg.

But she wasn't intimidated. The game had changed and she held the cards.

"I don't need to talk to him about this. I know what his answer is going to be."

"Well, why don't I just leave the offer on the table for twenty-four hours anyway."

248

Goldberg laughed. "How about this? You drop the assault charge because we still can plead self-defense, and we'll take the discharging a firearm inside the city, which is a misdemeanor anyway. Time served and no probation."

"We have a dead body."

"Actually, no, you don't. You have some photographs, you have some autopsy notes, but you have no body. It's gone, and the coroner is dead so all you have are pictures that could be of anyone."

Brisco took a deep breath and said, "I can make a case without a body. It has been done in the past. Oklahoma in 1912. Boston in 1856."

"My God," said Goldberg, "you're pulling precedence from the twentieth century and before?"

"Just saying that cases have been made without bodies."

"Yes, but those people disappeared completely, or nearly completely. They had bones in the Boston case. You don't have that anymore."

"I can make a case," repeated Brisco.

"No. I think we can prove that people have seen Miller since she was supposedly killed by my client. I do that and you have nothing."

Brisco took a deep breath and sighed. "I don't understand this at all."

"You should have listened to Tom. He told you he hadn't killed a human. He told you to cremate the body. He gave everything to the police, against my advice by the way, and now where are you? Had you cremated the body, you'd have some documentation. All you have is a missing body that no one can find and pretty soon you're going to have sightings. Miller is gone and the case is dead."

Brisco walked back to his bar and dropped a couple of ice cubes into a glass. He poured three fingers of bourbon in and took a healthy swallow. He breathed out slowly and said, "I'm not buying this nonsense that Miller wasn't human. Or that she is still out there."

"You don't have to. All you need to know is the body is gone and we have information in the form of a scientific paper that Miller was not a member of the human race. There is scientific precedence for this. I can bury you in science."

"You know I'll counter with my own scientists saying that there isn't another sentient species on Earth. There is no evidence for it."

Goldberg wanted to end this right now. She didn't want to go to court even if she knew she would win. Her partners wouldn't like it. They'd made that clear enough.

"It doesn't matter what your scientists say. We have the coroner's paper in which he describes it. He's your guy. If you impeach him, then all evidence of the autopsy is gone. If you don't impeach him, then his paper stands. Either way, we win."

Brisco laughed. "This is a tough one. I mean, we have him standing over the victim with the smoking gun in his hand, and here I am trying to get a plea for simple assault and discharging a firearm in the city, and you want to argue about it."

"I'll give you the firearm charge but not the assault. It was defense of another. He didn't stand on the sidelines and let this go down. He acted to save his friend and you want to put him in jail for it."

"I'll have to talk with the DA on this. I don't think he's going to like it."

Goldberg felt the tension drain from her. She knew that she had won. Brisco didn't have to ask anyone. He was free to make any deal he needed to, and if he was going to ask, it was a stall. There would be no charges filed. In the end, they wouldn't want to tell the world the best they could do was charge Johnson with firing a pistol inside the city limits.

She finished her Pepsi but found she didn't want to leave right away. She wanted to savor the moment. Her first major murder case with the evidence stacked a mile high against her client and there wasn't even going to be a trial.

Brisco, however, was getting antsy. She could see it. He wanted her to leave because she was a reminder that he had failed to get her to agree to a reduced charge. She was going to push it all the way.

Taking pity on him, she set the glass on the floor and stood up. Smiling, she said, "It was pleasant to see you again."

He thanked her and ushered her toward the door.

It seemed he had rushed her out but then she didn't blame him. She wouldn't want to keep her around either because of the results of the case. He'd be explaining for years how he had managed to lose it, even though it wasn't his fault.

She walked out onto the street, which seemed to be brighter, cheerier, cooler and just simply more pleasant than it had been for several days. She felt good, better than she had since Tom had called her from jail and she learned why he had been arrested.

She crossed the street, looked into the window of a diner whose specialty was hot dogs and French fries and was tempted to go in. She was tempted to eat hot dogs and French fries because today nothing could be bad for her, but she passed it.

She hurried up the street, falling in behind those who were leaving work and those who were looking for their evening dining experience. The street was clogged with cars, with busses and cabs and trucks, and there was a slight haze hanging in the air because there was no breeze. But she didn't care because she could call Tom and tell him that there probably would be no charges filed against him after all.

She entered the building that held her law firm and rather than waiting for the elevator, walked to the stairs that led to a mezzanine and then found the stairs that led up. She climbed them quickly, relishing the ache that developed in her legs, thinking about the health benefits of stair climbing as opposed to riding in an elevator.

She entered the lobby and one of the receptionists, a young, heavy girl who wore too much make up and sometimes wore blouses that revealed too many of her tattoos, said, "They've been looking for you. In the main conference room."

"Have they been there long?"

"Most of the afternoon. Partners meeting but they said to tell you they were there when you came in."

She felt her stomach turn over. Nothing good ever came from meeting with all the partners. They met to terminate the associates who hadn't lived up to their promise or to tell associates that they were no longer on the track to partner or to tell them that they might make partner about the same time as Earth developed rings or the Atlantic Ocean evaporated.

She took a deep breath, hurrying first to her office to get rid of her purse and her briefcase. She stopped long enough to inspect herself, glad that she had opted for a conservative suit with a light blouse for her visit to the DA.

Satisfied, she walked to the conference, tapped on the door and opened it.

There was a conference table of a finished, polished mahogany. Eight high-backed leather chairs surrounded it. A silver service with crystal sat in the center of it. Windows dominated two walls, giving a view over the city to the river and a railroad bridge that looked like an elaborate model. Trees and parks lined the far bank of the river and beyond that was the interstate. There wasn't much traffic coming into the city but there was a great deal heading out.

There were four men and two women in the room arranged along both sides of the table. The chairs at either end were vacant, meaning that no one had assumed the role of leader in the meeting. They were all operating on an equal footing here, which sent chills down Goldberg's spine. It looked like an inquisition.

One of the men waved at her and said, "Come on in and have a seat." He motioned to one of the vacant chairs at the end of the table so that she would be facing into the room rather than looking out at the view. They were saying that their futures were bright and expansive and hers was dark and limited.

If she wasn't reading too much into the seating arrangements. If they had actually thought about that. If they were about to fire her.

She took a seat and wanted to say something but nothing came to mind. She just said, "Good afternoon."

C. Richard Howell said, "Good afternoon. You know everyone here?"

"Of course," said Goldberg, but she didn't like the question. It implied that something bad was going to happen.

"We've been wondering what was happening with your murder case," he said.

Now she grinned. "Dismissed. Or will be. No charges brought, not even the ridiculous discharging a firearm in the city limits that Brisco talked about. I haven't told Tom yet because I came directly here."

"You're sure about this?"

"Of course. I just came from his office where I was seated on the couch and given a beverage. He wanted me to tell Tom, that is the client, that he would accept a plea for assault and the discharging the firearm. I pointed out that if it wasn't murder, it wasn't assault and we'd accept no plea. I think he was hoping to save face."

One of the women, Harriet Chambers, an older woman of forty-five with jet-black hair cropped short, leaned forward, as if wanting to comment. She had small, delicate features and once would have been astonishingly beautiful. Now she was merely beautiful. She was also the smartest person in the room and they all knew it but pretended they didn't.

She said, "Maybe we should have been a little generous on this. We could have given him something so that next time he will be generous with us."

Goldberg looked at her in horror. "You aren't suggesting that we take the plea putting my client in jail so that Brisco might not be as aggressive next time?"

"I'm merely suggesting that Mr. Johnson did, in fact, assault Ms. Miller and he did, in fact, discharge a firearm in the city limits. That he is not being charged with murder or manslaughter would seem to be quite a victory for us."

"But . . ."

"That Mr. Brisco did have a case against Mr. Johnson on those charges."

"I'm not going to sell my client down the river," said Goldberg, now getting angry. She stared at the woman, telling her that she wasn't afraid.

"And we wouldn't ask you to do that. We are only suggesting that there is a give and take in this business and we could have been generous here."

"Tom is off the hook as of this minute," said Goldberg. "I have done what you asked me earlier. I have ended the case without the firm getting deeply involved. The DA will take the heat and no one will be talking about cheap lawyer tricks. The newspapers will be full of the DA's office blowing the case. I believe that we all came out of this looking good, meaning, of course, we in this office."

Howell held up a hand to stop the discussion. He said, "Ms. Goldberg is correct. We didn't want the firm to get a black eye because of our defense of Johnson and we won't. If nothing else, we'll look as if we are quite good, having the charges dismissed, given the circumstances. I think we can allow Ms. Goldberg to go and we can finish the rest of our business."

For a moment it looked as if there was going to be a protest, but then Chambers nodded, as did the others. Howell smiled and said, "That will be all, Rachael. Very nicely done."

She stood up and glanced out the side window. It was getting dark now. She didn't know where the time had gone. She smiled and said, "Thank you."

She left the room.

CHAPTER THIRTY-SEVEN

"I don't understand how you plan to find Miller now," said Johnson, sitting in the front seat of the car as they followed the route taken by the bus. "You have no proof that she was on it and if she was, that she stayed on it."

Mitchell was tempted to turn up the radio so that he didn't have to listen to Johnson anymore. Everything that Johnson knew about Miller was now useless. Miller would have changed names and credit cards and identities. She would be a different person, though Mitchell knew that if he saw her he would recognize her. She couldn't change that much.

At least that was what he believed. Johnson had said nothing about her having the ability to shape-shift and while Mitchell realized he was accepting quite a bit as true today that he wouldn't have last week, shape-shifting was not among the things he now believed.

So to keep Johnson from talking, Mitchell said, "We're into the twenty-first century and Big Brother is alive and well. Everything we do, say, write, sing is recorded and archived. You walk down the street in any city and there will probably be a dozen cameras to record your passing. Drive down the street and there are cameras to record you. Walk into a store, a shop, drive into a gas station, a fast food place and everything is recorded. If you went to Popeye's Chicken yesterday, I can probably find videotape to prove it. Or a credit card receipt. Buy gas. Stay in a hotel, go to the bank, and I can find out about it. So, finding Miller will not be all that difficult."

"I don't see how that will help us," said Johnson.

"We'll get video of the people getting off the bus and if she has hooked up with anyone. We'll get video of her leaving the bus station and if it is with someone, we'll get the license numbers and if it is a cab, we'll get the hack license and see where he took her. Either way, we'll find out where she went in the city."

Johnson sort of laughed. "Of course the local police or the sheriff will cooperate."

"Professional courtesy," said Mitchell.

"And if that doesn't pan out, we just start hitting the clubs, looking for her."

"If she hasn't changed her hunting pattern," said Mitchell. "She might be afraid of us looking for her like that."

Now it was Johnson's turn to pontificate. "She won't know that we're on to her. She'll believe, given the situation, that we'll believe she's dead, so there is no reason for us to be searching the clubs for her. I mean, you give up the search once you're told that someone is dead."

Mitchell fell silent and stared out toward the horizon where it was getting dark. Clouds were forming for rain and the sun was dropping toward the ground. Be night soon. Hunting time.

"How far are we from the city?" asked Johnson.

"Twenty, thirty minutes," said Mitchell.

They rode on in silence, the only sound the rumble of the road under the tires. Johnson looked into the fields where there was corn or soybeans and sometime cattle standing around as if waiting for something interesting to happen. He looked down at the river beds as they crossed bridges, sometimes thinking about how it would look from the bay window of a house or a blown up photograph hung on a wall.

He knew, just knew, that he was about to meet Miller again.

He would see her, maybe with a small scar that the bullet had made, or maybe with longer, bigger scars from the autopsy, or maybe nothing at all. She might have healed completely by now. It had been long enough.

But he knew that he was going to see her, just as he knew that it would not go well and that the sun would come up tomorrow. He knew it and if someone wanted to call it a premonition or a prediction of the future that was fine, but he knew it. He almost said something to Mitchell and then didn't.

In the distance he could now see the city. Twilight had set in and lights were coming on. The high rises, such as they were, began to twinkle with light. Buildings were popping up along with signs promising nice places to stay and good food to eat. The outskirts of any town along an interstate highway.

"Bus depot coming up on the right," said Mitchell. "See if we can get some answers now."

He pulled into a long, narrow drive that opened into a sea of asphalt lined for both busses and cars. The bus terminal was a long, low building of glass and steel that couldn't be more than two or three years old. Fuel prices had driven some people to the bus who would have used the family car in earlier years. The atmosphere was family friendly rather than derelict driven. A clean place for middle-class travelers.

Mitchell ignored the parking places and the yellow lines on the curb, pulling close to the door. He shifted into park, turned off the engine and then, grinning, said, "We're home, dear." It was an out-of-character comment for him.

They entered the bus terminal and Johnson was astonished. It looked nothing like those he remembered from his college days. It was bright, clean with some kind of indoor–outdoor carpet on the floor to deaden sound, a game room off to the right and a TV room to the left. There was a snack bar stuck in one corner that looked like something at one of the newer ball-parks.

"This is nice," he said. "I might start taking the bus again." Mitchell made his way to the back, found a door that announced the manager and opened it without bothering to knock. It was a neat room with a couple of desks and a large flat panel screen that kept track of the busses.

A small, round, balding man looked up, annoyed and then saw the badge Mitchell held.

"Help you?"

"You have tape of the arrivals?"

"Of course. Keep the tapes for two weeks and then recycle them. Color camera and digital feed. You can zoom in on a button and get a clear image," he said, proud of the system.

"Everything that came in from the east," said Mitchell. "After about six to start."

"Give me a minute." He turned to a computer keyboard, typed and looked at the screen. He moved the mouse, clicked, moved it again and clicked and pointed. "Up there you'll see everyone getting off the bus."

They turned and in high-definition glory were the passengers getting off the bus. The picture so sharp and clear that it nearly hurt the eyes to look at it. The camera had been focused on the door so that it was simple to see the faces of each of the passengers as he or she got off.

Miller was the next to the last. She was dressed like a college girl in cutoffs and a T-shirt that hugged her curves. Her long hair was dyed and her face leaner, more angular than it had been, but it was clearly her. Even the light red of the dimpling where the bullet had penetrated her skull was visible, the screen that good.

Mitchell turned and looked at Johnson and said, "I didn't really believe it. Not until now. Not until this very minute."

"You see something?" asked the manager.

"Can you follow that woman?"

"Certainly." The manager moved the mouse and it clicked again and again.

The screen fragmented into four parts showing people walking through the terminal, people near the snack bar, people near the doors and then people in the parking lot.

"You have this well covered," said Mitchell.

"I can pull up a single car so that you can get the license number if you want it," he said. "Cuts way down on the crime when they know we see everything around here."

"Big Brother would be proud," said Johnson.

The manager apparently didn't understand the reference.

"There she is walking toward the doors. She's with those two men." Mitchell looked down at the manager and said, "I don't suppose you recognize them."

The manager laughed. "Why would I?"

"Just a thought. Can you track them?"

"Sure."

A moment later Johnson and Mitchell saw Miller with her two male friends leave the terminal. They walked across the parking lot and just as it seemed they were about to disappear, the scene changed and it showed them heading toward a light gray car.

They stopped on the passenger side and Miller waited for the door to be unlocked. When it was, and opened, she climbed into the front seat, smiling.

"License number," said Mitchell.

The angle changed slightly and zoomed in on the license plate. It was so close, so clear they could see the bug spots and the rust on the bolts that held it in place.

Mitchell wrote it down. He then pulled a cell phone out of his pocket, touched a number and said, "Mitchell here. Give me a name to go with XKE 902, state."

He turned and smiled at Johnson and then a moment later said, "Registered to Lionel Humphries."

"Tombstone name," said Johnson.

Mitchell wrote some more and then said, "Thanks." He snapped the phone shut. He looked at Johnson. "What do you mean, 'tombstone name'?"

"Just that it would look good on a tombstone, but it's not a name to remember. It doesn't sing."

The manager asked, "You get what you need?"

"Yes. Thank you."

"Always willing to help the police. Keep things calm that way. I like it when it's calm."

As they walked out of the office, Johnson asked, "Are we going over there now?"

"You have a problem?"

"Are we ready to meet Miller again?"

Mitchell laughed. "I've never met her. Just seen her in the morgue and running away from Blanchard's house."

"That doesn't really answer the question."

They reached the car and got in. Blanchard, as he started the engine said, "She doesn't know me, so she has no reason to be spooked, if she's still with them. I'll just ask a couple of questions, generic questions, about the girl who was injured and let it go at that. Just to size up the situation."

"She's quite devious," said Johnson. "She's very observant and she's very clever."

"But she isn't going to know that I know anything about her," said Mitchell. "That's if she is even there and if there, I get the chance to talk to her. If not, I'll talk to the boys about what they saw and did and if they gave anyone a ride from the bus terminal."

"Backup?"

"Not needed for this."

They drove in silence for a moment and then Mitchell turned from the main street. He grinned broadly and said, "I used to live here. My first job was here. I know most of the town. We're going to one of those new apartment or condominium places."

The streets, which had been narrow and tree lined, became wider with plantings that might one day be big trees. New construction. Houses that looked almost like mansions and then a strip mall with a coffee house, a BBQ house and a video store. On the right was a massive building, three stories high and with a parking lot that would have done justice to a major airport.

"Those boys are living well," said Mitchell.

They pulled into the parking lot. It was filled with new cars. Expensive cars that had all the options. And pickup trucks that had never been near a farm and that would probably never haul anything at all. Big tires and bright colors shined brightly in the security lights.

Johnson said, "We could probably find tape of her going inside."

"If she went inside."

"I think she would use those boys as a base until she found something else. She's gone to ground right now and isn't moving freely," said Johnson. "You might scare her."

"Maybe you should wait in the car. She does know you."

Johnson nodded. "Fine."

Mitchell got out and as he started for the door, Johnson followed. "I'll stay out of sight."

They walked into the building and looked for apartment numbers and a directory. It was set up like a mall with a big map that told them where they were and showed the layout of the whole complex including two swimming pools, a meeting house, a game room and management offices.

They walked up a flight of stairs into a wide hallway with carpet and paint that looked new and fresh. There was imitation art on the walls, some with tiny spotlights on it, making it look like a long, narrow gallery.

The doors were recessed so that each had a little entryway. Someone standing at the end of the hall couldn't look down the hall and see people at someone else's door.

Mitchell stopped at the door and raised a hand to knock. Johnson stood to the side, his back against the wall so that whoever opened the door wouldn't be able to see him.

Mitchell knocked, waited a moment and then knocked again, louder. When that wasn't answered, he hammered on the door. It opened a moment later and he held up his badge and said, "We're checking on a girl who was injured at a bus station up the road."

And as he spoke, Johnson realized that it was the wrong thing to say and that Linda Miller would immediately understand the flaw in his statement.

CHAPTER THIRTY-EIGHT

The man had died much quicker than Miller had expected. She had sapped his strength subtly and then pressed her lips to his throat, biting carefully, almost playfully and he had responded by reaching up to her breast. She squirmed, as if to press herself against him and then began to suck.

The man moaned, low in the throat and then his hand dropped away. He seemed to gasp, as if he had just run a long distance and then seemed to shrink. He went limp.

Miller finished and then sat up looking at him. The skin was a fish belly white, unhealthy, nearly inhuman. She reached out and touched his face, almost in affection, and then put a finger on his eye. There was no reaction at all.

"Damn," she said. She rocked back, away from him. He'd died too quickly and she wondered if he had been sick, not that it mattered all that much to her.

She stood up and walked to the chair pushed into a corner and sat down. She felt better, stronger, and she knew that in a few days, a week at the most, she'd be back to full strength. Healing had taken a little longer because the damage had been so extensive. Had the coroner been a little smarter, she would never have been able to recover.

Well, she wouldn't need to eat again until morning and the other one wasn't going anywhere. He was laid up in the other bedroom, his strength gone for the moment. She had been very hungry.

There was a rapping at the front door, but Miller ignored it. Friends of the men and she had no desire to see them. She knew that the men wouldn't be interested in seeing friends, at least they wouldn't tonight . . . or ever.

But the pounding became more insistent and she knew, just knew that whoever it was, wouldn't be going away. She'd have to answer the door or risk someone calling the building manager or the police.

She stood up and grabbed one of the man's shirts lying on the floor. She put it on and caught a glimpse of herself in the dresser mirror. The tails were long, nearly reaching her knee. She was covered as completely as if she was wearing a dress.

She left the room and closed the door. She glanced at the other door and knew the man in there wouldn't be getting up anytime soon.

The pounding came again, this time loud enough to wake the dead. She heard a voice but didn't hear the words. She reached the door and looked out the peephole. A man stood there looking back, over his shoulder, as if he was listening to someone standing in the hallway.

She opened the door and looked at the badge the man held. She had the impression she knew him and then remembered where. He was talking about the girl she had attacked and she knew suddenly that he knew who she was but he didn't seem all that surprised.

She let the shirt fall open and when his eyes dropped, she reached out and grabbed the lapels of his jacket, jerking him from his feet. She pivoted, threw her hip into it and slammed Mitchell into the wall. He dropped his badge and began to slide toward the floor.

She picked him up and threw him into the living room. He hit the back of the couch and rolled over it, landing on the floor on his hands and knees.

As she approached him, Mitchell reached back under his coat and drew his pistol. He pointed, aimed and fired three times in quick succession. She felt the hot metal strike in the chest, on the left side and staggered back. The rounds punched on through her and exited her back.

For a moment she was lightheaded, dizzy and close to losing consciousness. She staggered and then shook herself like a dog just out of the pond. She grinned at him, her teeth now bloody and her eyes bright.

"I'll dine again tonight," she said.

Mitchell fired again, but it seemed to have no effect.

Johnson looked around the corner just as Miller snatched Mitchell off his feet and threw him into the wall. He stepped forward and saw her pick up Mitchell and toss him into the living room.

He was going to hit her, but had no weapon and knew that he couldn't stop her with his bare hands. Then, suddenly, there were nearly a half dozen flat bangs as Mitchell fired his weapon. He saw Miller stagger but knew the wounds wouldn't stop her.

"Shoot her in the head," he shouted.

Miller glanced back at him and hissed, "I'll take care of you in a moment."

She sprang at Mitchell who fired again and then again. One round was wild, smashing into the wall but the second struck home, slamming into Miller's head. She staggered once and fell as if all the bones had left her body. She hit the floor solidly and didn't move.

Mitchell climbed to his feet, his weapon in his hand, still pointed at her. At her head. Waiting for her to move.

"We've now got about sixty hours," said Johnson conversationally.

"I don't get this," said Mitchell. His voice was high and tight with just the hint of a tremor.

"Regeneration," said Johnson. "They regenerate so quickly but a head shot slows the process. The only way to stop it is to burn the body."

"What about a stake through the heart?"

"Old wives' tale. The stake slows the process too, but the tissues grow around it like human tissue grows around a piece of shrapnel."

Mitchell wiped a hand across his face. He looked back at one of the chairs and dropped into it. "That was close. I hit her five times in the chest."

"Head shot is the only thing that will stop them." He moved closer to the body, looking for the offspring, but there was only a single, anemic worm-like creature that pulled away from her. It struggled to get away from the body and then was suddenly still, turning black. It didn't have the energy, the stamina to withstand separation from a body that was still trying to recover from massive injury.

Mitchell took his cell phone from his pocket.

"What are you going to do?" asked Johnson.

"Call the local police. We've got an officer-involved shooting and they're not going to be happy with me in their jurisdiction without letting them know I'm here."

"And they'll impound the body for autopsy and you saw how well that worked the last time."

"We can't just take her out of here and burn her," said Mitchell.

"Why not?"

"Because that isn't the way we do things. There are procedures to be followed."

"Which is how they can operate in our world with impunity," said Johnson. "We play by one set of rules that inhibits our ability to deal with them. They have another set that gives them all the advantages."

"I don't know why you're arguing with me," said Mitchell. He pointed at the body. "If we can establish that this is Linda Miller then you're off the hook. Obviously you didn't kill her if she is dead here and I'm the one who shot her."

Johnson looked down at the body now. The shirt had come open so that he could see her skin. There were the bullet holes in the chest that were strangely bloodless. There were faint, barely visible scars that marked the incisions of the autopsy. She was skinny now. She hadn't regained her full body weight but he could see the potential was still there.

"Sixty hours, you say."

"If the autopsy is done right we can expand that and try to get her body released so that it can be cremated. You'd have the authority to do something like that."

Mitchell looked at his cell phone and then dropped it back in his pocket. "We need to search this place."

There were sirens then. Far away, barely audible, but coming closer.

"Somebody else already called the police," said Mitchell and retrieved his cell phone. He dialed 9-1-1.

Johnson opened a door and saw a man sprawled on the bed. There was a smear of blood at his throat and some on the sheet. The room was hot and smelled like a bear pit.

"Got another one here," he said.

Just then there was a noise behind him and someone shouted, "Everyone freeze."

Mitchell was on his feet and held his hands up, palms out. He said, quietly, calmly, "I am a police officer and I will show you my badge."

Johnson didn't move a muscle. He just looked at the barrel of the pistol held by the second police officer. He didn't want to be shot by accident.

"Move very slow," said the officer, looking at Mitchell.

Mitchell took out his badge and held it up. The officer looked at it and said, "That's no good here."

"Why don't you get on that radio and call for a supervisor so that we can get this all straightened out. We're not going anywhere."

"Do it, Larry," said the officer aiming at Johnson.

Mitchell relaxed and then sat down. He said, "The woman is wanted in connection with a series of killings in our city. She . . . escaped and I tracked her here but I thought she would be gone. I wanted to talk to the men living here to see if they knew where she might have gone. Unfortunately, she answered the door and recognized me."

"Where are those men?"

Johnson said, "Back here." He didn't know if they were alive or dead. He suspected the one he had seen was dead.

"I think we'll all just wait right here until the sergeant shows up. He's paid to make the big decisions."

"Very wise," said Mitchell. "Might I suggest a medical examiner as well."

Johnson nodded toward the living room. "Maybe we should all sit down."

"Okay, but be careful."

Johnson stepped over Miller and then sat down. He smiled at Mitchell and said, "I never thought you'd get me off the hook by shooting the victim."

Mitchell wasn't amused. He said, "Let's not say anything that can be used against us. Let's see if we can't get an attorney in here. We have work to do."

Johnson leaned back in the chair. "At least it's over for me. Finally."

EPILOGUE

Tom Johnson sat across the table from Sarah Hartwell. There were no visible signs of the injuries she had suffered other than her blond hair was cut short and styled in a new way for her. There was a noticeable tremor in her hands but it was nearly invisible. She leaned forward toward her plate and looked down at the food on it.

"It feels so good to get out of the house," she said. "For a while I didn't think I would ever want to leave again."

Johnson had to laugh. "I thought, for a while, that I would be spending the majority of my life in prison. Seemed that the options were limited there."

She looked up and smiled. "I thought the self-defense would work out."

"I never really thought of that as the right plan. I thought if we proved that Miller was not a human, then the law had no jurisdiction."

"Cruelty to animals?" she said.

Johnson sat back and said, "I never thought of that. I guess if the DA wanted an indictment, he could have come up with something."

She put her fork down and said, "I don't understand why all the charges were dropped."

"There were too many complications," said Johnson. "No, that's not quite right. I think it had to do with a breakdown of the system here. I was arrested but it began to look like a botched case. They lose the body. The coroner steals it for scientific research and then he gets killed. So his testimony is gone."

"Yes, I understand that, but I don't understand what happened with you and Mitchell."

"He shot a woman who was attacking him. He killed her and it looked like that was Miller. DNA matched. Fingerprints matched. It meant that the body they had lost was someone else, at least to their way of thinking. Since I had been charged with killing Miller and I obviously hadn't, and since they could not prove that I killed anyone, they let the thing go."

Hartwell reached out and picked up her drink. She took a swallow and said, "But the charges were dropped before Miller was killed."

Now he shrugged. There were things that he didn't want to tell her. Things that were better left to the conspiracy nuts on the Internet, to the writers of paranormal books, to the historians who would someday learn what Miller really was. Now was the time to let all that go, though the thought of a book kept popping up in his mind.

Of course, no one would really believe it even if he managed to get Blanchard's paper or assemble the various published reports of the last century. People were always coming up with wild theories, often with some supporting evidence.

It was best to let it go. Miller wouldn't be killing anyone else. Mitchell had the body cremated and then the ashes were scattered over running water. There was no way that they would be able to regenerate from that. The offspring that had deserted her when he shot her had been destroyed before they could begin to grow into larger creatures and those seen as Miller were shot the second time were anemic, unhealthy and unviable. She hadn't had time to get back to full health. The trial was now ended, right there, in that apartment.

Hartwell took a breath and said, "I have never properly thanked you for saving me. I haven't forgotten what you did."

"I'm sorry that we got into that position in the first place. I never thought she would attack you. I thought we were both safe from her."

"So what are you going to do now?"

Johnson sighed and said, "I haven't worked it all out yet. I was freelancing magazine articles and had enough circulating that I was pulling in a steady income. But the backlog is gone, published and paid for and it'll take six months to recreate it, if I can. I don't know what I'll do about that. Maybe find a job. I can say, 'Would you like fries with that.'"

"You know, you have a house and I have a house and we could sell one. That would put some money in the bank. And I can go back to work now. My boss has called and asked me to return."

"Sarah, I don't think we should live together . . ."

"I was hoping to make it something a little more permanent than that. Something very long term."

Suddenly Johnson lost his appetite. He looked across the table at her, and knew, just knew that it was the right thing. He should have thought about it himself. It was something right and good and just a little frightening.

She reached into a pocket and took out a ring. "I always liked this one and thought maybe you should give it to me."

He took the box, opened it and took out the ring. He reached for hand and slipped it on. "Will you marry me?"

"Yes."

ABOUT THE AUTHOR

Kevin D. Randle has been writing all his life but has also found time to serve in the Army, Air Force Reserve and the National Guard, retiring as a lieutenant colonel. He has published over 100 books including science fiction, murder mystery and action adventure. When not writing, he is engaging in historical research, which often appears in his books. He has a PhD in Psychology and a master's in Military Studies. He makes his home in Cedar Rapids, Iowa.